It's a rare thing to find yourself between the pages [...] yourself, see your own thoughts and hopes an[...] you—but Sharon K. Souza manages to place he[...] with each chapter. *The Color of Sorrow Isn't Blue* pulls together the complex corners of grief, heartbreak, hope, and even humor in a way that will take your breath away. With a master hand, she guides us to the fragile place where all seems lost, and yet it's the place where we discover ourselves anew. A beautiful book by a gifted writer.

Bonnie Grove ~ award-winning author of *Talking to the Dead*

Where does a woman turn when the unthinkable happens? For Bristol Taylor, hope has dissolved inside a fog of grief and remorse, leading her to a place she never dreamed she'd go. With a truly skillful touch, Sharon K. Souza walks readers through that fog, reminding us that on the other side of even the darkest passage there is a Light to be found.

Jennifer Erin Valent ~ author of *Catching Moondrops.*

A beautifully written novel. Sharon K Souza has managed to delve into the darkest places of a woman's heart with finesse, dignity and touches of humor. Highly recommended!

Kathryn Cushman ~ author of *A promise to Remember* and *Chasing Hope.*

Sharon Souza takes the reader on a journey into the deepest questions the soul can ask. Beautifully crafted, perfectly paced, painfully honest. She offers no easy answers, but doesn't leave the reader in despair as she tells the wrenching story of a mother swamped by grief and regret. I will never react to a news story about a missing child in the same way.

Patti Hill ~ author of *Goodness and Mercy*

A beautifully written and gripping story about a mother's worst nightmare. It grabbed me on the first page and wouldn't let me go. Souza is a master of emotion and words. Her character development is wonderful and I found myself laughing and crying with the main character, Bristol, but also with some of the quirky and wonderful secondary characters. Highly recommended.

Linda Hall ~ author of *Night Watch*

One of the most achingly beautiful, achingly true books I have ever read. From the opening lines I was mesmerized. Souza is a writer who crafts an unforgettable story with a master's touch with language. This is a must-read for anyone who wants thoughtful, memorable fiction.

Latayne C. Scott ~ author of *Latter-Day Cipher* and *Discovering the City of Sodom*

A powerful story, real and raw. Souza's writing is beautiful, but it is also true … showing the depth of grief and the nearly insurmountable job of climbing out of the pit it creates. There are no pat answers in this story—only the reality of friendship and a gradual realization of God's constancy. This book will touch the heart of anyone who has experienced the pain of loss and show that doubting and despair don't have to be the end game.

Rebecca LuElla Miller ~ author of *Power Elements of Story Structure*

Sharon K. Souza's beautiful new novel guides you through the territory of The-Worst-That-Can-Happen so adeptly that you emerge with a clearer eye and a braver heart.

Kathleen Popa ~ author of *The Feast of Saint Bertie*

THE COLOR OF SORROW ISN'T BLUE

A Novel

Sharon K. Souza

ISBN-13: 978-1502446862
ISBN-10: 1502446863

Printed in the United States of America.

Most Scripture quotations in this publication are taken from the HOLY BIBLE: NEW INTERNATIONAL VERSION. Copyright © 1973, 1978, 1984 by International Bible Society.

This is a work of fiction. Names, characters, places and incidents are either the product of the author's imagination or are used fictitiously.

Cover design by Kathleen Popa, www.cottonbond.com

Author photo by Mindy Grant

Starfish photo by Jan Willem Geertsma

For Brian

who made it home

This story was inspired by the disappearance of Cyndi Vanderheiden, 25, from Clements, California, in 1998. I was acquainted with her mother, Terri, but that was hardly necessary to know Cyndi's family lived the worst kind of nightmare for 14 years, and continue to bear a sorrow that only those who have lost a child can understand.

To the Vanderheiden family, you remain in my prayers.

One

*G*rief, it is said, is a sea that ebbs and flows. Comes in waves that roll over the shore, then recedes in a dizzying, lose-your-footing-in-the-sand sensation, leaving you unsettled but standing. Well, whoever said that never felt the tsunami effect, the drowning, sucking, tidal wave of grief.

I know, because I haven't come up for air in five days short of a year. A suffocating, black hole of a year, each day collapsing in on itself like sand too long unwatered. Eighty-six hundred hours; five-hundred thousand minutes; thirty-one million seconds of a smothering nightmare I can't wake up from. A long slow terror, like free-falling in the dark with no cord to pull.

I don't plan to be here for the anniversary five days from now. Not after what I saw this morning.

"I'm going to the beach house for a few days. On Thursday." I ignore the shadow that flits across David's face and clouds his eyes.

He blinks, but I know it doesn't clear up a thing. "This Thursday?"

"Yes."

"Alone?"

I push down the pang of guilt that's taken up residence in my gut this past year. "Yes."

"But I thought ..." His words drift off with a head shake and a shrug.

I know exactly what he thought. He and I would do the interview together—because we aren't the only ones watching the calendar—then we'd, what, pay a public visit to the Find Kinsey headquarters, strike a pathetic pose for the cameras, make another plea for our daughter's return, then retreat to the cave that our home has become?

No, thank you.

The last printing we did of Kinsey's "Missing" flyer is still stacked up on the brown laminated table with the pressed board showing through where the edges have chipped away—the only one left out of a room full of such tables—the stacks of flyers as high as they were five weeks ago. There are two brown metal chairs now instead of fifty, and that's one more than we need most days. The phone seldom rings, and when it does it's one more dead end, one more dagger to the heart.

I mean, really, how many times do we have to die before it's over?

But my sister, Ainsley, puts her key in the lock five mornings a week. She straightens the over-sized posters that shift every time a train goes by on the tracks across the road from the strip mall that houses the headquarters. Posters of a beautiful little girl with strawberries on her sundress and a makeshift wreath of flowers in her hair. The leaves are wilted but the daisies still hold their own. We called her our flower child, David and I, because of that picture. She kept the wreath on the entire day the photo was taken, said, "No"—her favorite word at the time—whenever I tried to remove it.

Why would I? I mean, for God's sake, so what if she slept in it?

"Babe, are you sure?" David asks.

"Sure?" I have to think back to the antecedent of his question, which, I remember now, was my pronouncement. "Yes."

I know he's planned that we'd spend the day together, mingle our pain as it were, like strange bloodmates. The truth is, I have more than enough pain of my own. And what can we say that we haven't said an infinite number of times already? How many times can we send our sighs back and forth, like a ping pong ball masquerading as conversation?

Yeah, it's exactly like free-falling in the dark.

And, oh, how I've fallen.

David doesn't try to kiss me when he leaves. The Pavlov conditioning I've subjected him to this past year has seen to that. But he does give me one more glance, a final plea with eyes I can't look into anymore, and not just because they're Kinsey's eyes—though that in itself is more than enough. They're soulful eyes, David's are. They drew me in the first time I met him, even before he had the chance to flash his famous smile or turn on the charm. They're still soulful, but what I see in his soul is not what I used to see. Now his own sorrow brims at the edges, always there, on the verge of spilling over. He does his best to keep it in check. Still. For me. I've learned to look just past the eyes on the occasions we have something to say to one another. It's all about survival these days.

When he's gone I pick up the phone so I can transfer at least one of my lies of the morning to the truth column. You see, I've yet to procure my plans for Thursday. And beyond.

"'Morning, sweet thing." My stepmother's voice is way too perky for this time of day. I catch her just as she's leaving for school, the only way to keep the conversation short.

Sissy is the epitome of a morning person. I don't happen to find that in her favor. And I wouldn't think anything of her greeting, except that she doesn't have caller ID. Yet she's right more often than not, and that's just plain spooky. Unless, of course, that's how she answers the phone, regardless, which I would not put past her.

"Hey," I say, the best I can do at the moment. "I'd like to use the beach house for a few days."

"Why, of course, baby. I told your daddy this very morning that you and Davy should get away. And what better place?"

Sissy thinks she's a steel magnolia. And trust me, she would be, if she came from the south. But the South Bay is as southern as my stepmother gets. San Jose to be exact, forty-five miles from San

Francisco. Born and bred.

She's a superlative, Sissy is, the consummate everything. But if someone had to fill the gap our fleeing mother left all those years ago, well, it could have been worse.

"I meant me, Sissy."

She doesn't answer right away. "Just you?"

I can almost see her begin to slide her diamond S along the silver chain at her neck, back and forth like a tiny tram. It makes a whisper of a sawing sound I don't need to hear to experience, because I've heard it a million times if I've heard it once. She's already worn through one clasp, and is well on her way to another. Lucky the pendant fell into the cleavage of her bra and not down a storm drain, or toilet, or some other irretrievable place. The crease between her professionally perfect eyebrows deepens. I can see that too.

"Yes."

"Well, baby ..."

"I just need to get away, Sissy. Me, by myself. I don't want to be here come Sunday."

"No, no. Of course you don't. And of course, the beach house is all yours."

The beach house is not a beach house at all. It's a twenty-foot trailer on a cracked slab in Half Moon Bay, that comfortably sleeps four—if you don't mind touching. And that's what I mean about Sissy. She turns a sow's ear into a silk purse every single time. But it is on the beach. I'll give her that.

I thank her then hang up. No use giving her any more opportunity to decode the tone or content of my words, because Sheila "Sissy" Vanderpool is the 007 of stepmoms when it comes to that. She can see straight through to the truth better than anyone I ever knew.

How Ainsley got Sissy's skills without the benefit of her DNA is a mystery all its own. But she did. I don't even count to ten before the phone rings—not anywhere near enough time for Sissy to have called my sister.

"Bristol?"

"Ainsley. Hey." If there's one person I try to muster enthusiasm for on a regular basis, it's Ainsley. But I haven't yet buoyed from the bomb I dropped on David this morning, and the proof is there in my voice.

"How's it going?"

There's enough of a question within the question that I'm convinced she's talked to someone. Had to have been David.

"It's going," I say.

Gone is more like it, but I don't want to give Ainsley more to worry about. She deserves a break. She's carried well beyond her share of worry these past three hundred sixty days, continuing to pull yeoman's duty, by herself for the most part, at the Find Kinsey headquarters long after all the other volunteers returned to their safe and insulated worlds, and when I knew one more desperate minute there would push me over the edge I've been so precariously balanced on. But I've been on that edge long enough now that I no longer fear the plunge. In fact, I welcome it.

Before we go any further I hear a hitch on the line and know it's Ainsley's call waiting that's kicked in. "You want to get that?"

"No, no, that's okay. I'll call them back."

Them would be Sissy. I'd bet the rest of what I possess on it. But that's not saying much, since the rest of what I possess doesn't mean much of anything to me now.

"About this weekend." Ainsley handpicks every word for the idea she's about to present. Ainsley, the diplomatic one. "I think we should get out of town, all of us. Avoid the phone, the media, go to the cabin, and just ... be together. Forecast says there may even be snow." Her voice crackles with hope. "What do you think?"

The cabin, in South Lake Tahoe, belongs to Grady's brother Colin. Grady, my brother-in-law. It's big enough to sleep all of us and more. Unlike the beach house, which would never do. Eight is not four, and never could be when you're talking about places to sleep.

"I'm going to the beach house. On Thursday." This has become my mantra.

"Listen, I just dropped the boys off. Can I come by for a quick cup of coffee? Better yet, how about I hit the drive-thru and grab a couple of mochas and maybe a muffin?"

I sigh. I'm going to get exactly what I deserve for my lies and other bad behavior. "Sure."

The boys are Ainsley's ten-year-old twin sons, Sam and Eli, identical only so far as their epidermis. Beyond that, they're as different as my world before and after Kinsey. Sam's the mischievous one, the prankster, the entertainer. You know him by the energy that bursts out of him like sunspots, as impossible to hold back as a sneeze. Eli's the—well, I call him Braveheart, for more reasons than I could cite. Not that Sam isn't good; he is, and I love him as much as it's possible to love. But Sam will succeed by the wit with which he's been gifted; Eli by his character. They're not bookends, these two. Rather they're the yin and yang of brotherdom.

Jaclyn comes next in my parade of callers, and right on time. She and Ainsley couldn't have spaced their calls more perfectly if they'd tried. I had no clue such a network existed between my stepmom, sister and best friend. But now I see they're worker bees in a common hive, with me—Queen Bee apparent—coddled and insulated, and not even knowing it.

Till now.

It comes as news, because Sissy Vanderpool and Jaclyn Papier meld as well as fire and water. Get them together and there's a whole lot of steam. Don't ask me why. It just is and always has been. But they've buried the hatchet—hopefully not in each other's back—for the sake of my, what? Sanity? If so, they're too late. By a light year.

"Bristol. Hey, girl."

"I'm going to the beach house. On Thursday." I'd be nicer but I'm put off by the falsetto of Jac's voice. She's trying much too hard to be blasé and we both know it.

"Well, some of us were talking—"

"Some of us?"

"—about going to the cabin for a few days."

"Uh huh. Some of us who?" I already know, of course, but there's something satisfying in hearing her squirm.

"Well, let's see. Ainsley. And, um, Sheila." Not Sassy—which is what she's called my stepmother for years instead of Sissy—but Sheila. And even at that she garbles the name as best she can so I might somehow miss it. "They say there could be—"

"Snow." I say it with her.

"Exactly." The falsetto continues. "So what do you think?"

What do I think? "I think things are desperate if you and Sissy are willing to hole up in a snowed-in A-frame for a dangerously long weekend just to babysit me."

"Bristol, come on." Her voice is her own once again. "No one wants to babysit you."

"Uh huh. I'm going to the beach house. On Thursday." I don't tell her the rest—meaning the fact that I'm not coming back—because I'm still trying to fool even me.

"Well, since I've already cleared my calendar, how about if I come along?"

"And where will we put David?" It's mean to yank her chain like this, yes, but it's the new me. The not-so-improved model.

She stammers, so out of character for Jac, who usually has it so together. "David's going?"

I hear the hope and surprise in her voice. "Since you've obviously talked to Ainsley and"—I can hardly believe this—"Sissy, you know I'm going by myself."

"Then why—"

"Jac, I need to be alone for this. I don't mean to hurt anyone, but that's how I want it."

Even as I say the part about not hurting anyone, I know it's not true. Because right now, David, the one I'm hurting most, is not even on my radar. I should feel awful about that. I really should.

"I'd stay out of your way, an invisible sidekick. I'd just be there if you wanted someone to talk to."

"Besides myself?"

Jac's silent a little too long.

"Kidding," I say. But I'm not. "Anyway, if you came with me, what would Loren do for Valentine's Day? You don't want to let him get away, do you?" It takes all the energy I can muster to sound as upbeat as I do.

"Daryn." Her voice takes a dip. "And he'd understand."

"About being alone on Valentine's Day? Not likely. We all know guys like the romance of it even more than we do." By romance I really mean sex, but Jac isn't the kind to dabble. Not till she's rightfully occupying a honeymoon suite on a tropical isle somewhere. Which is why a woman as beautiful as Jaclyn can't seem to hang onto a man.

The question she leaves unasked—the one about David being alone, and we're not just talking about Valentine's Day here—is a testament of her devotion to me. There was a time I'd say I deserved her friendship, but I've not pulled my weight for some time now. Three hundred sixty days to be exact.

"What'll you do?" she asks.

"Listen to the waves. Pretend things are different than they are." I've gone too far with that, so before she can say one sympathetic word I say goodbye.

I've added the morning mugs to the dishwasher along with a dab of soap and turned on the machine, when Ainsley wrestles her way through the back door, cup holder in one hand, pastry sack in the other. She sets both on the kitchen bar, then gives me a hug. Her cheek touches mine, and I hear the kiss that doesn't quite make contact.

"Spice," she says, referring to the muffin. My favorite, not hers. She tolerates spice, but lemon blueberry makes her smile. I sigh again. She pulls a knife out of the drawer, and puts the halves on the two plates I set out. I slip onto the stool across from the one she's scooted onto. "Thanks for letting me barge in."

Barge? Ainsley Marie Vanderpool O'Neal has never barged, not once in her whole life. Now me? I barge, I push, I stomp, I bully. Talk about yin.

At least I used to.

"Decaf," she says, reading the markings on the cup, and hands it to me.

I hate decaf, but I take it anyway, as I have for three hundred sixty days, and lust after the real thing in Ainsley's cup. What we do for love. Or maybe peace. My family, who are rightly convinced that I don't need anything else to stimulate body, soul or spirit, are protecting me from myself. I sigh again, and promise myself it's the last sigh till Ainsley's in her car, backing out of the drive. Then I can sigh my way to oblivion if I want to.

I know I should bring up the subject for which she came and make this as easy for her as I can, but these days I lack the energy to confront even Ainsley, as mild and undemanding as she is. As it turns out, David's the only one I can still dig my heel into. I break off a piece of muffin, and wait. I'm buying time and we both know it.

"So, Bristol, what do you think about all of us going to the cabin? Sweetie?"

What do I think? Besides the fact that they not only colluded on this whole thing, but they scripted it too? I think of the last time we were at the cabin, twelve, no eleven days before Kinsey disappeared. I see the little pallet I made for her to sleep on, beside the bed David and I shared; see the pink jacket she wore, with the white fur around the hood tied up tight around her face to keep her warm in the snow. See the pink of her cheeks. The pink of her nose. Too much pink.

The mocha is too cool and too sweet, but I drink as if my life depends on it, even though my stomach wants to throw up what I've already swallowed. I think for a moment I just might let it, but then I pull in enough air to settle things down.

Ainsley reaches across the counter and touches my free hand. "I know this is a hard week for you." Her gray eyes glisten and threaten to spill over with the compassion she harbors. "We all want to do what we can to get you and Davy through it."

Through it? Am I the only one who has seen the news this morning?

I ease my hand from beneath hers. I can't muster so much as the hint of a tear as I turn away, though there are so many inside I slosh when I walk. I know it's the drugs they have me on, the antidepressants meant to quell every ounce of feeling inside. For my own good, they say.

To get me through. I'd tuck it in my cheek and spit it out when no one is looking, dramatically, like in the movies, if I thought I could handle the fallout. But fear is the one emotion it hasn't annihilated.

As it is, I've been taking half as many as they think I have for a couple of weeks now, enough to keep the darkness at bay, but not enough to make me feel more dead than I already do. With the new refill David just picked up for me I have a nice little stockpile going. What accidental foresight, because the thought of going to sleep and never having to wake to this nightmare again is so compelling, so comforting.

I inch the cup out of my immediate space with the back of my hand, across a grout-line in the tile. There. Off limits, I tell myself, and pretend there's a barrier I can't reach through. I'll dump the rest when Ainsley's gone. When the barrier dissolves.

"I'm going to the beach house. On Thursday." I nod as if that settles it. But I know it doesn't. I know that Ainsley, the peacemaker, is here to do battle.

"Well, but sweetie, it would be so much better for us not to be alone."

I catch the *us* of her argument, but of course she means me. Not even David. Just me.

Two

*M*y eye lands on the calendar that hangs by the fridge. Its heading spells February in quirky letters, its big lavender squares show the phases of the moon and all the special days of the month. Nine in all, including Waitangi Day, which has some significance in New Zealand I know nothing about. There are notes scribbled here and there, dates circled for this appointment or that one. But the calendar is from last year. We never turned the page, not once in twelve months. And here we are again. A million times I've thought, if only it were that simple to stop time. But time doesn't stop. And it doesn't march. What it does is draw out every possible fraction of a moment, to wring as much suffering out of you as it can, more than you ever thought you could live through. And that's the worst part of it: you do. Live through it, I mean.

Thursday is two days away, a long time to wait now that I've made up my mind. I should just throw my bag in the car and leave right this minute. I mean really, what's so special about Thursday as opposed to Tuesday? It's not like there's one single thing to keep me here. Not since— God, oh God, I still see her face, Zachary Martin's mom, standing deathly quiet beside her husband as the Pennsylvania sheriff made the announcement before the spray of microphones this morning. I could not turn away, no matter how much I hated myself for watching, as the camera zoomed in to a close-up of her eyes, capturing that last speck of hope—the one thing holding her together—as it dissolved into a pain infinitely worse than what she already carried.

I can't be Zachary Martin's mom, can't endure one more degree of pain. Not one more. It will take only a minute of strength to fill my mouth and swallow. Surely I can muster that much courage. Surely even I can do that.

But as much as I'd like to leave right now, I see David's eyes and I know I won't leave before Thursday. They haunt me, those eyes, as intensely as they used to draw me in. I know I will hurt him even more than I have before this is over. And I know I should care one way or the other. I really should.

After a long shower I pull on my best jeans and favorite sweater, reach for my perfume, then think better of it, my heart thrumming all the while with the decision I've made, feeling like it's written all over my face. I don't wait for my hair to dry. I pull it up into a clip, toss my purse onto the passenger seat of the oxidized Saturn that used to be David's, and head for the city. I'll be late for my appointment because of Ainsley's visit, but I don't bother to call.

An accident on I-580 brings traffic to a standstill. California drivers don't slow down for anything, fog included. I think about taking the approaching off-ramp, going back home and trying for another day, but now, what other day could there be? So I inch my way forward with the herd until the opportunity to turn back is behind me. The culprit is a United Rentals truck, stopped and facing east in the middle of the westbound lanes, the open trailer it was hauling tipped on its side, its load sprawled across the interstate. The number one lane remains open, but it takes forever for all the lanes of traffic to merge into that one, especially with the many rude drivers who don't understand the etiquette of merging and want to take their Tonka toys straight to the head of the line. But finally I'm through the toll booth and onto the Bay Bridge where there's no turning back.

I'm so relieved I consider turning on the stereo system in the car, something I haven't done in nearly a year. I consider it, but even before that familiar wave of fear puts me in check I know I won't do it. I haven't a clue what CDs remain hidden inside the mouth of the player. All I know is they'll stay there forever if I have my way. I don't want to hear and remember a song that Kinsey would ask me to play again, "One mo' time, Mama," because she liked the beat or the chorus. And not yet four years old. That would indeed plunge me over the edge, but now that I've decided on the time and place, that's something I don't want to relinquish control of.

The sun breaks through the fog, which has rolled back on itself on both sides of the bridge as if a heavenly snow plow has blown through, and the bay is suddenly ablaze with the reflection of sunlight. In my former life it would have elicited a happy response, but now I only narrow my eyes to minimize the glare. It never occurred to me to bring sunglasses as I waded through the fog on my departure from home. My stream of consciousness, which never takes a break, jumps from the snow plow analogy straight to the cabin in South Lake Tahoe. The one I won't be at this weekend. My left hand tightens on the steering wheel.

My cell phone rings, jarring me. I forgot to put on my Bluetooth, mostly because I hate the thing, but I answer the phone anyway. And why not? There are worse transgressions I'll commit before the week is out. What I didn't do was check caller ID first.

"Hey." It's David. Yay.

I think about hitting the End button, faking a dropped call. There'd be nothing to it, considering how much I've faked this past year, but my mouth gets ahead of my thumb.

"Hey."

"I didn't know you were going out this morning." David tries hard not to sound as if he's checking up on me, but we both know he is. He does every day, several times a day. I don't know if he hopes I'll answer, or if he hopes I won't. No. I know that's not true. I'm projecting again.

"I'm—" What do I tell him? I don't think as quickly as I used to, not at all. I haven't told him about my appointment with Jeff Girard, and I'm not sure why. Maybe because it matters so little now what comes from that appointment. "I have errands."

"Are you close enough we could have lunch after?"

"No," I say. "What do you need?"

Well, if that isn't the stupidest, most open-ended question I've asked in a while. What does he need? The list is endless.

"Nothing," he says after a moment. "It can wait."

Not for the first time I wish he'd yell at me. Call me bad names, any one of which I'd deserve, just do something to kill the lethargy. But I imagine he too is projecting, thinking he can navigate me through this if he's only careful enough.

"Well then," I say.

"Okay. See you tonight."

I drop the phone into the gaping cavern of my bag. I'm not taking another call today. Not one.

Within thirty minutes I'm at Embarcadero Center in the financial district of San Francisco. It may be the darling city of the West Coast, but I'm not a city girl. It is, at least, a glorious day, but at this time of year it won't last long. I hope to get home to Walnut Creek before the fog returns. I wind my way down to the fourth and final level of the parking garage of Embarcadero One before I find a spot for the Saturn. I park and walk to the elevator, and push the button with the gold 34. I hold my stomach, alone in the car, but only until it makes the first of nine stops on its way up. By the time it reaches my floor I have to press through a mass of bodies, brief cases and shopping bags to exit the car.

The decorators of the offices of I'm Just Sayin' Greeting Cards adhere to the minimalist, less-is-more style that I love. But when you have a view of the glistening bay, the bridge, Treasure, Yerba Buena, and Alcatraz Islands through the glass wall, capped as it is today by a perfect sky, minimalist is the way to go.

The receptionist, like the office she graces, is a striking beauty of the minimalist variety. Perfect hair, perfect makeup, perfect everything, with nothing overdone. Her hands are striking, with long, musical fingers, though why I think of them as musical or why they capture my attention in the first place I don't really know. But I love that her fingernails are real and unadorned except for a light, blushing gloss. They too are long and not quite squared at the ends, which I also love. I hate the thick, boxy look that everyone wears these days. She has a thin gold band on her left pinky finger, that goes to just below the middle knuckle. There's no other jewelry besides that tiny ring. The minimalist in me can hardly draw my eyes from those hands.

Like the flash of a movie scene that's gone in a blink, I remember a velvet-lined box that smelled of forest when you opened it, and a ring, almost identical to the one on this young woman's finger. The box was the centerpiece on a round-edged dresser in my grandmother's bedroom—my maternal grand-mother, oddly enough—the ring in one of its diminutive drawers. I couldn't have been more than three the last time I was in her home, now all of a sudden I wonder about that ring, can feel it on my three-year-old finger. But I know for sure it wasn't mine.

"I have an appointment with Jeff Girard," I say to the receptionist, who really should be doing something grander, more visible to a world that would adore her. The pronouncement sounds more like a question. I feel a bit off kilter from the flashback.

She doesn't pick up a phone, press an intercom button, or refer to an appointment calendar. Instead she rises to a height I have to look up to, a height enhanced by the heels that seem like appendages, she wears them so well. She walks to one of the four shell-like foyers and taps on the door. I'm astounded by her perfection, every time.

"Ms. Taylor," she says in a voice exactly as you'd expect. She ushers me through the doorway where Jeff Girard stands waiting to greet me. I feel things I haven't felt in forever as his hand touches my back to usher me deeper into his office. I sit in the chair he offers, while he leans against his desk, facing me, his ankles and arms crossed. His smile is seductive. Everything about him is.

His office could be used for a movie shoot, maybe something with

Michael Douglas, it's that spectacular, especially enhanced as it is by the view. Even the smell is spectacular, a blend of plush carpet and the subtle spice of cologne.

"I was beginning to think you might not come," he says.

"My sister"—I shrug—"stopped by."

"It's alright. We don't need reservations."

"Reservations?"

He glances at his watch. "Since it's gotten late I thought we'd make this a lunch meeting. It's that or I don't eat till dinner, and quite honestly I'm famished."

"I'm not—" my hand sweeps down the front of me, taking in my sweater, my jeans, completing my thought.

"We're good," he says, he who is dressed to perfection.

And I know he's right. This is California, after all. And as much as I don't want to, I feel compelled to relent.

We ride the elevator down to street level and follow the curve of the sidewalk to Fisherman's Wharf. It's such a remarkable day for February. Gulls swoop and swell over the water like miniature kites. The breeze is salty, fishy, delicious. It seems everyone is out, enjoying this window on spring. Occasionally my shoulder brushes Jeff's as one or the other of us dodges other pedestrians or rollerbladers. I can hardly stand the current this sends through me, unused to feeling anything as I am.

"Don't tell me you're one who can come into the City and not have a bowl of clam chowder," he says as we walk.

I reply with a weak smile. He seems not to notice my discomfort.

We don't wait in line at Castagnola's, but are immediately shown to a window table with a perfect view of the bay. The waiter fills our water glasses, sets the carafe on the table, then unfolds my napkin and drapes it across my jeans. Behind that practiced smile I bet he's thinking, *what a slug*. When he's gone, Jeff folds his hands, leans toward me and smiles. It's the smile, I believe, that safeguards his position at I'm Just Sayin' in spite of the overwhelming downturn in the economy. I bet it continues to see him through.

"We like the line," he says. "Very original. There are how many cards in all?"

"Thirty. For now." I don't feel nervous or excited, not like I did eighteen months ago. When it mattered. "Get well, birthday, baby shower, baby congrats."

"Mother's Day?"

I feel as though I've been whacked in the heart, and it takes all my willpower not to flinch. "And Father's Day."

"Appropriate for a line called Baby Talk, which we also like."

"I'm continuing to add to each of the categories."

"And you're sure I can't tempt you away from freelance?"

He's offered me a job as a staff designer twice before. I turn him down a third time for a couple of good reasons. One, I don't care enough anymore. And two, I don't care enough anymore. He smiles and my eyes are drawn to his mouth, then I tell myself the truth. It's the mouth that keeps me from accepting the job. For I'm afraid he surely could tempt me, but it has nothing to do with giving up freelance. I compare his lips to David's lips, trying to remember when my husband's had the same allure. It's only the arrival of our waiter that draws me back to safe ground.

Jeff nods at me and I give the young guy my selection. A bowl of clam chowder, though I'm not the least bit hungry. Jeff orders and we're alone again, relatively speaking.

"I'll have Brooke draw up the contract." Brooke is the bling in the outer office at I'm Just Sayin'. "I'll have her send it to you next week."

"Next week?"

That won't work. At all.

"Is that a problem?"

"Well, I— I just—"

As he waits for me to complete my thought, I get the sense that he relishes the control he wields over me.

"... hoped we could get it nailed down this week."

He retrieves his phone from his shirt pocket and opens his calendar. "Let's see. Could you come in Friday morning? Nine-thirty?"

"Friday, no. No, I'll be out of town."

"Well then, Monday morning is the best I can do."

"I'm going to Half Moon Bay on Thursday." I don't know why I offer this.

"Hmm. I realize it's a bit of a detour, but maybe you and your husband could stop by on your way? I'd like to meet him."

I bite the inside of my lip before I say, "David won't be with me." Too late I remember it's Valentine's weekend, and how odd is that?

He studies me long enough that I grow uncomfortable. "You know, I'm heading to Carmel on Saturday. I go right through Half Moon Bay. I could bring the contract by for you to sign."

I look down and brush imaginary crumbs from the napkin in my lap, then look across the table at him. "I'll come by Thursday morning."

His smile is practiced as he checks his calendar again. "Oh. I'm afraid I spoke too soon. Looks like I'll be out of the office Thursday."

And why does that matter? I want to ask. Must you be here for me to sign the stupid contract?

"So it looks like it has to be Monday."

But Monday won't work and I know he knows that. I draw in a breath, let it out slowly. "What time on Saturday?"

"Why don't I call when I know for sure?"

I feel myself go rigid, then reach for my purse to find something to write on, but he slides his business card across the table and hands me his pen. "Just jot your number on the back." I comply, and he smiles again as he slips the card in his pocket.

I'm not stupid, not clueless. I know what's going on here, know when I'm being played, though why Jeff Girard would be the least bit interested in me I can't begin to imagine. He lives for the conquest, I decide. It's that and nothing more. Well, fine. I'll play along, at least until I get that contract signed. But buyer beware, I tell myself, because Jeff Girard is that enticing. In another time and place I could get myself burned.

I don't know why I care so much about this contract, this sale that doesn't matter now, but I do. It has nothing to do with David and everything to do with Kinsey, and I guess that's all the reason I need.

My phone sounds from deep within my bag. It's not my ringtone, signaling a call; it's the series of beeps that announces a text message. It's David, I know without looking. He's taken to doing this lately, texting me these little phrases you might read in a Hallmark card between lovers. My jaw clenches and I swear under my breath, using words I never used to employ.

Jeff leans back in his chair, watching me. "You want to get that?"

I reach down, snap shut the opening of my bag, and make myself relax. "No."

There's a look in his eyes as if he knows exactly what's going on here, though he couldn't possibly. The smile never leaves his lips as he makes small talk during the lunch I barely touch. When he walks me back to his building, he offers to walk me to my car, but I insist we part at the elevators. I've been humiliated enough for one day. He doesn't need to see the heap I drive now.

"I'll see you this weekend," he says as he steps into the executive elevator. The last thing I see as the doors slide closed is that smile. That dangerous smile.

Three

*H*ow do you lose a child?

It's not so hard, really. You simply make one irredeemable choice. You ignore the warning bell that rings in your head, because it's not a bell at all, you know? It's just the gnat of a thought that's too easily brushed aside. But in the scheme of things, it turns out that it's the mother of all bells, made up of all the noise in the universe. You just don't happen to hear it. Can you imagine?

Since that first irredeemable choice was so easy, I'm planning another. But I'm finding the serendipitous ones, the ones that are completely spontaneous, are so much easier. It's one of those mysteries of the universe, like blinking out your last contact lens into the sink just as the water is swirling down your vanity drain along with the toothpaste you swished out of your mouth. You could try to do the same thing on purpose for a hundred years and never manage to do it.

As David and I sit across from each other at the dinner table, he pretends not to enjoy his meal. He downplays everything on my account these days. He toys with every bite, as I do in earnest, but he manages to clean his plate, while I don't even come close. I rebuke myself for every morsel I swallow, for going through the motions of normalcy when things are so colossally abnormal.

I try to remember what dinner was like a year ago, the day before *that* day, when a little girl's laughter was always on the menu. I try to remember how much I loved the three of us at the table back then, together again after a day apart. What I remember instead is how much I hated being apart in the first place. When you're trapped in the dark, it's hard to remember the light. Still I try. Try to recall what our last supper was, and whether Kinsey liked it. I've wracked my brain for three hundred sixty days now to remember all the details of the last good day of our lives. There are so many gaps. It's a puzzle I work at even in my sleep. Occasionally I find a missing part, and it's like a gulp of air in my drowningness. I just want to remember the last 3:02 my daughter and I were together, the last 7:49. The glow of Kinsey's skin in the last bath I gave her, the last bedtime story I made up—because made-up stories were the ones she liked best. Is that too much to ask, I ask? The detectives, who now call this a cold case—as they called the Martin case until this morning—tell us as kindly as possible to accept that our little girl is not coming home. Well. How do you do that? How the—

"Did you get your errands run?"

The tone of David's voice, the look on his face, exudes hope, not for anything so mundane as the completion of my errands, but that maybe this time, with this question, I'll toss him the smallest of bones along with my words. That I'll care. For him, his question, anything at all would be enough for David. But the thing is, I don't. His head rests in his left hand, a familiar pose these days, and I know he's as weary as I. How he summons the energy to put one kind word in front of another is beyond me.

I'd hate me if I were him. As much as I possibly could.

"I did, yes. It was nice to see the sun."

A cloud crosses David's face. "The fog didn't lift all day. Not here."

I want to clamp my mouth shut at such a stupid slip-up. The best I can do is clamp my jaws, which I do. I could tell him I went into the city. After all, I have the right to come and go as I choose. Instead I pick up our plates and carry them to the sink. Guilt flushes my face with a broad brush. Guilt because of the feelings stirred up by that impossible smile of Jeff Girard's. "Maybe it was yesterday."

David clears the few remaining items off the table, sets the salt and pepper shakers back on the stove top, puts the butter in the cupboard, a helper I could do without. "Thanks for dinner." He touches the small of my back, a gesture to go with his words, his hand covering the print of Jeff's hand.

"Sure," I say. I feel nothing for David. Nothing at all. No, that's not entirely true. For I know there's a seething so deep inside it barely registers. But when and if it surfaces it will be with the force of a hurricane.

When he's gone I center the salt and pepper shakers, just so, on their little platform. He never gets it right. Doesn't even know there's a right to get wrong. Isn't that the story of our lives? Of my life? The one innocent mistake I didn't know could go so terribly wrong? I drag that thought around like my own corpse, naked before God with the knowledge of my sin.

Since the public frenzy died down two or three months after Kinsey's disappearance, with the abduction of another child in another place—a child with the name of Zachary Martin—and I no longer need a protector, I've had one goal for the few waking hours David and I spend together: keep our words and contact as minimal as possible. I do that by staying as occupied as I can in any room where he isn't. Yes, I know how bad that sounds, to use and then discard for my own selfish needs. But you don't know what it is to see your own pitiful reflection in eyes like David's eyes.

Because they're Kinsey's eyes too, remember.

But tonight he seeks me out. He taps on the door to my office, which I mistakenly didn't close all the way, and takes a couple of steps past the threshold. His hands are loosely tucked into the pockets of his jeans. I recall for an instant how I used to love the way David wears a pair of jeans.

"Working on a new design?"

It's a rhetorical question, for it's clear that's exactly what I'm doing. Not just because Jeff requested a set of Thinking of You cards to go with my Baby Talk line, but because it's the best excuse I have for being alone. I want nothing more than to get out of here Thursday morning with my plan still intact, without my discerning husband discerning the notions of my heart, which feel as visible as the mark of Cain on my forehead.

"I sold the line today."

He takes another step toward me. "Well, babe, that's, that's great." I don't need to see the question on his face to know he's wondering why I didn't say so before now. "With—"

"I'm Just Sayin'."

"Really? I didn't know you were even—"

"I wanted to wait till I knew for sure."

"Well, that's great," he says again. But I know the fact that it comes much too late to matter hasn't escaped his notice any more than it has mine.

Without invitation he sits in the only other chair in my office, rests his elbows on the arms, and folds his hands. So, this is not a casual visit, as if there were the slightest chance it would be. I don't even try to stifle the sigh that comes from that deep place within.

"I know you want to get away this weekend, Bristol. I get that, I really do. So do I. And if you don't want to go to the cabin, we could go wherever you'd like." I tense at the word *we*, and he hesitates, but only for a moment. "The beach house if that's where you want to go. Anywhere. You name it."

He has that "come on, Bristol, please" tone to his voice, the same tone Kinsey began to use at bedtime shortly after we moved her from her crib into the youth bed Ainsley gave her, that had belonged to either Sam or Eli. Once she realized she could get out of her new little bed anytime she wanted, she did. At first she'd just plunk her way down the stairs and show up, happy to be back among the wide awake, certain we'd be happy too. It wasn't long before she realized she needed a reason to get up, and that's when the fun began. It was fun for a while, anyway.

We hear her pj'd feet scuffling down the oak stairway. I love that the stairs aren't carpeted, because who wants to vacuum stairs? I remember thinking this as I listen to her progress. She's slower making her entrance now that she knows how swift our reaction can be. I lean forward to look around David's chair, to see the doorway she'll appear in any moment now. David and I exchange a mirth-filled glance. We haven't yet grown weary of Kinsey's bedtime shenanigans. Sure enough, she inches her way from the foyer into the living room, silent as a shadow, her pjs splashed with balloons in all the primary colors. When we both turn our eyes on her she says, presenting her hands in a palms-up display as if making her case, "Guys, can I just hang out with you for a little while?" Can I just ... ? My brows disappear beneath the bangs that swoop across my forehead, I press my lips together to keep from laughing. It's still four months till she turns three, and she says such a thing? I write this down on the ledger of my mind to add later to her baby book as I scoop her up and carry her back up the stairs. "Please," she wails, stretching it into at least three syllables. "Daddy! Help!"

My hand grips the pencil I've been sketching with, and I'm suddenly cold. I can't stop the tremor that rises up through the void that used to house the vital parts of me, the parts no human eye can see. Where do they go, those parts, when you die inside? Is there a boneyard for souls, do you think?

"I do want to go to the beach house," I say. "Alone."

"Bristol, I know things have been off between us"—he's looking everywhere but at me now—"for a while."

"A while?"

He falters, then finds his footing again. "But somehow we have to get things back to normal."

"Normal? Really. How, David, do you suppose that is ever going to happen? Shall we ask the Martins about normal?" I see by the shadow that crosses his face that he's heard the news, news he'd hoped till this moment I hadn't heard. "Yeah, we can all call it the new normal. How's that?"

"Bristol, don't. Don't. It's sad what happened to that little boy, but there's no connection between him and Kinsey. None."

"Sad? Sad?"

"Okay, it's tragic, horrific, whatever you want to call it, it's all that and more. I get that. But Kinsey isn't Zachary Martin." He severely punctuates each word.

"Yes. All that and more. Do you know what happened to him? He was—"

"Stop. Just stop." David stands, his arms drawn close to his body as if he's as cold as I am. His hands are interlinked at his mouth like he's about to whistle with his thumbs the way boys will do. Of course he won't, but that's how he looks. And young, he looks young. And scared. Well, I can't help that now.

He drops his arms and takes a step toward me, though he maintains the buffer between us. The DMZ as I've come to think of it. He's smart that way, David is. "Bree, come on, we have to talk about this. We have to figure out how to get back to us. You and me."

It's all I can do not to cry out with the pain as his words slice through the shell that's supposed to protect me. "There is no you and me, David. It stopped being you and me the day Kinsey was born. No, the day Kinsey was conceived, David. We don't just erase the fact that We Have a Daughter."

"I know that, Bree." He takes another step closer. "But we can't lose *us* while we're looking for her."

He's in my space now, down on one knee as if he's about to propose. It would strike me as funny, if anything could. I push back in my chair, withdraw as much into myself as I can. "Looking? Looking?! Who's looking, David? Not the cops, who think we ought to just plan the funeral first thing in the morning. Not you. Not me. No one is looking."

He leans away from me, his head in his hands again. "I look. Every time I leave this house, everywhere I go. The same way you do. Ainsley's at the headquarters every morning Monday through Friday without fail, and Sheila's there three afternoons a week and most Saturdays."

What he doesn't say but clearly implies is that I'm not at the headquarters. Haven't been for months. And with all that time on my hands. But he's not the one who took the calls, the ones that generated so much hope, and the ones that ... didn't. It wasn't his heart that raced every time the phone rang, and all but stopped when the crazies called. So many crazies.

"We're looking," David says, "all of us. And we'll find her."

The way his eyes look off to the side when he says those last four words tells me one thing: he does not expect to find her alive.

"I don't want her found," I say, making my meaning painfully clear. "I want her home."

———————

When he's asleep, or pretends to be, I do what I've done every night for the past three hundred sixty nights. I slip out of bed and go to Kinsey's room. She was born at a time when chocolate brown was added to pink to become the new baby girl hue. Her room is still done in those colors. I step over the carpeted threshold and close the door behind me with just the whisper of a sound. Not that David doesn't know I'm here every single night, and not that I might disturb him with my outpouring of sorrow—never mind that it's a block of ice inside me that never melts—but because I don't want to share what's left of Kinsey with anyone, not even her father. Especially not her father.

On Kinsey's fourth birthday—the one *we* missed, but not *her*. I pray in the deepest place within me that she didn't miss it—I tripled up on my soul-killing drugs, darkened my bedroom as best I could, and slept through the worst part of the day. It was three weeks after what would have been Christmas. Late that night when my eyes finally opened and wouldn't shut again for hours, I crept into her room—I don't know why stealth is so important to my ritual, but it is—lay my head on her pillow, and held her blanket close to my face. It was all that kept me breathing. In the near darkness I could hear her. So very clearly.

"Want get cothy, Mama," Kinsey says in her two-year-old voice.

"Would you believe," I reply, "that I was thinking that very thing? I want to get cozy too, baby girl." I'm sitting just long enough for the kitchen floor to dry. It's Friday morning, and on Friday mornings, among other cleaning chores, I mop. I lift her onto my lap and tuck her blanket around us. She leans into me.

"Cothy," she says again, wearing the most contented smile, but her voice fades even as she speaks the word.

And here I am again. I stand in the dark, getting my bearings, taking in what's left of her essence. The scent of shampoo I'd wash her baby hair with lingers, as does the scent of her skin, soft and pure. I don't imagine this, I know I don't. It's real. It's strongest on her pillow. I'd know it anywhere, that Kinsey smell. A mama knowing her cub. I try as I do every night to remember who gave her the blanket, the white and yellow one, crocheted, or maybe knitted, I don't know, that she's slept with forever. I'm assaulted with this one thought every time: does she cry for it? At night, does she cry?

Lord, I wish I could. Wish I could void myself of the misery I've brought on us all.

I pray here, and only here, as I kneel beside her bed. I'm strong by day in my agnosticism, a hypocrite by night when it's just me and truth. And so I plead, I beg. And promise. Oh the things I promise. The list is desperate and endless. I won't do this, I will do that, if only. Oh, God, if only. We've yet to strike a deal, he and I, but I keep trying to find that one persuasive vow, that thing that will turn his ear in my direction. The problem is my heart. You'd be appalled at the things it tries to hide. I'm not fooling anyone, not a soul. Certainly not an omniscient God. And still I bargain.

But the way I see it, a mother has a right to her baby, plain and simple. That should give me the advantage in the answered prayer category. Any right-thinking person would agree. But here we are three hundred sixty days later, and Kinsey's bed is still empty at night. I'd never thought of God as arbitrary before this. Or capricious. Now, it's hard to see him any other way. Because if I were God this is one prayer I wouldn't have to think twice about before granting. And I'd make real sure the beast that took my baby girl never took another child. Or another breath. Oh, the things I would do if I were God.

Four

I've been to Dante's inferno, to that "deep place where the sun is silent," with no rescuer in sight. Not that I want a rescuer. I want more than anything to pronounce my own judgment, to work out my own damnation. I know of no other way to find relief. But for a while, the DA was bent on helping me along with the process.

Filicide. I had to look up the word the first time I heard it. Obviously it has to do with taking a life. As do the words homicide, suicide, fratricide, sororicide, matricide, genocide, uxoricide—which is the murder of a wife by her husband. Oddly, I can't find the word for the murder of a husband by his wife. One might surmise it's always justified, but that's just my own opinion.

I'd have selected matricide on a multiple choice test as the thing they thought me guilty of, rather than filicide. But when you look at all the words together you realize the prefix refers to the one killed, not the one doing the killing.

The word came up repeatedly on the non-stop news shows as talking heads bandied about my name and Kinsey's along with that word, so sure they'd figured out the whys and wherefores of what happened that morning. All that remained was to find the body and the answers would fall into place. Clips of me talking about the disappearance of Kinsey were constantly compared with clips of Susan Smith talking about the disappearance of her two young sons back in '94. And of Casey Anthony, regarding the death of her daughter Caylee. I learned early on not to speak within a hundred yards of a camera or microphone, but not soon enough. With two or three statements the damage was done, and there we were, Susan, Casey and me, crying for our children in that panicked, falsetto voice, birds of a feather in the public eye.

I'd known Susan was guilty the moment I heard her speak. Knew she tried hard to be convincing, and she was. Only not in the way she intended. It made me sick to my stomach, then and now, to think that a mother could intentionally drown her own helpless boys. Just strap them into their car seats and send them into a lake, their frightened, trusting eyes watching her every move, the last undying face they'd ever see. And stunned that I—a woman who loved her daughter as profoundly as one can—should be equated with a woman like that.

Or with Casey, whose not-guilty verdict did nothing to dispel my opinion.

That's when they went to my doctor for the antidepressants, David and Ainsley. When all those comparisons were being made.

I was twenty-two at the time of Susan's crime, and had graduated from USF a few months before. David and I hadn't yet met and I was only casually dating another guy or two. Marriage and motherhood were things I planned for the future but was in no hurry for. Still, even a woman who hasn't given birth has a strong maternal instinct, and I was as horrified as the rest of the world when the truth came out about Susan Smith.

I was far more horrified when the spotlight of the investigation of my own child's disappearance homed in on me.

I was thirty-six when McKinsey was born. And. Oh. My. Lord. I was a rare bud suddenly blossomed open, full and fragrant, like it was my day of birth as well as hers. All my senses came fully alive the moment she left my body in a baptism of water and blood. And yet the resplendence of it was as much pain as it was ecstasy in its immensity. I was as near death as I was glorification, right at that spot where both ends of the spectrum unite.

I'd come alive in degrees: my pubescent body morphing me from girl to woman—not nearly soon enough or fully enough for my satisfaction; the feelings awakened by my first real kiss; my first clumsy interlude with David. But when they placed the naked little body of my daughter on my heaving chest, the groans of childbirth still in my throat, I knew this is what I'd been created for.

And they thought I could kill that.

The polygraph is what absolved me. Odd, considering the weight of my guilt.

The street lamp that casts a hint of its subdued light into Kinsey's room every night shuts off at the earliest sign of dawn. I separate two slats of the blinds that cover her window and peer out through the gauzy gray of morning at the resurrected memorial mound, as we've come to call it, that collection of candles, cards, balloons, etcetera, that people leave on our front lawn in honor of Kinsey. In the early days of losing her it's all we could do to keep up with the mountain of items. Dad and Sissy, and Ainsley and Grady would take carloads of dolls, toys and stuffed animals to area hospitals, until the pediatric wards were drowning in them and they asked us not to bring any more. After that they went to the various Goodwill stores throughout the Bay Area. We'd toss the balloons after the helium seeped out, gather up the wilted flowers in time for the trash collection each week, and toss the candles as well. But I've kept the cards, every single one. I just haven't read them.

I tell myself I will, but now, well, now I won't have time.

It was a relief when people stopped coming, stopped bringing their children to deliver their offerings or light a candle for the lost little girl. But with the anniversary looming, they've begun to come again. I know they have the best intentions, but to me it seems a morbid fascination. And what of the fear *the lost little girl* must incite in the hearts of those children?

I close the blinds on the depressing image, a constant reminder of what we could never forget in the first place, and turn away from the window, feeling as though there are weights attached to my heart.

"Let her be cared for. Please."

I think or say that out loud a thousand times a day at least. Let her be cared for. I don't consider it a prayer, which I do consider a complete waste of whatever hope I have left, or had left before this morning. No, not a prayer, but a reasonable request, considering. And yet, even now I remember that girl in Utah, the one they found, and the hope that swells within me nearly breaks me apart.

But Zachary Martin now trumps everything. Zachary Martin with his trusting brown eyes and his short, spiked hair that makes him look like such a little man. But he'll never be a man, not now. He'll never be again, period, except in the heart of that woman whose eyes I watched die. And why? Why? For some sick devil's pleasure?

What an irony my life has turned out to be. On one side there's a mother who ran fast and hard out of my life even before I could say her name; and on the other, there's a daughter who's just as gone. A magnet in reverse is how I feel. What would that be, I wonder? Is there a word for such a thing? I suppose I should invest some time in the search, to learn more about the thing that I am. Oh I know there are antonyms for what a magnet does: repel, repulse, reject; but for the repelling magnet itself? That's what I'd like to know.

Dad tried hard in the early years of my and Ainsley's lives to convince us it was perfectly normal to have a mother stuff everything she owned into the front of a Bug and never look back. But the pathetic, pitying look in the eyes of everyone else we knew told us otherwise. Starting with Grandma Vanderpool, who became caregiver to one- and two-year-old girls overnight. In no time at all she looked as if she might like to find a Bug of her own. That thought may have sprung from my own toddling insecurities. Suffice it to say, there's never been much of a bond between us and Grandma. No wonder Dad yielded to Sissy's overtures without a fight. And you could say it's worked out for the best. You could say that.

I leave Kinsey's room and slip into bed. I'm asleep before David rises for the day. The nightmare, of course, is always the same, though I don't think it qualifies as a bona fide dream, because what it actually is, is my unchecked mind refusing to pause the video of what happened that day. Unlike some people who remember dreams as though they were a DVD they could play at will, capturing the fine points of a dream for me is like trying to hold smoke in my hand. But every part of this memory is painfully clear. I'm running toward the space where I left my car idling in the parking lot while I hurried back into the preschool to get Kinsey's Amoxicillin, forgotten in the office refrigerator. They'd called only an hour after I'd dropped her off that morning, her fever spiking again. And so I'd left work to get her, because David was working across the bay.

I left Kinsey in the backseat, strapped in her safety seat, because she'd already nodded off, her cheeks cherry red from the effects of the fever. Leaving her in the car was so much easier than taking her out and starting all over again, when I was merely running into the office, just through those double doors, where I could still see my car if I craned my neck just so. It's not more than thirty yards total. And the monitor who was right there on the playground with the recess kids gave me the A-OK sign when I called to her, asking her to keep an eye on the car if she wouldn't mind. Afterwards, when the police questioned her, she said she didn't remember any of that, but I swear she gave me the sign. I swear it.

She did remember seeing a small, dirty-white truck on campus for several mornings previous to the stealing of Kinsey. She didn't, however, think it was worth reporting to anyone. But it was there, abandoned by whoever stole my car with my daughter inside. It too had been stolen a few days before. My car was found a day or two later, abandoned in a remote part of the Delta, found by a farmer plowing his cornfields. It's been parked at my dad's house since the police released it back to us, because I can't stand the sight of it. There were no fingerprints or anything else to help identify the kidnapper. No trace of where he'd gone with our baby girl. No trace at all.

It's surreal, in the dream as it was in real life, when I come out of the office to an empty parking space. I look around, thinking I'm sure that's where I left the car. But it had to be a different space, because it isn't there.

Oh, God, it isn't there.

The panic that surges through me is the most horrible thing I've ever felt. Someone has taken my car? With my daughter in the backseat? Do they not know my child is in the backseat?

"Oh, God. Oh, God!" I scream.

The monitor, whose attention is on the three boys tumbling down the slide, turns with a startled look on her face and begins to jog toward me.

"My car! Where's my car? Kinsey's in my car!"

The monitor—I can't remember her name—acts confused, shakes her head, raises her hands, palms up, in a what-do-you-mean manner.

"My car! It's gone! My daughter—"

My heart is beating fast and hard, my breath comes the same. I'm gasping for something with which to fill my lungs.

"What do I do? What do I do? A phone! I need a phone!" Because my phone is in the missing car, in the pocket of my purse.

But there isn't a phone. The monitor hesitates a moment, looking back at her charges, then runs to the office. In no time at all Mrs. Perez, the director of the preschool, is at my side, trying to calm me down, trying to make sense out of something that can't possibly make sense.

The dream is always the same. Only a deeply drug-induced sleep offers a respite for a few blessed hours at a time—though I can't remember the last time I rewarded myself with that. When I wake, the nightmare continues.

The coffee smells fresher than it should for three hours old as I follow its aroma to the kitchen. I retrieve my mommy & me mug out of the dishwasher—it's the only one I use now—and reach for the coffee pot.

"'Morning."

I jump like a fool and clutch my heart with my free hand as I respond in the typical startled manner.

"What are you doing?" It's ten o'clock, two and a half hours after David should have left for work. I don't even try to hide my irritation. If he had caused me to break that mug, that would have been it. The more informed talking heads would have for sure been bandying about that word in association with my name, the one I can't find, the one used when a wife kills her husband. Okay, maybe not for real, but trust me when I say I've committed murder in my heart, and more than once. See what I mean about the secrets it hides?

"We need to talk, Bree."

Every nerve in my body is on high alert. I leave the mug by the pot and turn back toward the stairs, but David gets up and follows me. I stop in the middle of the hall and turn on him like Bilbo Baggins in that scene with the ring. I remember when I could really pitch a fit. So does just about everyone who knows me well. That kind of fit would take more spirit than I possess these days, but I give it my best shot.

"Don't make this a bigger issue than it is, David. I'm going. Leave it alone."

He takes a tentative step toward me. "I haven't asked anything from you during this whole ordeal, not anything. But now I'm asking that you let us get through this together. Babe, we need each other, now more than ever." His eyes plead more than his voice.

"Haven't asked for anything? Are you kidding me? What more could you ask for?"

That stops him cold. "What do you mean?" He appears to be puzzled. I must say, it's a good act.

"Why do you think this happened, David? Why did we lose Kinsey?"

I get this picture in my head all of a sudden of Ainsley and me. We're young girls pricking both ends of an eggshell with a large safety pin, and blowing. Sissy is there, cheering us on as the mucous-white and yellow contents shimmy into a bowl. Had to have been a science project for one of us, though I can't remember if it was Ainsley's or mine. But I can practically see David's heart and soul being blown right out of him, just like that egg, as he stands here before me. That's how my crazy mind works these days. The rabbit trails are peculiar and endless.

"What are you saying?"

Lord, I swear I can hardly stand to look at his eyes. "She should not have been going to preschool. She should have been home with me."

"She was better," he says, so missing my point. "The doctor said—"

"Not for the day, David. Forever. We talked about that before we ever had a family. I would always be home with our babies. Always. I was thirty-five before I got pregnant for a reason. This is not new information."

"Things happen, Bree, beyond our control. You can't blame me for the economy. I mean, what—"

"I can blame you for the second loan we took out on the house, which sent me back to work."

"Bristol, you could have been going to the grocery store, or to your dad's."

"But I wasn't. I was going to work, and that's your fault. If I'd been going to the store, or my dad's"—I don't even try to camouflage the sarcasm—"I wouldn't have had to go back in for Kinsey's medicine, now would I?"

My voice is one of those voices that sounds perpetually like I'm going into or out of laryngitis. It breaks all the time. There are singers whose sound is actually enhanced by that vocal imperfection, sort of their stock in trade. But I bet they hate it as much as I do. David says it's one of the first things he noticed about me. Says he thought it was sexy. I wonder what he thinks now.

"We had to keep the business going."

"We could have sold the house."

"Bree, we talked about that, about the importance of holding on." He sounds more desperate than frustrated. Me, I'd be furious.

"And you decided."

He shifts from one foot to the other. "You've been carrying that around all this time?"

I know the part he's left unsaid, the part about my culpability. I'm the one who left our daughter in the car, after all. David's never once brought it up. Not so much as hinted. He's by far the better man, I know that all too well. But I'm not the only guilt-bearer here. I just can't figure out which of us is the splinter and which is the beam. "Yeah, I'm the one whose stupidity is to blame, but you broke your word to me and that's why this happened. We did this. To each other, to Kinsey, we did this."

He stands there for a moment or two, giving me a chance to recant, to say it's all okay. Peace, love, and all that stuff. But it will never be okay. Not ever. He leaves without another word. And I can breathe again.

Five

I'd cut off my hand for the chance to sketch Kinsey's portrait. Why I waited until it was too late is a question that will haunt me as long as I live. And beyond, I fear. I know it's because I could never keep her still long enough, but I should have tried. I should have. I could use a photo now, sure, but what's the point of that? I tuck my sketch pad between the few clothes I've packed for the trip to the beach house. This weekend I intend to design the cards Jeff asked for. I want the package complete when I place it and the signed contract in his hands. I hate loose ends.

I haven't heard the mechanical hum of the garage door as it rolls open, so I know David is downstairs waiting. Again. Know he wants one more chance to change my mind, to keep me with him this weekend, to share the intrusive spotlight of the media and anything else that will mark this horrid anniversary. The focus on our family has intensified in the days since Zachary's body was identified, so that spotlight burns hotter than ever. There's not enough left of me to hold up under the scrutiny. If that's unfair to David, so be it.

I get this burst of whatever it is that's released in a moment of fear when I recall how close I was to turning toward him during the night when he reached for my nightgown. It's a thing with David, he likes to rub the fabric with his fingertips when he thinks I'm asleep, like a child with the edge of its blanket. Like Kinsey.

I used to think it was sweet, this connection he craved, but I've come to think of *sweet* as a juvenile term, very junior- highish. Nothing is sweet. And if it is, keep it away from me. As for David's cravings, keep those away from me too. Please and thank you. But last night, wow, all I can say is my defenses were down. Or something. When I felt his fingertips so near my back, with just the lightness of the fabric between my skin and his touch, I can't tell you how much I wanted his arms around me, to be in that safe place that David used to be. He felt my body tense, and, misreading the sign, his hand moved away. The moment was gone. Thank God, it was gone.

It's so much better this way.

And now he's downstairs waiting. Well, there's nothing to do but get it over with.

I take one last look around, though I've packed more than I need, even for this trip. Then I slip into Kinsey's room and sink to my knees by her bed. Lord, I'd do anything for a spigot with a handle I could turn to release the river of tears dammed up inside. But there's no spigot, no release. Every cell in my body bulges with the fullness of my misery. I'm bloated with grief. Kinsey's blanket is soft against my face. I hold her scent in as long as I can. On a whim I unzip my bag and slip the blanket inside. I'm so glad I thought to do that.

I'm on the bottom stair when a loud knock sounds at the front door. Three loud knocks to be exact, with a ta-da-DAH beat. Sissy's trademark greeting. I can't believe this. I swear I can't. I'd just go straight to the garage, ignore David and the knocking that continues, but Sissy has my car blocked in with that stupid Land Rover of hers. I'd bet anything she has. Before I gather the sense to respond one way or the other, David is at the door. He turns the deadbolt that only gets locked at night because he remembers to do it. He gives me a puzzled shrug as he opens the door, but I don't know who he thinks he's kidding. Certainly not me. If he thinks this is going to work, he doesn't know how determined I am.

"'Morning." Sissy steps past David into the house. "What a day, huh?"

From what I can tell the coastal fog that's hung over the town for days hasn't gone anywhere, but you couldn't tell it by Sissy's greeting. Or by the capris and flip flops she's wearing. What in the—

Ainsley steps in behind her. "Hey."

Her level of enthusiasm doesn't quite rise to Sissy's, but our once-a-sixth-grade-teacher-always-a-sixth-grade-teacher stepmother would give her an A for effort. Me, I have something else entirely in mind.

David is about to close the door when Jac sticks her head in. "Hi there." She lingers half in, half out, the only one smart enough to be afraid.

"What is this?" There's no mistaking the tenor of my voice.

My eyes take them all in, then land on David for the answer, but he holds up his hands and shakes his head, so like the preschool monitor it gives me the creeps. "I don't— Really, I have no—" He shakes his head again.

I look to Sissy and repeat my question.

"Girls' getaway." There's not a hint of an apology in her voice. "This all you got for three days?"

I squeeze the handle of the bag nearest her and pull back as she reaches for it. "Girls' *what*?"

"Getaway." Sissy uses her teacher voice and I falter just the slightest out of habit. She crosses her arms and smiles. It's the exact look and stance that always followed the words "You're grounded" in my younger years. Not that Ainsley would recognize it, the brat. But I do. Sissy was the disciplinarian in our house, a very collected one.

I assume the same stance. "Well, have a good time."

As if on cue my sister and best friend step up to flank my stepmother. I see at once their solidarity, right down to their beachwear, and if I weren't so angry I'd laugh, because if there's one thing these three have never been, it's united. Sissy and Ainsley, yes. Ainsley and Jac, for sure. But Sissy, Jac and Ainsley? Not on your life.

In spite of myself I heave out a breath. "What is this?" I ask again.

"We're not letting you go alone," the spokes-teacher says.

I run my eyes over the quartet staring me down, clutch my bag tighter, secure the other one on my shoulder, and head for the kitchen. "See you," I say. David alone attempts to follow, but I stop him with the nastiest look I can muster.

I toss my bag in the backseat of the Saturn, climb behind the wheel, and stab my finger on the button that activates the garage door opener. I miss twice before I make contact, then hold my breath as the door rolls open. And just as I knew it would be, Sissy's Land Rover fills the half of the driveway not occupied by David's work truck. Sissy's stupid Land Rover. Her stupid, stupid Land Rover. My fingers drum the steering wheel as I try to think what to do. She's way too close for me to edge around the behemoth—by design, I'm sure. Sissy's no dummy.

Well, I can wait them out.

And I try. Twenty-three minutes by the Saturn's digital clock I sit and huff. What in the world are they doing in there?

Sitting around the kitchen table eating slices of Sissy's homemade coffee cake, that's what.

"What is this?" I say for the third time. "I need you to move your truck."

I see right away that David has become the fourth Musketeer. Well fine. I know where he keeps his extra set of keys. I'll take *his* stupid truck.

But they aren't there.

"David." The look on my face does the rest of the talking.

He draws on each of his *compadres,* like a straw sucking up their strength. "Sorry, Bree."

"Sorry? *Sorry?*" He chooses now to grow a backbone? "Sissy, move your monster truck out of our driveway or I swear I'll drive over the top of it. Please."

"Why does everyone call it a truck? It's not a truck. How about some coffee, baby? We saved you a cup." She pulls out the empty chair beside her.

"I do not want coffee. I want to get on the road."

"Well, let's just load up your bags."

"Alone! I'm going alone." I'm whining. Forty years old and I'm whining.

Sissy stands up, looks at her watch. "We're never going to miss the traffic." The others join her.

"This'll be fun, Bree. No husbands, no—" *Kids* is what Ainsley's about to say, but that, of course, would just be tacky, considering. Her lips turn white as she bites back the word. "Husbands," she says again. "Sorry, Dave."

"No problem."

I'm losing here, I see it. My mind races for a plan. "Alright, alright. How about if Jac and I go? I won't be alone over the weekend, if that's what this is all about"—and of course it is—"and the beach house won't be so crowded." Ainsley is actually the easiest one of the three to manipulate, but just going with Ainsley wouldn't make sense to this group. So Jaclyn's the next best thing. I'm pretty sure I can work my way around her. But Sissy, no way.

Jac and Ainsley look uncertain, as if they might acquiesce, but Sissy shakes her head. "The Rover's packed, gassed and ready to go. We just need you and those bags of yours, sweet thing."

I could really dislike this woman ... if she hadn't been so good to us, to Ainsley, Dad and me. She's pushy, so freaking pushy, everyone says so. It doesn't bother her in the least what everyone says. Not in the least.

"Are we going?"

I launch one more protest, but we all know I'll never get out of the garage on my own. I throw up my hands and utter a curse for good measure. "I'll get my bags out of the car."

"I'll get them." David's back in a flash with my one puny suitcase and my carry-on bag.

I'm angry, really angry at him, because he's the easiest target right now. But I know the plans I have for the weekend, so I don't turn my face away when he leans in to kiss me goodbye. It surprises him, I know, that I let him. He tries for a second kiss, but that's just pushing it.

"Bye," I say.

"Love you." It's what he always says, and he means it. He'll have far fewer regrets than most of us because of it. "Call me?"

Sissy directs her charges toward the front door. "Sorry, Davy boy, not allowed. Not on a girls' getaway."

Ainsley, the peacemaker, pats his arm. "Maybe on the way home."

Not likely. My stomach makes a bungee dive when I think of how traumatic their return trip will be. I catch it on its way up again and take one last look around. "Shotgun," I say, and head to the Land Rover with not an ounce of enthusiasm. There's not an ounce of argument from anyone about me taking shotgun. Ainsley just retrieves her purse from the front passenger seat and slips in behind the driver. Obviously, they all want to keep an eye on me.

My crazy stepmother has a Chihuahua named Spike. And yes, he's in the Land Rover waiting for us, his wicker bed strapped into the middle of the front seat, where he loves to sit guard. If anyone should hit us or we them, the bed will be safe. Spike, on the other hand, is on his own. I buckle myself in next to the pampered beast and warn him with a low whisper, "Growl at me one time and you're road kill."

———

I haven't uncrossed my arms, spoken a word, or looked anywhere but out the side window thirty minutes into our drive. My kidnappers have tried to engage me, including a Starbucks they ordered against my will—a caffeinated Starbucks, at that— which I have yet to acknowledge, but I'm not giving them the satisfaction of that something-or-other syndrome where victims develop an affinity with their captors. Stockton, Stockdale, Stock*holm* Syndrome, that's it. It doesn't bother me one bit that they're getting on fine without me. Besides, I have a lot to think about, a lot of plans to alter. I've spent the past two days thinking about how I'll do it, scripted it with precision. Now this.

Finally, there's a lull in their non-stop chatter. I heave an exaggerated sigh and rub at my temples, but it does nothing to alleviate the headache. The caffeine would help, and I'm tempted. I really am. But no.

"Clarissa," my sister says all at once, and Sissy smiles.

No, no, *no*. Don't do this, Ainsley. Don't. But they're off and running.

"Desiree," says her backseat partner.

I look over my shoulder, throw Jaclyn a scowl, and mouth the word *traitor*. But she just smiles.

"Esmerelda," Sissy says from my left.

"Shouldn't you be driving?"

She laughs and lifts my Starbucks out of the cup holder. "Here. You need this. Badly."

I take it, though I will not be bribed. It's barely warm, but it is caffeine. I practically slurp as I drink. Almost immediately my headache begins to recede like an ebb tide.

Jaclyn pokes me in the shoulder from behind. "Your turn."

"I'm not playing."

"Come on, Bree. Your names are the best," Ainsley says.

"We're at F, darlin'," Sissy chimes in. "It might be wise to let her pass, at least till we get to a safer place in the alphabet."

"Well then, Felicia."

"Felicia?" I turn around as far as I can to give Ainsley one of my best *looks*. "You can't be more original than Felicia? And besides, how many times have you used it?"

"I like Felicia."

I turn back around and hike an eyebrow at Sissy. "Freda, Fanny and Fifi," I say.

"Triplets. Well. Who knew?"

"Does she come with a pooper scooper?" Jac asks from her corner in the back.

Ainsley feigns a sympathetic pout. "Poor Fifi."

"I meant Fanny."

Everyone laughs but me.

"Okay, okay—"

"Do not say Gertrude," I say to Ainsley.

That stops her, but just for a moment. "Okay then—"

"Or Glynnis." There's another moment of silence. "The idea is to be original."

"I haven't used Glynnis for at least ten years, Bree. Maybe twelve."

Sissy glances at Ainsley through the rear view mirror. "You know she has a memory like an—"

"Do not say elephant."

"I know, I know. Original."

"So what else has a long memory?"

"God," Jac says. "But only for those things he chooses not to forget."

Okay then, game over. I give Spike a look that starts him quivering, and go back to staring out my window.

The silence in the car is heavy. But then my sister, who is braver than she ought to be, says, "Guenevere?"

Alright, even I have to admit that's a good one. And new. I don't say so out loud, but I do give a nod. And the game goes on.

It's a peculiar game when you think about it, one we've played for years. For what these are, are names for all the sisters Ainsley and I never had. The nonexistent sisters that made our mother run away. At least that's how we view it, Ainsley and I. It's better than thinking she left because of us.

And, really, who could blame her? Two babies in two years, names beginning with A, then B, and a husband who read baby-name books like the Farmer's Almanac, with a bookmark stuck in the Cs? Dad insists it was a coincidence, that he really had no intention of the two of them procreating their way through the alphabet. Teri wasn't waiting around to find out, just in case. And again, who could blame her?

Actually, me. Now more than ever. I mean good grief, it was the age of women's lib and birth control, you know? She could have put her foot down and said, No more babies! if that's what she wanted. Our dad is not and never has been a bully. And that's exactly what Sissy did. Even before she proposed, she said, "Marty, I love you to pieces, but between your two babies and my thirty students, we have enough kids." End of discussion. That's how it was with Sissy.

I don't remember who started the name game, though I can't resist a glance to my left, but when most families sang "Ninety-Nine Bottles of Beer on the Wall" on road trips, we made up names for our make-believe siblings, starting at C. Always at C. Chloe, Desiree and so on. X always stumps us. I mean, how many times can you use Xena? And the image it conjures can flat poke you in the eye. I guess because we're a family of girls it never occurred to us we might have had brothers, so the names might be off the charts in weirdness, but they're always feminine.

We never played Slug-Bug for obvious reasons.

"Horatia."

"Horatia?" Ainsley, Jac and I say it in chorus.

Sissy only shrugs. "It beats Fífí."

"By how wide a margin?" This from Jaclyn, my friend, my defender.

Sissy's eyebrow arches. "Was that you, Puff?"

Ha. I knew the solidarity couldn't last. Wondered how long before the barbs and claws came out. It's Sissy who throws down the gauntlet with her pet name for Jac. And it all goes back to Peter, Paul and Mary. The musical group, not the biblical one. Their most famous song, of course, is about a dragon and a boy named Jackie Paper. So what else do you call a girl named Jaclyn Papier, but Puff? If you're Sissy Vanderpool, that is.

"It was me, Sassy."

So, it's tit for tat.

"Ivanka." Ainsley picks up the gauntlet, tosses it out the window, metaphorically speaking, and does her best to get us back on point.

"Well, doesn't that just trump all?" I give a wicked chuckle, quite impressed with my little pun, but it's met with a carful of groans.

The opponents hesitate, weighing this moment in the balance. "Juliet," one says; "Janae," the other, both calling a momentary truce.

Which leads us to K.

And I swear under my breath. Whose dumb idea was this?

Six

Sissy loves to make fashion statements, the more outlandish the better. She's taken to wearing these garish glasses that match her clothes. The frames are big, with lots of surface for artistic expression. Some even have wings, like Cat Woman. I don't know if she shops to match her glasses or vice versa, but she definitely matches. She hasn't always done this, thank heaven. It would have mortified me in my teenage years. She says age has liberated her. Swell. Today she's wearing red polka dots. Even her flip flops are polka-dotted. Can you say funky three different ways?

She also loves to make an entrance. I've personally seen her make an entrance as many as three times at the same event when the first two went unnoticed. And with Sissy, everything's an event. Flamboyant is nothing more than code for S-I-S-S-Y.

One entrance is plenty when we arrive at the beach house, considering the lack of audience. It's a cold, windy day on the coast, but we prop open the door and slide back the aluminum windows to displace the stale air with that which is fresh and sea-laden. Sissy lights the pilot on the stove, though it takes three tries before a match finally stays aflame long enough to get the job done. She turns on the burner under the tea kettle, while Ainsley, Jac and I haul in the luggage. And the food. From the looks of all the baked goods and casseroles, this getaway has been planned since my announcement on Tuesday.

Well, fine. I hope they have a great time.

Within minutes the beachcombers have changed into heavy sweats and socks, with the exception of Sissy who refuses to give up her fashion statement, and the door and windows are shut tight. We sit around the table, shivering, drinking Darjeeling tea. Spike is in a plaid sweater and thinks he owns the place.

"How exactly did you get today and tomorrow off?" I ask the teacher among us.

"Winter break," Ainsley says for Sissy, who has a mouthful of tea.

"Then who's keeping the boys?" I ask Ainsley.

"Grady."

"Grady?

"He traded shifts."

"And you?" I say to Jac.

"I'm the boss," she reminds me. "Left the shop in Trudy's capable hands."

Well. I've caused quite the domino effect, I see.

"So, NNTW," Sissy says.

Jac and Ainsley mouth the letters, trying to figure them out. For that's another thing about my crazy stepmother, she uses all kinds of funny acronyms, and loves to make a guessing game out of them. For example, WASP is not what you think it is when Sissy uses it. No, with Sissy, WASP is *what a strange person*. Or maybe *wink and say please*. Context is everything when playing her game. Ainsley says she does this because, as a teacher, she's got this thing for the alphabet. I say it's simply because she's Sissy.

"No Need to Worry." I say it as drolly as I can.

"You've heard that one before," Ainsley complains.

"And so have you."

Sissy nods her confession. "Yes, well, my bad. I'll have to watch that."

Nothing new under the sun, that's for sure. I bet most people don't realize that's a Bible verse, not that it would stop them from using it. It doesn't stop me.

Sissy reaches over to the stove for the kettle and adds hot water to her mug. "I made a pot of white bean soup for lunch. Shall I heat it up?"

Ainsley's eyes go wide. "White bean soup?" In this confined space? That's the part she doesn't say.

Jaclyn's eyes go wide as well. "Is there anything more ... aggravating than white beans?"

I go ahead and ask the question on all our minds. "Sissy, really, what were you thinking?"

She laughs. "That we'd spend lots of time on the beach. That's why we came, right?"

I catch the sideways glance she sends my way.

"And for dessert," Ainsley says, "I brought the stuff to make S'mores. With chocolate graham crackers."

"Chocolate?"

"Well, why not, Puff?" Sissy says. "I'll give 'em a try."

Honestly, you'd think it was summer vacation the way Sissy's dropping letters all over the place. Not to mention the sentence fragments. That's what comes of being raised in the home of a teacher, you notice these things. And spelling, oh man.

"Hey, I know," she says. "Why don't we get tickets for that little theater in town tomorrow night? I just love that place. Not a bad seat in the house."

"I wonder what's playing?" Jaclyn says.

"What does it matter? It's the theater." Sissy says it with a dramatic flair. But then she says most things with a dramatic flair.

"Sure. Yeah. You all go ahead." I wet my finger and rub at a pencil mark on the laminated table top and try not to sound too eager.

Sissy eyes me suspiciously. "Hmm. Well. We probably couldn't get tickets this late anyway. Especially on a holiday weekend."

Not that Valentine's Day is really a holiday. I sit back and decide not to push.

"So, who wants soup?"

———————

The lunch bowls aren't even dry before someone—Ainsley, I think—breaks out the Triple Yahtzee. "I have pencils for everyone," she says. They're all new, sharpened to fine points, with different-colored erasers stuck on top.

"I want red," Sissy says. To match her dots.

I head for the tiny bathroom in the back of the trailer, mostly just to find some space. "Go on without me."

My sister follows me with her eyes. "No, no. We'll wait."

"Really, Ainsley, I'm fine. Go on ahead."

"We'll wait." Jac adds her voice to my sister's.

I see right away that if solidarity were combustible this place would go up in flames. "Well then." I turn back from the bathroom and take the fourth chair at the table. "Chartreuse."

Not one bit of this is lost on my stepmother. As always, she's the one I have to watch out for.

We have our own rules for Triple Yahtzee, no surprise there. We have our own rules for lots of things. But these have been our rules for as long as I can remember. We play all six games on the sheet—in one sitting. If you roll anything in one roll that requires all five dice—full house, large straight, even a Yahtzee—you double the points. And believe it or not, we roll Yahtzees in one roll more often than you'd think. If you get four ones, twos, threes, fours, fives and sixes in any one of the upper columns, instead of just the normal three, you double your bonus. And if you get more than six Yahtzees during the course of the game, you add a one in front of the fifty, making that Yahtzee worth a hundred fifty points—which could be doubled or tripled—instead of just fifty, and then you use the extra Yahtzee as a three or four of a kind, a full house, or in the corresponding number in the upper column. Naturally, you put your best rolls in the triple-score columns, then fill in the rest of the score card.

We never use the clunky white dice that come with the game. Ours are tiny wooden dice, a third the size of standard dice. Sissy found them at some craft store years ago, and so we all have a set. If nothing else, they're quiet.

Sissy, Ainsley and I were playing Triple Yahtzee when I went into labor with Kinsey. My pains had been mild throughout the day, and once they found out, there was no way either my sister or stepmother was going to sit at home and wait for a call. Not on your life. They both came by after work, along with my dad, and kept watch with David and me. The game helped pass what seemed like an uneventful evening. Then all of a sudden my water broke, right there at the kitchen table, and Kinsey was with us three hours later. She's the most accommodating child you can imagine.

My unfinished score sheet is still in Kinsey's baby book.

I don't like the memories drudged up by the plinking of the dice on the laminated tabletop, and I get this wave of nausea I have to swallow back. I hate that they've put me in this position, even though I love them. All of them. I do. But this, this I hate.

I'd give anything for a back door to this place, to get away on my own for a little while. Then I stop and think, would you? Would you really give anything? As if there were anything left to give. I'm not so cavalier with my words these days. Not even when it's me I'm talking to. By the way, if that's the standard of having lost it, talking to yourself I mean, I've lost it to the moon and back. You should hear the conversations I have with myself. On a good day I— No, strike that. There haven't been any good days in three hundred sixty two days now. So believe me when I say you mostly wouldn't want to listen in.

"Bree? Bree." Three sets of eyes study me as though I'm a specimen in a lab class. "Your turn."

I wonder how many times they've said it. I pick up the dice and toss them on the table. There's not a trace of potential anywhere. I roll two more times. "Scratch," I say, and draw a big fat zero where my pink Yahtzee would go if I had one.

"Oh, Bree, not there."

"The white one," Jaclyn says, as if I've never played the stupid game before. As if I don't know I'm giving up three times the points if I were to throw a Yahtzee.

I give them a look that silences them both, and draw a diagonal line through the circle as if it were an exclamation point.

Sissy wiggles her pencil between her fingers. "You know what? We could finish this later. How about a walk on the beach?"

Spike's ears twitch at the word *walk,* and he lifts his head. The minute Sissy pushes back her chair he's up and out of his basket, dancing at the door, his manicured toenails clacking on the linoleum.

He's nails on a chalkboard to me, Spike is.

Sissy slips a leash onto his quivering body. "It's not fear that makes him tremble," she always says. "It's anticipation."

But I've seen him jump a foot in the air at his own shadow. I know fear when I see it. *Do you, Sissy?* I want to say this to her. *Do you know fear?* Because you can't possibly know fear till you've walked into a morgue expecting to identify the body of your baby girl.

———————

Walnut Creek was gloomy with fog when the Land Rover roared out of the driveway back home, but it's like we drove through a veil when we hit Highway 1, leaving the damp gossamer behind. It's spring in Half Moon Bay. Cold, yes, and windy, but clear as Kinsey's eyes when she smiles.

Lord. The deaths I die a thousand times a day.

I love layers, things that build. Layers in clothing, layers in the plot of a book. I especially love them in music. One singer, then two, then four, then a dozen. Like "Hey, Jude," or that old Coke commercial they used to show during the Olympics. You know the one. I'd like to teach the world to sing ... My sorrow is like that, layer upon layer upon layer, and the layers have gotten so deep I can't dig my way out.

Sissy exaggerates the drawing in of a sea breath and throws her arms wide open. "WAGD."

"What would God do!" Jac says, as if this were one of the flash card quizzes Sissy-the-sixth-grade-teacher is so fond of.

The teacher rolls her eyes at her former student—and probably gives her a D in her mental grade book for good measure—while Ainsley laughs and says, "What a glorious day, is my guess."

"Grand is actually the word I had in mind, but close enough."

I know all about Sissy's mental grade book. Not that we've ever discussed it as if it were something real, not with Sissy at least. But Ainsley, Jac and I, we've discussed it. At length. If the truth were known I'm probably what got it started in the first place. *Bristol, love, our dirty socks go in the laundry hamper when we're through wearing them, not under the bed.* C minus. *Sweet thing, our teeth are not brushed by osmosis. We must actually put the brush to the teeth and scrub for it to do any good. With toothpaste.* D plus. *Bristol Rae Vanderpool, we do not pick our nose and wipe it on the sofa. Ever.* F minus. Squared.

But to be fair I have to ask myself, would I have resented those corrections any less from a mother whose womb had incubated me? Of course the answer is no. I was much too insolent, saucy and opinionated for that. Not much has changed.

Ainsley's the sweet one.

Sissy stops walking, and watches as Spike squats in the sand to relieve himself of his morning tea. Yes, squats. Yes, tea. He thinks he's all that and more. When he's through, he shakes his hind leg, a sign that he's finished his business and is ready to continue on. Though we walk, he prances. He stops again to yap at a seagull that's perched on a small rock jutting out of the sand, and pulls at his leash with a menacing growl. As if he had even a little testosterone, the fraud. If Sissy ever called his bluff and let go of her end, he'd be shaking his hind leg for a whole 'nother reason.

I don't mind dogs. But a dog that's worse than a cat? Yuck.

This is not how I pictured my last weekend on earth. But then I look around, and like Sissy, I can't help but breathe in the scent of the sea and give my face to the wind. There are worse places to spend your last hours, that's for sure.

Seven

*M*y keepers won't let me out of their sight. They think I'm going to fill my pockets with seashells like a wannabe Virginia Woolf and walk into the Pacific as if it were the River Ouse. But they needn't worry. That isn't how I have it planned, though they've pretty much crashed my site when it comes to the logistics of just how I'm going to pull it off now.

I hate women who meddle.

Okay, that's a strong statement even for me. I just wish I'd forgone the request to borrow the beach house and come without anyone knowing. Broken in or something, a stealth trespasser. But I wanted them to know where to find me when this is over, and I'm paying the price for it now.

I cast a glance at my red-polka-dotted stepmother, who stops every few feet to shake the sand off her flip flops, not caring how ungraceful she looks. A sand crane she's not. But she is the organizer in all of this meddling, I'd bet my life on it. Ha. Not much of a bet. I bark out a laugh at my secret joke, and I swear I hear a seal bark back a reply.

Sissy turns her face my direction, and covers her eyes with a cupped hand against a sun that's dipped past its zenith. "What's that, Bristol love?"

I pretend her words get lost in the wind, like a kite sailing off without a string. Oops, there they go ... As a diversionary tactic I reach down, pick up the remains of a starfish and hurl it Frisbee-like into the waves. My efforts are as lame as everything else in my life, as the very next breaker brings it back to my feet. I bend down and pick it up again, this boomerang starfish. And I'm pounded with the thought, where is my boomerang baby? Oh, God, where? And why doesn't she come back to me?

Sissy reads minds, I've been convinced of it for years. She's at my side as soon as the thought draws blood, propping me up like a walking stick, though she pretends it's she who needs my arm. Sissy, a woman who never stumbles.

"Do you know what my least favorite verse in the Bible is?" She tethers each of us with a mystery smile as surely as she tethers Spike with his leash, and waits. She knows we'll never guess, of course she does. I mean, honestly, it's not like there are only a handful to choose from.

"That one about women keeping silent in church?" Jac tries but doesn't quite manage to stifle her smirk.

"Okay then, my second least favorite." Sissy steals Jac's thunder with an air of indifference that I know from experience aggravates like a thorn in your sock. She waits only a second before she says, "And there was no more sea." She gives us a moment to feel the weight of her words as she inhales a sea breath, her nostrils opening wide for better passage. "No more sea. You know, I sometimes think John stepped out of divine inspiration for those few words." She looks as if she's waiting for one of us to cry blasphemy.

Well, don't look at me.

"I mean, think about it." She holds out her arms toward the farthest horizon, like Moses with breasts and red polka dots. All she lacks is a budding rod to make the waters part. "This is the closest thing we have to heaven on earth, and we're to believe some people will live throughout eternity and never dip their toe in the foam?"

Jac squints at her. Ainsley does too.

"There are people," she explains, "who have never seen the ocean, never felt the spray on their face." Sissy closes her eyes and leans into the wind, and I get this weird vision of Kate Winslet. When next Sissy speaks she employs her sixth-grade-teacher finger to strengthen her point. "People who love God and are going to heaven, who, we're to believe, will miss out on this forever. Does that sound like God?"

"I'd jump onto Travelocity right now if I were them." Jac says this with a perfectly straight face.

"Does it?" The teacher in Sissy waits for an answer. "Sound like God?"

"Well why does it say it then?" Ainsley really wants to know.

Sissy steps out of the drama she's been casting, and shrugs. "Of course it means what it says and it's there for a reason. I just don't understand it."

"Wow," Jac says. "Something you don't know. Imagine."

One thing I'll miss is books. Elizabeth Berg especially, *What We Keep* in particular. I have to get through it between now and Sunday, and I still have a hundred and eighty-eight pages to go. It's not a long book by any means, only two hundred seventy-two pages. Not a problem if I were here by myself, which was the plan after all. But how I'll find enough quiet time now, between Yahtzee and chick flicks, to finish the read has me perturbed. As I said, I don't like loose ends.

Why it's taken me a decade to read this novel by my favorite author, when I've read all the others, I don't quite understand. Well, that's not quite true. The subject matter had a lot to do with it. Okay, everything to do with it. It sat on my bookshelf, face out, begging attention, year after year. But like the task you never get to, the closet shelves you can't quite reach, it remained undone. Till now. I decided I had to conquer it.

Kinsey loves books. She can say her alphabet with hardly a slip. I can't take all the credit because David's a reader too. Biographies mostly, but that still counts. One of my favorite things was that hour every night between bath time and bed time, all of us huddled in one big tangle on the living room sectional, Kinsey fresh in her pajamas, smelling like bubbles and sunshine, half on my lap, half on David's. We'd all have our books, but David and I ignored ours while Kinsey read to us. We called it reading, even though what she did was recite the story as well as she could remember it. If it was a story she'd never heard before she'd make up her own from the pictures, and David and I would clap and clap.

He was Davy then. Such a long time ago.

I know, to call it reading isn't quite the truth, but it certainly isn't a lie. It's just another thing that falls into that universe of gray—like so much of life—that's bordered by a thin, sharp line of black on one side and a thin, stark line of white on the other. I know there are things that fit neatly into those minuscule strips of black and white. I just don't happen to know what they are anymore.

He was Davy then.

Out of nowhere those words begin to churn in me, to stir up a sympathy I don't expect and cannot afford. A sympathy he doesn't deserve.

And yet.

He was so much fun in the early days. The carefree, early days. He brought something out in me that might have been there all along if life had been different. If there'd been no name game to play, no dark edge that tempered everything about me. And he was kind. Is kind. Way more than I've ever been to him. Through that first miscarriage, then the second.

And then he was Dave, because the newness had worn off. Because life was back to its old tricks of taking things away. Not that any of it was his fault, but the fallout has to land somewhere. It just has to. And once he went back on his word to me, he was David, said with a sharpness I didn't have to work to cultivate.

And still he was kind. Even on that day. When he finally realized what

I was telling him in my hysteria, as he raced across the bay to the preschool, breaking every traffic law, even then he was kind. He kept me on the phone and told me over and over it would be okay, that Kinsey would be okay, instead of telling me what a foolish, lame excuse of a parent I was, as he should have, as I would have to him if the tables had been turned. Believe me, I'd have spewed at him every vile and hurtful thing I could think of, just as I've been doing in the privacy of my own head for the past three hundred sixty two days. To him and to me.

Once the adrenaline wore off and hope began to seep out of us that Kinsey would be found quickly, unharmed and unscathed, that's when I expected the backlash. I waited for it, waited for the accusations, the contempt. But it never came, and I hated that it didn't. That lack of contempt felt like burning coals heaped on my head. I know that wasn't his intention, because of all that kindness he carries around. But kindness can wear on you. Trust me. You want to be challenged once in a while. You want the cleansing—and the connection—a good fight can bring, like a sudden deluge that washes away all the crap. A spring cleaning of the soul, so to speak. You breathe so much better after. But David was never a fighter. He still isn't.

What's in a name, the old saying goes? Just ask my husband.

I keep a few paces behind my keepers as we continue along the shoreline, my way of rebelling against their presence. They're wise, and give me my space. The broken starfish is rough as a loofah in my hand, but I can't let it go. It's mine now, for good.

A few brave souls in wet suits straddle their surfboards and paddle out past the breakers. They bob on the waves, growing smaller with every swell they crest, until they're a black, odd-shaped dot on the vast silver-blue backdrop. And then they stand and ride the sea like conquerors. I envy their daring, even as I grip the edges of my jacket a bit tighter, and think of all the things I'll never do.

Lord, I miss her voice. Miss how her words end on a high note, as if everything is a question to be answered. They say four is the age of why. *Why is that there? That* is the freckle mole on her collarbone; the one in the exact place as mine. *Why does Lily have a brother and I don't? Why can't I hold water in my hand?*

Why do You keep her from me, You who have the power to make this right?

I have my questions too.

"Grady." The word wafts back to me as Ainsley snaps her phone closed and sighs out a breath. "Sam broke a tooth. He tried to catch a DVD. With his mouth." She smooths out her eyelashes with the back of her index fingers, as she's done all her life when something goes wrong. A preening bird is my sister.

I'm hoping this means they'll leave. But when Sissy breaks into a snorting laugh, I know better. "Wait till he's eleven." Sixth grade is what she means. It's no accident she'll say goodbye to thirty-six years of teaching just as Sam advances from fifth grade to sixth a year and a half from now. She'd make it to forty if it were just Eli, she's made no secret of that since the day Sam learned to run. He skipped walking altogether, just went straight from an army crawl to sprints.

"I thought we weren't talking to husbands," Jac says.

"You have to have one first." Sissy says this as if she's explaining the periodic table to a moron. Spike, who's in her arms now, licks her chin as if to say, "Way to go."

"He added 911 to the end of his text," Ainsley says. "I had to—"

"911? For a chipped tooth?" Sissy's tattooed eyebrow hikes above her polka-dotted frames. "I wouldn't send him to the school nurse for a chipped tooth."

"Forget the tooth," Jac says. "Why would you text 911? For any reason?"

"Well ... because ..." Ainsley looks to me for help.

To me.

For help.

And I'm suddenly tempted to stuff my pocket with rocks. "Leave her alone," I say. It's the best I can do.

"What do you want to do?" Sissy says this to Ainsley, but the compassion of her words doesn't match the look on her face. Not at all, no. It says, We're not leaving here, tooth or no tooth.

Ainsley's eyes take us all in. "Grady can handle it." Her voice is grossly unconvincing.

Sissy gives her an atta-girl wink. "Of course he can. He's a fire-fighting EMT. A captain, no less. He's got it covered."

Ainsley smooths her lashes again, nods.

For three hundred sixty two days my sister has faltered every time she mentions Sam or Eli's name, as if apologizing that she still has children and I—

I grip my starfish until it digs into my hand.

Ainsley feels guilty for wanting to have her babies and work, I've known that for years. To each her own, I say, but what I really think in my heart is that she wants to have her cake and eat it too. "But what the heck does that mean exactly?"

Three pairs of eyes turn my way. Sissy peers at me from behind her glasses. She has eyes like an owl, and this slow blink that makes you second guess every word you say to her. It tells me what I fear, that I've said this out loud.

"Well, I guess it means that Grady has it covered."

"Mmm," I say. "Well okay," and we resume our walk, only now I take the lead. I scan the seascape before me and plot out an escape route. If I could make it unseen to those rocks jutting out into an overly-aggressive surf I could maybe find a crevice to hide in, no matter the spray, until the others pass by. But there's the problem of all those footprints I leave behind, a veritable bread trail to out me. You can run, but you can't hide, I tell myself. I cough out a laugh, because it helps to know someone's on the receiving end of my thoughts—even if it's just me.

Sissy would know the answer to what I was really asking back there. She could dig things up before there was Google or Bing, like no one you ever knew. It's this uncanny ability she has to know things. Don't ask me how. That's why she almost went to work for the CIA. Seriously. Sort of. It was about the time Teri was loading up her VW Bug to make her escape from the baby mill known as the Vanderpool household. Sissy walks right in to the Federal Government Offices in downtown San Francisco to apply, says she has a gift and should be hired right away. It doesn't matter they're not advertising. While she's filling out the application she gets to talking with the receptionist there. Talking's a whole 'nother gift Sissy has. Well, she and Nadine Proctor, the receptionist, hit it off so well they decide to go to the Wharf for lunch. Just leave the application right there on the clipboard half complete. By the time that lunch hour was over, they were good friends, and have been ever since. We didn't know Sissy then, of course, but when you've heard a story often enough, the facts become familiar as old friends.

Can you imagine Sissy with the CIA? Yeah, so can I.

But to prove my point to myself, that Sissy would know the answer to my question—and I'm fully aware of the psychotic sand sinking beneath my feet—I stop, turn and throw out the question. "What does it mean, to have your cake and eat it too?"

Sissy stops, becomes contemplative, and waits, as if Jac or Ainsley might manage to pull the answer out of the crisp sea air. The cry of the gulls is all the answer I get, but then Sissy, who never disappoints, gives me a sly smile, then passes it out to the others. "There was a man named John Something—give me a minute and it'll come to me—in, I believe, the sixteenth century, an Englishman and an author. What he wrote went something like this: 'would ye both eat your cake and have your cake?' "

Jac rolls her eyes away from my stepmother. "Well, that certainly clears it up."

Sissy ignores her and goes on. "So what it really means is you can't eat your cake and keep your cake. You can't have it both ways, whatever *it* is. Sadly."

"Isn't that the truth," I say and resume plodding through the sand.

I squint into the dipping sun, which has set the afternoon sea on fire. It's so dazzling it's painful, but I can't look away. I squint until my eyelashes veil the view, and watch. This tells me what I need to know, and what I dread, that the world keeps spinning, time keeps its frantic pace, and you can't go back. Ever. Not ever. The thought starts a panic that begins where my womb belongs and moves up through my body, a liquid hurt that seeps into every cell, until it reaches my heart, and squeezes. I should be used to this by now, this take over, this coup, but I'm not. I feel so off kilter I don't think I could ever find true north again. Not in a million years. Certainly not in two days.

My foot collides with a piece of driftwood, punishment for not watching where I'm going, and a different type of pain jars me from toe to tooth. I stumble, catch myself, squinch up tight in defense, and swear.

"Won't help," Sissy says. Sissy, our morality cop.

"Doesn't hurt," I mumble, and spit the word out a second time to make my case.

"Sit down and let's have a look, make sure there's no blood."

Sissy really expects me to pull off my sandal and show her my toes. "I'm not in preschool," I say. I catch the petulance in my voice and offer a convoluted apology. "I only act like I am."

It's a knowing smile Sissy gives me, one you'd think came only with motherhood. But then, what is motherhood? Is it a woman who flees in a VW Bug, leaving her genetic fingerprint behind in a pair of matching cribs? Or a woman who wouldn't know a labor contraction from a grammatical one? Who knows? All I can tell you for sure is that it's not a woman who leaves her baby girl in a car to be taken.

Not so much was known about the baby blues way back when, which may or may not excuse Teri. Me, I have no such defense.

Eight

*A*ll my life I was angles and planes. The only knobs on my body protruded from my elbows and knees. When other girls in sixth and seventh grade were wearing bras to cover their burgeoning chests, I wore mine to cover the evidence that nothing was going on beneath the stretchy cotton. I let the straps show just to prove I had one on. One mortifying day the end of sixth grade I succumbed to temptation and stuffed the cupless thing with bathroom tissue, and ignored the startled look from Sissy, who did a double take from the blackboard. What I couldn't ignore were the dual wads of tissue that fell out of my top as I hung upside down on the monkey bars. Especially when Kenny Branson picked them up, stuffed them inside his own T-shirt, arching his back to keep them in place, and yelled, "Hey, guys, look! I'm wearing Bristol Vanderpool's boobs!"

So when I actually began to develop a chest worthy of the word during my second trimester of pregnancy, I couldn't believe the transformation. No wonder women pay money for this. I mean, I had mounds. Large mounds. Three of them when you counted my belly. And that was beautiful too. I treated myself to a Wonderbra. I know, what a ridiculous waste of discretionary funds, which were meager as lace in a nunnery. But let me tell you, I felt decadent from the moment I strapped it on. I'd never had anything to put in one before, and counting the four months left of my pregnancy and the twelve months I planned to nurse, I had sixteen months of decadency ahead of me. I'd get my money's worth, yes I would.

I'd stop in front of the mirror a hundred times a day, unable to believe that was really me in there, that those were really mine. Reflective windows, the paint job on my car, anything that would throw my image back to me was my friend. I could hardly get enough of myself.

And Dave. Let me tell you, he was attentive.

Oh, I know. Once I stopped nursing they'd deflate like a pair of chili peppers in a hot skillet, hanging flat against my midriff. But for now, it gave me quite a lift. Ha.

I had three days of morning sickness during my pregnancy with Kinsey, just three, but in truth that might have been nerves while I waited to see my OB-GYN. There was no dignity in peeing on a stick over my toilet, so I chose to wait ... and pee in a cup over the john at my doctor's office, as I had twice before. I'd expected something more profound that first time, some better, more dignified way to discover that a life was growing inside of me. But that's always been my problem, high expectations.

I knew within days I was pregnant with Kinsey, had no doubt, but it was different that third time. There was no mucousy spotting in place of a period, no cramps. There was just no period, along with that telltale aching in my breasts. I still feared the worst through that first trimester, but hope was making a comeback. One thing's for sure, from the moment my pregnancy was confirmed, Kinsey never disappointed. Not ever. It comes as a stake to my heart that she couldn't say the same about me. Not now. And that's where I have to leave off my thoughts. I've never projected beyond that last glimpse of her sleeping face in the car seat. I can't. I just pray she's alive, and she's well.

If there's a God in heaven.

In all fairness I've no doubt there is, but we had this falling out, you see.

It's not easy being an infidel when everyone in your circle is a believer. Or when your former pastor is your father-in-law. But I've managed. Because relationships are all about mutual regard, and if God didn't care enough to cover for me the two minutes in my whole life when it mattered most, that tells you where my standing is. I've heard it said until it's cliché that God doesn't have grandchildren. Well, he doesn't have in-laws either. I won't get anywhere on the coattails of my husband or his pastor dad, and I'm resigned to that. It does give David one more thing to worry about, my fall from grace, but that's not my problem. I am not my husband's keeper, and he's not mine.

I didn't plan my great falling away. I just wanted to hide out that first Sunday after Kinsey disappeared, from the media who were camped out in front of our house, and from the people in our church who would never be able to keep the pity out of their eyes—or the blame. Though I begged him to go without me, David stayed by my side. He didn't understand that it was for my sake, not his. That I wanted to be alone, and as far away from him as I could get. He didn't know how angry I was. He still doesn't.

But one thing is clear, a year without Kinsey is quite enough. I want to quit feeling as though my heart and soul are missing. Short of that, I want to quit feeling, period. I want the comfort of not having to live through another day. There's only one way I know to achieve that, and I'm armed with what it will take to accomplish it.

I'd toyed with the idea all along. I mean, who wouldn't? Zachary Martin's mom maybe, because I always saw more hope in her eyes than I did my own when I could bear to look in the mirror. But when they said remains—not a body, but remains—had been found in Cuyahoga Valley National Forest ten days ago, I bet she toyed with it then. More than toyed. For ten long days, during which there was no end to the media coverage, she clung to that last shred of hope like the lifeline it was. But she knew. And I knew too. I prayed, oh, God, how I prayed. And when they announced on Tuesday morning that they had ID'd the skull through DNA as belonging to young Zachary Martin, I watched her light go out for good in the span of a blink, and I knew in that moment I could not be her. I cannot be her.

I sit in a nylon chair in the "front yard" of the beach house, pretending to read *What We Keep.* In truth, I'm working on Plan B, which irritates me to no end considering I had a perfect Plan A. Yes, you could argue that a perfect plan doesn't need a follow-up plan. I'll skip my initial response to that and just say, "Maybe so, in a perfect world. But this is so not a perfect world." So. Not. And now I'm trying to figure out how to make this work, and with as little trauma to my handlers as possible. I'm not completely heartless. Okay, that too is arguable.

I can't help thinking how grand it would be if we could all choose the time and place for our exit. I mean, what if you don't like the script as it's written? Do you still have to play the part? Doesn't quite seem fair to me. Not that things are. Fair, I mean. If there were such a thing as an understudy to a person's life, I'd give up the starring role and let her take over in a nanosecond. Wishful thinking aside, I won't let the fact that there's not deter me.

My trio of guardian angels are inside conspiring. Every now and then one of them will yoo-hoo me through the open door of the trailer to ask how the book is or if I'm not too cold yet, and pretend there's no other dialogue going on. But I hear them murmuring inside, a dead giveaway. There was a time I would have cared, would have demanded to know what they were up to, in a fun way of course, especially here at the beach house with all its looming possibilities. But I have my own conspiracy to contend with, and not enough mental energy to worry about theirs.

I'll have to give up my ruse of reading any moment now, for there's hardly any light left, even with the porch light throwing its pink illumination over my shoulder. Amazing how quickly some-thing as spectacular as a sunset can fade. It paints the sky with unearthly hues so lovely it hurts, then almost before you can blink twice the horizon is sucked clean of all its color, as though a cosmic eraser in the hand of God has wiped it all away, and the world is caught in that vast universe of gray I was talking about. Another reminder that the really good things don't last.

My heart catches painfully at that last thought, and I remind myself for the gazillionth time that just because I can't see Kinsey doesn't mean she no longer is. And I don't just mean in the spiritual sense. She's here, somewhere, alive and well. I know it. I do. I did. Now, God help me, my confidence wanes, and I can barely handle the fear. I look out at that far away horizon that melds with the sea beneath and the sky above in striated shades of silver, the farthest point I can find, and I know that the huge bowl that holds what I can see of the sea between myself and that far off point, stretching wide and deep, couldn't begin to hold the tears I'd cry if I could even start. I'm drowning, I swear I am.

"Bristol? There can't possibly be enough light left to read by. Why don't you come in now? Besides, dinner's nearly done, and— Oh, love, it's freezing out here!"

Sissy's right. Every bit of warmth got sucked out right along with the color. I've been shivering for an hour, even though I'm tucked under that awful throw I pulled off the sofa. Kelly green and chocolate brown in a boring plaid are not my idea of *haute decor*. Sissy's tastes and mine have always been at odds. Jaclyn's proof enough of that.

In spite of the cold, I'd much rather stay outside where the song of the surf nearly drowns out the wail of my own relentless thoughts, though I wouldn't mind another pair of socks.

And there I am, off and running again.

It's not every night Kinsey slips out of bed the minute I get back downstairs, or David, if it's his night to put her to bed. No, there are those nights we let her fall asleep snuggled next to David in his chair, or on the sofa beside me as I read and absently tickle-rub her back, those nights we're both too tired to make the stairs more than two or three times. Apiece.

We don't hear her until she's beside David's chair. That's not because she's become adept at descending the stairs in silence. It's because both pairs of her footed pjs are in the wash. Now that I'm working I don't have time to keep things up the way I used to. The way I want to.

"Guys," she says. "We got a problem here."

As exasperating as bedtime can be, I find her statement amusing, though I keep that fact to myself.

"What problem is that, sweet pea?" David swoops her up and sits her on his lap. He's trying hard, David is, to take the high road in our relationship. To be the civil one. And so his voice is oh-so-annoyingly civil. Me, I'm content to skulk along the low road, because I haven't come close to punishing him enough for the position we're in. Yes I know, we and the rest of the country, in this, the worst economic downturn of our lives. But I don't care about the rest of the country.

Kinsey points to one bare foot then holds up a lone sock. Its mate is snugly on her other foot, tucked up under the elastic edge of her pajama bottoms where it belongs. "It came off."

I immediately wonder how long it took her to tug off the sock she holds, to even come up with the idea.

"Ah," David says. "That is a problem. What do you think we should do?"

"Put it on," she says. Then she works her way off his lap and into the space between him and the arm of the chair. She looks up at her daddy, eyes wide and hopeful, while he looks at me, civilly inviting my input.

Well, I don't feel civil.

"Okay, Kinsey, here's the deal," I say. "I'm going to put your sock back on and put you back in bed. If you get up again"—I wag a finger at her in a way that disgusts me now—"you have to give me your toy. Every night, if you get up, you have to give me your toy."

I'm talking about the toy she takes to bed with her at night, the one she selects from all her other toys. We've done this since she was old enough to appreciate the privilege of this. Which coincidentally fell on the exact day we moved her into the youth bed.

She scrunches her shoulders up toward her ears, looks to David as if to say, 'Can she do that?' He shrugs, because he knows, yes, she can.

She can, indeed, do that. But the look on his face tells me how much he disagrees.

And so I tug on her sock, not nearly as imperturbable as I ought to be with a child who's barely three, and snatch her out of David's chair. I tuck her back in bed and don't even bother going down for my book. I'm showered and in bed before David knows I've finished with Kinsey, feigning sleep when he finally comes to find me.

I can see her now, still see the grape-colored pjs, the stark white sock on one foot, the other in her hand, negotiating her way into a few more minutes of time with Mommy and Daddy. I grow dizzy with the breath I can't expel.

I know feelings, emotions, are not tangible things, but honestly, it feels like Miss Pacman is inside my gut, if that's where such intangible things are stored, feasting away. If there were a physical door I could open, a spillway of sorts to let out all the trapped emotion, the moment the seal was breached I'd deflate like a windsock in a high pressure front.

I don't want to go in, don't even want to move, but if Sissy taught me anything it's to pick my battles. Whether or not to leave my solitary place in the sand and go inside the beach house isn't worth the fight. There will be bigger ones before this get-away is over. I know that only too well. I close my book with a sigh. I'm not going to finish. I know it. But I'll give it my best shot. I don't even want to think about the cards I'm supposed to design.

Sissy stands in the open doorway, clutching Spike in one arm, inviting me in with the other. That stupid dog doesn't know whether to advance or retreat as I pass. I can't help tossing him a look that sets him to quivering. A low growl wobbles his throat, so brave he is in the arms of his mistress.

"Oh, baby, it's okay." Sissy, who missed the exchange between Spike and me, runs her hand down his back and kisses the top of his head. "There now."

Ainsley is setting the dinner table. "How's the book?"

"It's Elizabeth Berg," Jaclyn says. And she's right. It's Elizabeth Berg.

My sister gives me that smile I've always loved.

I look down at the book, taking note of the pages still unread. I won't be sleeping much this weekend. And that's fine with me. But then I look around at the tiny parlor—Sissy's term, not mine—just off the two tiny bedrooms, across from the tiny bathroom, adjacent to the tiny kitchen, and wonder how I'll pull it off. Forget the fact that there's nowhere to go that won't bother someone, the real problem is the three mother hens clucking over this chick.

"I'll have to borrow it when you're through," Ainsley says.

Jac touches my arm in that familiar way. "It's one I wouldn't mind reading again, so dibs after her."

"With all the books in the world," Sissy says, "how can you even think about reading one a second time?"

Jaclyn's lips turn up in a victory smile as she sends a gotcha look to my stepmother, and I know exactly what she's going to say. "My sixth grade teacher once said a good book is as worth revisiting as your favorite friend." Jac's eyes cut to mine for the briefest moment before looking back to Sissy.

Sissy doesn't miss a beat. "And here I thought you never listened to a word I said."

"Would you like me to diagram a sentence, or name the planets from smallest to largest, or vice versa? I can, you know."

I straighten the silverware Ainsley has placed on the table until each piece is perfectly aligned and equidistant from the plates. I eye them and straighten the knives a little bit more. Jaclyn gets a devilish grin on her face and, when she thinks I'm not looking, nudges a fork. I slap her hand and straighten the handle until I'm satisfied.

She gives a little laugh. "Has she always been such an annoying perfectionist?"

Ainsley fills another glass with ice. "Are you kidding? If we had company and had to sleep together so one of our rooms could be a guest room, she'd get up in the middle of the night and make the bed around me."

"Oh come on." I roll my eyes. "I was ten." As if that makes it better.

"Yeah," Jaclyn says, "She did it to me, too."

Okay. I have issues.

"But back to the book," Ainsley says. "I'd love to read it."

Yes, okay. I must remember to put a sticky note on the cover before Sunday, leaving the book to my sister. That leads me to think of all the things I've left unbequeathed. Not that there's a single thing of any value. Still. There are those among us who are sentimental. I'll have to squeeze in a hand-written will this weekend, on top of finishing the book, when I had more than enough time to do both this past year if I'd only thought about it beforehand. But it was the identification of little Zachary that pushed me over the edge, that's given me the courage to do what I couldn't have done otherwise.

And now that I am thinking about it, there are two things I want to be buried with. Kinsey's blanket, of course. And her Handy Manny tool set. Yes. Handy Manny. She got it from Sam for Christmas just weeks before— Before. It immediately became her favorite cartoon and her favorite toy, the one she took to bed with her every night thereafter, Handy Manny, the tools, the whole set. We caved in to the one-toy rule, because a) you really could look at the set of tools as one toy, and b) we make the rules, so by rights we could breach them. But the caveat remained. Once we'd said prayers with her, if she got up even once, she lost the toy for the night. And once she began taking Handy Manny to bed the stakes increased exponentially, because it wasn't a single tool she had to give up, it was the whole darn thing. Harsh? I know. Lord, wouldn't I do it differently now.

David and I weren't sure she really understood the concept until one night—a Thursday I'm pretty sure—we heard her pj'd feet padding down the stairs. David and I rolled our eyes at one another, and I was just about to say, "Your turn," when Kinsey ran into the room, handed over the tool box without a word, then hurried back to bed. That was all, just gave up her toy for the chance to come downstairs one last time before sleep. A worthy trade in her mind. Davy laughed himself silly half the night, and though I tried not to, I had to laugh too. Of course, we returned the tool set to her, along with an impotent warning that she saw right through.

"Smells good," I say when I trust myself to speak, as Sissy pulls a casserole out of the oven, in which the nine-by-eleven dish barely fits. I have no interest in food, no appetite, but I do crave a diversion.

"Tater tot surprise," she says. "Your favorite."

Yes. When I was six. I resist the urge to say, "Yum," knowing exactly how it would sound coming out of my mouth. Instead I do my best to smile. I can just imagine how unpleasantly that comes across.

Sissy is so in her element, right here, right now. "Tomorrow morning we go clamming. I already have the chowder made, just have to add the clams and the sand."

Ainsley seems surprised at this, which surprises me, because I'm certain they've scripted this whole weekend. But her reaction says otherwise. "Wow. Fun. It's been years since we clammed."

Jaclyn, on the other hand, glances at her acrylic nails then gives me the look. The one that says, are you kidding me?! "You can't just get them in a can?" she says.

Sissy laughs, and I can't help thinking she did this on purpose. "Shall we pray?"

————————

Jaclyn and I share the room with the twin beds, though it's not like it was when we were twelve. Then, we'd sleep in one bed, no matter the size, and giggle till the early hours of the morning, smothering our faces with pillows when the fun got out of hand to keep from being reprimanded yet again, not caring if our bare toes touched. Now, I turn my back to her and face the wall. I can't believe I got roped into sharing this two-bedroom sardine can with three grown women, this weekend of all weekends.

I'm only waiting for Jac, and everyone else, to fall asleep. Then I'll creep into the *parlor* and read in peace. All night if I can.

"You still do that?"

Jac's voice is a whisper, the edges of which are laced with sleep. She's almost gone.

I look back over my shoulder. "Do what?"

"Rock."

Rock? How could she tell that from way over there? "I—" Haven't in years, though I always did. I'd lie on my side and rock myself to sleep. It took a while for David to get used to. Not that it bothered him, or if it did he never complained. No, he'd just grin and say he'd never slept with a rocker girl before. In all fairness, he'd never slept with anyone. David was that kind of guy.

I always rocked, and not just in bed. Sitting on a sofa or a porch step, it didn't matter. I'd rock. And Jac was right, I was doing it now. That's me, never still. Always restless.

"Sorry," I whisper.

"No, it's all—"

"'Night, girls," Sissy calls from the other room. "We have an early day ahead of us."

I can feel Jac bristle, even from my side of the room. "Eleven. She still thinks we're eleven."

Nine

*T*here are rules to clamming, the worst of which is that you can begin your clamming day one half hour before sunrise and clam till one half hour after sunset, if you choose, and if it takes that long to get your limit. Sissy has other plans for the evening slot, though she's not saying what. Sissy's all about surprises. But with the teacher in her still living large, she's also all about promptness.

It's a gray universe we venture into, without anywhere near enough coffee, after a night without anywhere near enough sleep. The fog dramatically shrinks our universe, and masks a raucous sea. But seen or unseen, the vigor with which the breakers hit the shore tells you of its intensity.

"Okay, listen up." Sissy uses her outdoor voice—a silly specimen of teacher-speak if ever there was one—but even then she's hard to hear above the crash of the waves. "We're here today to dig for razor clams." She lines us up like a D.I., Patton style, and paces back and forth in front of us. She taps her free hand with a clamming fork with every other footfall. All she needs is bloused pant legs stuffed into military boots and the backdrop of an enormous American flag for the image to be complete. "For those of you who don't know"—she pegs Jac with that look she has—"this is a clam fork, also known as a clam rake. It's used to dig the clams out of the sand."

It looks like an instrument of torture. I've always thought so, always rejoiced that I'm not a clam.

"We'll stake out our place along the shore," Sissy says, "and look for squirt holes—"

"For what holes?"

"Squirt holes, Puff. S-q-u-i-r-t. They tell us where the clams are hiding."

"Wow. Seems like a case of David and Goliath if you ask me. The poor little guys don't have a chance. I mean how fair is—"

"Once you locate the clam, you insert the fork, and ..."

Jac brings a hand to her face and says as best she can without moving her lips, "Good grief. The mental image this conjures."

"...must be four and a half inches long. Not four and a quarter, mind you, four and a half. We use this"—Sissy pulls a tweezer-like device out of the pocket of her flannel jacket, a device I haven't seen in years—"a caliper, to measure the"—she shoots another look Jac's way—"little guys. If they're too small, put them right back in the hole you dug them out of."

"This is grotesque," Jac says. "Obscene." Her words are for my benefit alone.

"But if they're keepers, put them in this bucket—I'll fill it with seawater—and we'll take them back to the beach house to clean. And eat. Oh." She closes her eyes and smiles as if she's in heaven. "Just you wait." She looks to the drizzly sky and gives her hand a final tap. "Let's go. We're burning daylight. Oh, and if a shell is slightly open, tap on it." She gives a mock demonstration. "If it closes, the clam is alive; if it doesn't, discard it."

"Knock, knock," Jac says.

Ainsley gives her a sideways look and smiles. "Who's there?"

"And remember, only ten per day per clammer." She passes out a fork, which truly does look like a brutal thing, to Ainsley and me, keeping one for herself. "Oh, no, did I only bring three?" She's a terrible actress, Sissy is.

"No problem," I say, "Jac can use mine."

"No, no, that's alright, I'll—"

"I insist." And I mean it.

She takes it as if it might turn to a snake in her hands, like Aaron's rod of old, and falls in line behind Sissy and Ainsley. I think again about making my escape into the gauze-shrouded morning, but there's still the problem of all those footprints.

We haven't gone far when Sissy drops to her knees. "Here we are!" She crouches in the sand and waves us into a circle around her. "A squirt hole."

"Bonanza," Jaclyn says at a level Sissy is sure not to hear.

Her caution is wasted as the word is swallowed by the wind that whips all around us. That eternal, seafaring wind. The others hunker down against it, retreat into their jackets like turtles. Not me. I love the wind. I was a kite in another life, I'm sure of it. A butterfly kite, purple and green, soaring higher than all the others. Okay, I admit it, I don't believe in reincarnation, though I can't tell you how appealing my life as a kite sounds to me right now. It's just that I've had to defend this weird obsession for so long when it comes to the wind. It's easier to say I wish I were a kite, and leave it there. People laugh at that, and it's the right kind of laugh.

The wind is the reason I don't cut my hair ... that and the fact I wanted to look exactly the same when Kinsey came home. If Kinsey comes home. I wonder how long it will take her to forget me, for the slate of her memory to be wiped clean, the way mine was, for I have no actual memory of Teri. Not one. That makes it easier, and if it makes it easier for Kinsey, that will be good. That's what my head tells me, but my heart isn't buying a word of it.

I turn my face to the gusts, throw myself wide open. I've thrown myself wide open to a lot of things these days. In a surprising moment,

Jeff Girard comes to mind, but of all the deadly sins I've committed in my heart these past three hundred sixty three days, adultery, or at least the temptation, is not one of them. I have no intention of playing into his hand. I just want my contract signed.

"...like this." Sissy inserts her fork like a pro and digs out a clam. It's closed up nice and tight, but she knocks just the same. I strain to come up with a punch line for Jaclyn and Ainsley's knock-knock joke, but nothing comes to mind.

Speaking of Ainsley, she wants to rescue the clam, I can see it in her eyes. It isn't long before she confirms this. "Don't you just know its little heart is pounding like crazy in there?" She turns to Sissy. "Maybe what we want is potato soup."

That's Ainsley, the kind one.

Sissy measures it with the caliper and tosses it in the bucket. "If we don't get 'em, love, someone else will."

"Don't we need a license for this?" Jac thinks she's found her way out. Ha. She should know better.

"Got it." Sissy doesn't even look up from her work.

"Got *it*? Meaning ...?"

Sissy looks at Jac as if she's a slow learner. "I have a license."

"That we, what, split four ways? Well, three anyway."

"Trust me. We've been doing this for years, never once been asked to show our license, never once seen a warden."

"'Morning, ladies."

He's materialized out of the fog, this guy in a khaki green shirt. Most of his long golden-brown dreadlocks are tied in back with other dreadlocks, but a silver ring decorates one that hangs down in front. His eyes are stark as glaciers, and his smile is, wow, sensuous. I swear I don't know what's gotten into me. There was a time I wouldn't want to romp in the same acre of the Garden as Eve, the mother of disobedience. Now I'm right there beside her, mentally plucking all the fruit I can manage.

The patch on the ranger's shirt says A.J.

Sissy stands and brushes the sand off her knees. "'Morning, Officer."

Oh, this is just too good.

"You're off to a fine start," A.J. says. His smile reveals perfect, white teeth.

Sissy looks at the clam in her hand, and fingers the caliper in her pocket. I can read her mind as if it were a neon sign: Is it really four and a half? "Chowder," she says.

He nods and the smile grows wider. Life is a game for A.J., I say to myself. But give him time.

"You know, your license really should be visible. Most people pin it to their shirts or jackets. You do have one, don't you?" A laugh lurks behind every word, as if he doesn't have a clue how to take himself seriously. It's a huge turn on, I bet. He's a girl slayer, this one.

"I do." Sissy opens her jacket, and there it is, pinned to her thermal shirt. Her jacket drops closed and she begins to slide the S back and forth on the chain around her neck.

"Perfect," he says. He shifts his gaze to Ainsley and Jac, and raises his eyebrows. That's how he puts the question to them, with raised eyebrows, like an old friend asking another old friend. He's smooth, A.J. is.

They shift from one foot to the other and fidget with their clam forks. I know Jac is steaming beneath her cool veneer, and maybe thinking of places to put her clam fork, places that involve my stepmother, but Ainsley, ever hopeful, turns her heart-shaped face to Sissy. "Do we?"

"Well, the thing is"—A.J. shrugs, and it seems like an apology— "that's something you have to get yourself. So if you didn't, you kind of know it." He turns his face to the wind to get a runaway dreadlock out of his eyes, then turns back to us and clears his throat. "What I see here is one license, one clam, and one clammer. Probably should keep it that way." He salutes with two fingers. "Good luck, ladies."

We all watch as he walks away, back through the foggy veil. Ogle is the more accurate verb. Only Sissy has the good grace to call out a thank you. He waves without turning around, though I wish he would, wish I could see that smile one more time.

"O.M.G." Sissy is the first to speak, and sounds exactly like a sixth grader, no surprise there. The G is for goodness, I know without question. My stepmother would never say God out of context. She raises her zebra-striped glasses to her forehead for a clearer look at the retreating figure. "Wouldn't you just love to see that poured into the right pair of jeans?"

"Sissy!" Ainsley's eyes are big with surprise.

"Good grief, you're old enough to be his grandmother."

Sissy gives Jac her best detention-hall look. But Jac's used to it. It hasn't phased her since the first quarter of sixth grade.

"Aunt maybe, grandmother never. Besides," Sissy says, "every woman over forty is eternally seventeen in her heart. The further away you get, the more like seventeen you feel."

"You'd know," Jac mutters, but the words are carried on the wind so that only I hear them.

So now we stand with our backs to the sea and watch Sissy dig for our lunch. She's a pro at clamming, she's a pro at everything. And that's the problem with Sissy. Perfection gets old mighty fast. But within a short time she has her ten clams. Not a lot in terms of chowder, but not even Sissy dares to exceed her limit after our near miss with A.J. the ranger.

I carry her clam fork back to the beach house while she carries the bucket, the ten clams rolling around like huge, misshaped marbles in the last sea water they'll ever know. I'd think it was morbid if I didn't love her chowder so well.

Sissy turns into Martha Stewart the moment we arrive, the bossy version, before prison knocked off the edge. But if you ask me, that whole thing was a bad rap. I'm glad she's made a comeback. Oh, how I believe in comebacks.

"Grab that colander from the cupboard up there, will you Ainsley, love? And Bree, we need a big pot of boiling water."

She's already turned the fire under the soup so it's ready for the clams. She stirs it absently as it warms up, and we talk the way girls do. About A.J. mostly. Man. I can't get over that smile.

Then the water boils, and Martha Stewart Vanderpool goes to work. "As you can see, the clams are in the colander. First we rinse off the sand." She plucks a vegetable brush out of the silverware drawer. "And scrub when necessary." Jac and Ainsley flank her, watching over her shoulders as she works her magic. Not me. I've seen this before. "All clean. Now for the boiling water."

"Ooh." Jac takes a step back.

"Can't be helped," Sissy says. She pours the water over the clams. "Voila and hurray! They all opened. Oh, all but one." She tosses that clam into the trash. "Never try to open a clam that refuses to be opened. Now—"

"Why?"

"Well, for one thing, it could be dead in there. For another, you'll never get it opened anyway. Where do you think the term clam up came from? Okay—"

"You won't want to watch this," I say to Jac.

"—we put the edge of our scissors under the zipper and snip upward toward the end of the neck."

I swear, she's such a teacher.

"Once we open the body of the clam, we pull out the digger and gills. See here?" She has to know not one of us is watching, but that doesn't stop her. "Squeeze gently and pull to separate the digger from the body. Rinse and it's ready to go." She lays one mutilated clam the color of putty on the cutting board.

Jac looks like she might lose the breakfast she didn't have. "Who was the first to eat these things?"

"Otters." Sissy doesn't miss a beat as she reaches for the next clam. She holds up her filet knife. "Anyone want to try?"

Ha. Right.

She goes back to work, and in a matter of minutes nine clam bodies are lined up on the butcher block, chopped and ready for the pot. Sissy admires her handiwork, then cocks her head and studies the pile of diced clams. "It's a shame there aren't more."

"I know!" Ainsley claps her hands to punctuate her idea, whatever it is. "Maybe we could wait till tomorrow to have the chowder and you could go clamming again in the morning. Ten more clams would be just about right."

Ainsley's exclamation ignites a once-sweet memory of Kinsey, vivid as a picture, now one more stab to the heart. I'm never ready when they come. Not ever.

 She's a week past her third birthday, though she speaks and reasons better than any of the other kids in her Sunday school class. She always has. She wants Auntie A to bring the twins over to play. But they're in school, I tell her. She sighs at the news and cups her face in contemplative hands, then her eyes brighten, she raises a finger in the air, and simultaneously declares, "I know!" And I can't wait to hear her idea. "Let's text them!"

Let's text them? I stoop down, laughing, and gather her into a hug, then retrieve my cell phone from my pocket. "That's what we'll do, baby girl. We'll text them."

And we did, but not before I snapped a picture of her, which is still saved in my cell phone, the one that was stolen along with my car and my daughter, but, thank God, I'd had the foresight to download my pictures and save them on my laptop. That was one of my favorites. But then, they all are. I can see it so clearly. The top part of her hair is pulled into a tight little pony tail that sticks straight up like a palm frond. And wrapped around it is a big bow, green as spring grass. I thought her hair never would get long enough for a real pony tail. It was slow growing for the longest time. In that regard she took after Ainsley, I'm told. But then, like bamboo at year three—the first year it sleeps, the second year it creeps, the third year it leaps—it just took off.

Even now, Ainsley's hair grows like third-year bamboo, but it's been ages since she let it get long. I was with her the day she cut it for good. She needed moral support. And help convincing Jamie—who'd done Ainsley's hair since high school—that Ainsley was serious.

"I want you to cut it," she says, "and err on the side of shorter."

"No. No." Jamie shakes her head. "You don't want me to do that."

"Really. It's okay. I know what I asked—"

"What you made me promise, you mean. 'Give me hair like Jennifer Aniston' you said—which is exactly what I did—'and no matter how hard I ask, don't let me cut it.' "

"I know. I know. But I can't have her hair right now because I don't have her life right now. What I have are three-year-old twins who drive their fire trucks through my hair."

"And what's wrong with that?" I ask, forgetting my role.

She frowns at me. "It gets tangled in the ladders." She snaps her fingers at her firstborn. "Sam, Sam! Do not bite your brother!"

The boys are here because I'm here—the babysitter for Ainsley's appointments.

"No wonder I felt like a wrestling match was going on inside me all those months. You," she says to Sam, "I should have named you Jacob."

Then she snatches up the scissors and cuts six inches off the right side before Jamie can snatch them back. I suck in my breath, but Ainsley doesn't flinch, not with all that beautiful hair lying on the floor at her feet. Ainsley, the brave one. Jamie says she'll straighten up the mess, but no more. "Then I'll leave right now and tell everyone that Jamie Beckman does my hair." So Jamie fixes it. She has to. And since she's fixing it, she goes right ahead and does everything Ainsley asks. And, of course, it's perfect.

The vision recedes, taking another chunk of my soul with it. I feel it spill out of me as surely as Jesus felt virtue flow out of him when the woman who couldn't stop bleeding touched his robe. A ridiculous comparison, I know, but there it is.

"... logical idea," Sissy is saying, "but the chowder smells so good, who wants to wait another day?"

"Not me," Jaclyn says. This surprises us all. "What?" she says, defensively.

And not even me. A lunch and dinner of Sissy's clam chowder is the perfect almost-last meal. I'm not saying I'm glad they're here. I'm not saying that at all. I'm just saying the chowder smells incredible.

Ten

I'm just sayin'. It reminds me that I'm meeting Jeff Girard in less than twenty-four hours here in Half Moon Bay. I need to work on card designs, need to have them finished when the contract is signed, but my well of creativity dried up long ago. I'll work on them later, I tell myself, the protagonist. And about our meeting, when he calls I'll suggest we meet at that drive-thru coffee kiosk up on the road, since it's within walking distance of the beach house. He'll know the one, I'm sure. I suppose I'll have to take Jac or Ainsley with me, because it's apparent they don't plan to let me out of their sight this entire weekend. I still don't know how I'm going to get around that. So many things to re-figure.

"You're making progress." Jac taps the cover of my book, then scoots the other Adirondack chair closer to mine. She rubs a sleeved arm across the wood and watches the blistered paint fly off like so much dandruff.

I stand and hand Jac the sun-bleached cushion that belongs with her chair.

"What are you reading?" I ask only because it's the polite thing to do, not because I care. I don't mean that quite like it sounds. There's just so little I care about these days.

"*Persuasion*, by Claire Ogden Connors. Oh, how I love her. But the thing about Claire is that she titles her chapters."

I hike an eyebrow as if to say *so?*

"I always say I'm going to remember the title of the chapter, then see how it applies. I always say that. But I don't remember, not ever. I always have to go back and look at the title again. And then I say, oh yeah, that's right."

"The titles should be at the end."

"Exactly! I've always thought so. And thus ends such and such a title, chapter twenty-one. I mean, that would work." She opens *Persuasion* to where her book mark is and begins to read. "I'm not very far into it, but I like it. Maybe not as much as *Final Storm,* but not much could top that."

I make a little grunt of agreement, then look at the cover of my own book. "I have to finish this by Sunday morning." I regret the words even before I finish saying them.

"Why? What's the hurry?" Jac's eyes are that particular shade of green you find in a shady brook in spring, and right now they're fixed on me, drilling me.

I shrug and look away, guarding what I can of myself. "It was my goal for the weekend. I don't see that it has to change just because you all crashed my party."

"Are you saying that amazing chowder wasn't worth a few spoiled plans? And, Bree"—she waits until I turn back to her—"that's our secret. No way do I want Sassy to know how much I loved it."

"Sorry, Jac, I think the third bowl was a dead giveaway."

"They're small bowls." She holds my gaze for a moment, then laughs. "Well, not so small. But how you ended up such a—" She stops all of a sudden and scrunches her lips closed, then zeroes in on a hangnail.

"Such a ...?" I lift my eyebrows, like Ranger A.J., and wait for an answer that doesn't come. "Such a ...?" I prompt again.

"Well, Bree, it's just that, well, you know what a—"

"—bad cook you are, love." Sissy's in the open doorway, with that ridiculous excuse of a dog cradled in one arm. There's no mistaking the pleasure she finds in Jac's discomfort, even when it's at my expense. "Think how boring it would be if we all had the same gifts."

Gifts, in the plural, is a stretch because "cooking" and "skills" ordinarily are not words you can use in the same sentence when talking about Sissy, which is probably why I'm not the great cook. I mean, who did I have to teach me? Yes, she makes great chowder, but that doesn't make her Julia Child. If you don't believe me, try her pot roast.

She descends the steps and deposits Spike on the sand. He turns in a circle, then lifts a leg and pees on it.

"That is not what I meant." Jac arches the brow only I can see. The thing about Jac is that she can arch both brows at will. Not me. My left is the one that cooperates. "You have your"—she thinks a moment—"specialties."

"Macaroni and cheese comes to mind. The kind that comes out of a box."

"And your art. I'm certainly no good with a pencil."

Sissy laughs. "Which is why you always got Cs in penmanship." She wipes Spike's leg on the sand, and picks him up again. "But as far as your cooking, Bree, I blame it on volleyball. You know, all those missed opportunities in the kitchen because of sports. And that's perfectly okay. You always could spike, love." She looks at that stupid dog then sends me a slow wink.

And my heart takes a tumble. I'm such an idiot. It's *Spike*, not Spike. My prowess he's named after, not his. Well, she could have said so. In all this time, she could have.

"And thank you. It'll be our secret." The smile she offers Jac is purely theatrical. "Now, I know you're all on pins and needles about tonight's surprise." She turns back toward the open door. "Ainsley love, it's time. Ainsley?" We hear the toilet flush through the hollow-core bathroom door, so Sissy tries again. "We're ready for the surprise!"

"Oh, okay. Just a sec." A plastic bag rustles and a cupboard door closes, then Ainsley's at the door, holding graham crackers and marshmallows.

"S'mores?" Jac says. "We already know about those. And the chocolate graham crackers, we know about those too."

"Yes, but what you don't know about is the bonfire. What, you thought we'd make them over the stove top?" Sissy laughs, and shivers. The fog has dissipated, but the air is still crisp and cold, and her bare arms have erupted in goose bumps. "I brought Presto logs and a hibachi, but a bonfire must have driftwood. So, let's spread out and gather what we can." She unties her sweatshirt from around her waist and slips it on, then attaches the leash to Spike's collar, and off they go, north, judging by the position of the afternoon sun.

I snap my book closed and send a silent string of oaths at Sissy's retreating form. But then an idea comes, and I smile. It's not a real smile, of course. I haven't known one of those in three hundred sixty three days. But it's enough to bring a frown to Jaclyn's face. And to Ainsley's.

"What?" they both say. It's an accusation, not a question.

I shrug and slip out of my chair. "There's nothing like a good bonfire."

Jac and I are matching mittens, the kind that connect with a cord to keep one from getting lost from the other. We have been since the day we met back in elementary school. If you don't believe me, send us to two different malls in two different cities and we'll come back together with the same funky purse. It's just how we are. So it's not the least bit surprising that we have identical cell phones, make, model and color. I'm glad, because in my haste to leave home I forgot my charger, but Jac's is connected to the wall right beside the toaster. Her burgundy phone is attached.

I point my thumb in its direction. "Can I use that when yours is charged?"

Sissy lifts her eyes from the pieces of jigsaw puzzle spread all over a table too small for its gigantic frame, pulls her glasses toward the tip of her nose, and studies me over the rim. "Why? Who are you going to call?"

Ainsley, who I know for a fact is dying to check on Sam, closes her magazine and waits for my answer.

"No one." My tone has an edge, but I can't help it. "It's just dead."

"Of course you can," Jac says. She's dying to smirk at Sissy as she reaches for my phone and attaches it to the charger. I know that for a fact too.

I could scream with the strain I'm under, trapped as I am in this strait-jacket of a situation. There are things I need to do, things that can't wait, yet I can't exactly sit here and write out my will in front of everyone. That would be, pardon the pun, a dead giveaway. I'd thought about this very thing since the day Kinsey's case went cold. I swear, who gives up on a child? And what gives them the right?

I'm not sure I'd have really gone through with it, but a skull found in Cuyahoga Valley National Forest changed all that. What I didn't have was a backup plan. And if there's one thing Sissy the sixth-grade teacher taught every student that came through her class, it's Have. A. Backup. Plan. If your dog eats your homework, it better be saved on your hard drive. If your hard drive crashes, it better be saved on a floppy disk. Now, of course, it would be a flash drive. If you lose your flash drive, your best friend better have a copy on her flash drive. Back. Up. Plans. She's famous for them.

As you might have guessed, my relationship with Sissy is complicated. Like the relationship I currently have with God. They both want to save me. I just don't want to be saved. Not anymore. It's been that way with Sissy since the day she moved in. I knew nothing about marriage at the age of three, obviously. I just knew this person was spending way too many nights in our house, and I liked it better before this arrangement. I liked that it was Dad and Ainsley and me. Liked that he rubbed our backs before sleep, and played Lite-Brite better than anyone else. That he knew about peanut butter, that it had to be smooth on white bread with a sprinkle of sugar.

That we had his attention.

I knew about mothers, because kids in our preschool had them. I knew that we had one too, and ours was named Teri. There was a picture on the wall. But pictures don't sing, they don't laugh, they don't hug. That's what dads do.

Then Sissy arrived with her rules and her charts and her schedules. And a quarter-inch curling iron with which to curl our dad's hair. Nice tight curls that covered the tops of his ears. Even he will tell you it's a mercy he went bald at such a young age. Not that Sissy was a tyrant. Just a teacher. And no matter what I did, she didn't leave. Not even when I asked her to. "Go home?" she said, with that laugh of hers. "Why, Bristol love, I am home."

All these years later I remember the feel of her hand cupping my cheek, softer than I expected, and the upthrust of the *inside me* as it revolted against her words.

"You seem a million miles away."

I turn and look at my sister. If I'm not careful, she'll see far more in my face than I want to reveal. My keepers are intuitive. All three of them.

I admit I'm secretly amazed that Teri didn't call or come after Kinsey disappeared. Okay, she wouldn't have come—even I know that—not when our cataclysm was the mainstay of the cable news shows for weeks on end, and not after it no longer was. But you'd think she'd have called. "She must be dead." She had to be. "Otherwise..."

Ainsley looks confused, then stricken, but quickly recovers. "No, sweetie. No." I can practically see her draw from that well of optimism deep inside her, that confidence she has in all things good. "We have to believe, Bree." She touches my hand to make the point. "She'll come home. She will."

"Teri," I say, and hold my sister's eyes with my own.

"Teri?" There's no missing the surprise in her voice.

I turn away and look out to sea. "You forget how big the world is till you see the ocean again." Forget how many places there are to be lost in. My boomerang child is just a grain of sand in the scheme of things, blown away on an adverse wind and unable to regain that elliptical path that brings her home again. While God was looking the other way.

"Yes," Ainsley says, "you do. Don't you love it here?"

Yes, I love it. Not the breadbox of a beach house or the touristy feel of the town, but the surf and the tide, the beginning and end of all things as it bleeds on the shore then pulls back again in its eternal cycle. That's what I love. The surf is the last earthly thing I'll hear, and I'm begging there be nothing beyond that. Just a nothingness void. But I know the risk I'm taking. Because what if I'm wrong?

Eleven

We've had our second meal of chowder and sweet French bread. Next comes the bonfire. The ancient hibachi, peeling its blistered paint to expose worn cast iron the color of ashes, strains beneath three Presto logs. It's ringed with the pieces of driftwood we drug back to the beach house, though our labor didn't yield much to speak of. But it's ambiance Sissy's after, so this should keep her happy for a while. We're only waiting now for the sun to fall off the edge of the world. From what I can see past the yellowed chiffon curtains that cover the front window, tonight's sunset will rank high as a spectator sport.

I'm reading like mad the account of *What We Keep's* Ginny Young. To get to the end. But I've still one hundred eighty two pages to go. This would have to be one of Elizabeth's lengthiest books. Naturally. Not that two hundred seventy-two pages is a long book. It's not, as novels go, but just now every page counts. For some it wouldn't be a problem, they could skim their way to the final page. But it is a problem for me, because I don't skip words. Not even one. I know there are readers who pass over description as though it were garnish on a plate, there, like a human appendix, for no good reason. They're also the type of people who chew Life Savers. Really, if all you want is dialogue, pick up the phone. Me, I want to feel the texture of Jasmine's silky under things in Ginny's twelve-year-old fingers. I want to know the smell of a hot summer day. Elizabeth Berg gives me that.

Not that it matters now.

I'm sacrificing comprehension as I read this book, because, honestly, who can concentrate on the levels of this story with all the chitchat and dice throwing and Spike yapping going on in this place? Though I do look at Spike with a different eye, now that I know.

I mean, she could have said, couldn't she? When she bought that mote of a puppy from out of a box at the grocery store entrance from an eight-year-old boy with freckles and tears, and brought it home and gave it such an in-your-face name. She could have said, "Bristol, love, his name is in honor of you," in that way she has, that rankles and soothes all at once, like pressing a gum swollen with the hidden skin of a popcorn kernel. She could have. But she didn't. No, she just announced his name, "Spike," and wreathed his neck in a black studded collar, a pimp of a dog.

But that's Sissy.

I mark my page with the I'm Just Sayin' business card I've been using as a bookmark for a while now. It's not the one with Jeff Girard's cell number on the back, that he passed to me after I'd given my number to him. That one's tucked inside my wallet amidst the credit cards I don't dare use anymore, not with interest at twenty-one percent. This is a generic one I took from the receptionist's desk after my first appointment. Well, the first appointment of my second go-round with the company a few weeks ago. Timing is everything, as they say, and what I don't have is timing. Because if I'd sold my Baby Talk card line to them the first go-round, I wouldn't have been at a preschool picking up Kinsey, leaving a job I didn't want to be at, three hundred sixty three days ago, with Kinsey in the backseat of my car, left unattended for the two minutes in the universe that mattered. Mattered. I'd have been home with my daughter where I wanted to be. Where I belonged.

"Bree?"

Sissy and Jac and Ainsley are in a semi-circle watching me, and once again I haven't heard one or all call my name.

"We're going." My sister holds out her arm to me, and I have this flash of a vision of a branch over quicksand. I take her hand, though I know in the real sense I'm too far gone for whatever strength she has to offer to pull me out of this mess. Still, I love the feel of her skin on mine.

Sissy and Spike lead the way down the reinforced aluminum steps and onto the beach. Followed by Jac and then Ainsley. My compatriots stop, in turn, at the landing and wrap their jackets more tightly around them. Ainsley raises the hood of her collar. It's miserably cold out here. Whatever warmth was gained by two hours of sunshine this afternoon was absorbed by the sand then relinquished as soon as the sun went down. But the fog is holding offshore and the wind has gone home for the night. Even I'm glad for this.

Four aluminum-framed patio chairs have been placed in an arc before the altar of our bonfire, equidistant apart. A straightened metal clothes hanger sticks out of the sand six inches beside the arm of each chair within easy reach of our right hands. If I look hard I bet I can see the end of a tailor's tape hanging out of Sissy's pocket. Growing up, the four chairs that circled our butcher block dinette were always set back from the table four inches, give or take a millimeter, and centered perfectly on the place mats that were aligned evenly with the edge of the table. Not that Sissy is OC. No. Of course not. But for fun I'd shift a place mat and push in a chair on my way by, then hide around the corner and watch her go back through the ritual of righting things. That's a strong suit of Sissy's, righting things.

Odd that I'd be the one to do this. Me, with the same compulsive flaw.

"We'll light the logs," Sissy says, "then add the driftwood once the fire is going strong." By *we*, she means *she*. "Then, of course, the S'mores."

The logs are already in the hibachi awaiting the flame, two on the bottom, the third on top, resting in that concave space between them.

Sissy lights her Scripto wind-resistant utility lighter. She's made a point to mention the wind-resistant part two or three times. To show again how much she plans ahead.

"Hmm," Jac says. And I think *here it comes*. She licks a finger and sticks it in the air. "Not a ghost of a breeze. Anywhere."

"BSTS," Sissy says as the log catches.

Jaclyn is as smart as anyone I know. She's a sharp businesswoman who's invested wisely enough to never have to work again—though she'll be the first to tell you The French Market, her specialty shop in Walnut Creek, isn't work, it's a labor of love. But as smart as she is, she's never caught on to Sissy's acronyms.

"Better safe than sorry." Ainsley and I say it in unison.

Jac rolls her eyes my way.

"Be right back," Sissy says.

Ainsley is just about to take a seat, but stops. "Can I help?"

"Nope. Got it."

So we sit in our arc. Jac, then me, then Ainsley, with the empty seat at the end for Sissy.

Spike, in his sweater, shivers a few feet away from the infant fire. He looks from face to face, his eyes pleading for a warm lap. Well, every face but mine. He knows better. Ainsley pats her leg and Spike makes a perfect leap.

"Here we are." Sissy drapes a throw over each of our shoulders and tosses one over the back of her own chair, then she's off again. By the time the logs are ablaze she's back with large, covered Styrofoam cups of hot chocolate. Ghirardelli's.

One thing about Sissy, she always did have the best class parties of the entire school.

"Is this perfect or what?"

Perfect, no. Still, I give Sissy her kudos. She deserves that much.

Ainsley savors a sip of her chocolate. "Wonder how Sam is." She's kept it in as long as she can, I know.

Well, Sissy only said she couldn't call home, she said nothing about talking about home. So I reach over and squeeze Ainsley's hand. "I'm sure he's fine."

"You can't even see the caps they make these days, they're so natural," Sissy adds.

Like that's a help.

Jac, the only true motherless one among us, asks, "Why would he try to catch a DVD with his teeth?"

"It was *Pirates of the Caribbean*," Ainsley says, and for Sam that was reason enough.

"Well then, thank God it wasn't a sword."

Ainsley starts to laugh, then changes her mind. Instead she moans.

"How are things at the station these days?" I ask. My brother-in-law is a battalion fire chief in Contra Costa County, his twentieth year in firefighting.

"No more layoffs, so that's good. It kills Grady to see these firefighters, even the ones without families to provide for, lose their jobs. And once we got through the traditional Christmas fires, things settled down."

"Things couldn't be worse for David," I say, though I know they're about to get worse. For the first time since planning this weekend I get this pang in the pit of my stomach. Not dread exactly. Certainly not remorse. It's more like anticipation, of just wanting it to be over. It must be that I'm relaxed out here. Or exhausted. I don't trust a thing about my feelings anymore. If I could check them at the door and just exist, amoeba-like, maybe then I'd stick around. There are ways to achieve that, of course, synthetic ways. But I'd prefer to be dead in the real sense than the kind of dead that comes with addiction. As it is, this pain is eating me alive. I can't take any more.

"Do you mind?" Sissy says. "Let's have some girl talk."

A weird silence falls on us then.

"I know," she says, "let's talk about summer. It's my last vacation before I retire"—she actually stands and does a happy dance—"and I want it to be memorable. Let's do a cruise, to Cabo or Alaska, all of us. The boys, and, and—all of us." Sissy folds in her lips and turns to stare at the fire, and this time the silence is blistering.

I know what she's thinking. I should have stopped after the first "all of us." Stupid, stupid, stupid me. That's what she's thinking.

They've all fallen into the Kinsey trap at one time or another, mentioning her as they used to, as though she were up in her room asleep. As though she still existed. Then they clam up—a perfect analogy now that I know what it means—and change the subject as quickly as good manners allow. Well, she does exist. She. Does. Exist. My unspoken declaration is followed by an unspoken flurry of words, like ricocheting bullets, I never used to use. That hollow place inside me has become a war zone.

"She might be home by then." I say it to the fire, and to the sea. I'm amazed at how calm my words are considering how explosive I feel. I look straight ahead, but I know their fretting eyes are on me. They think I'm delusional, all of them. Even David. And now I think even me.

"Bristol, love, you know I didn't mean ..." Sissy leaves off in a rare loss for words.

I stand before they have a chance to converge on me with their smothering arms, and I add the first piece of driftwood to the flames, craving the destruction, then pull my hanger out of the sand. "Who has the marshmallows?"

Chocolate on chocolate is one too many chocolates for my taste, but I nibble away at my S'more for Ainsley's sake. The gooey marshmallow sticks to my front teeth. I rub it away with my tongue, then take another bite.

The fire has grown enough to throw its heat in our direction, as the driftwood burns atop the Presto logs. Who else but Sissy would build a bonfire in a hibachi? Honestly. Of course it's only our front sides that benefit from the blaze, but the throws protect our backs to a point from the cold night air.

"Let's talk about Sunday," I say. There. The moose is on the table.

There's another span of silence broken only by the tireless surf, but then the strains of a guitar in the hands of a god, somewhere up the shoreline, reach our circle. I turn my head to better hear the notes and wish I'd held my tongue a moment longer.

My life has been defined by the worst of all timing for the past three hundred sixty three days. This moment is one more reminder. I just want to close my eyes and lose myself in those minor chords as they color the atmosphere around me, pushing back a little of the monochromatic pall I live within. You'd think I'd be beyond disappointment by now, but I could cry at the interruption I've created for myself.

If I only could.

I don't have to wonder for long who'll be the first to pick up my gauntlet as Jaclyn buries one end of her hanger in the sand and wipes her hands on the thighs of her jeans. "Okay, let's. We've been dancing around it for two days already, and it's not helping a thing."

Then all three of them are speaking at once.

"Couldn't we maybe wait until ..."

"... always were about confronting things head ..."

"... only want to help you ..."

"'Evening, ladies."

Twelve

A.J. the Ranger crouches in the sand on the other side of our bonfire, that compelling smile of his half-engaged. "Nice night." He plays with a thin branch of driftwood, and continues to smile as he looks from one of us to the other.

The hubbub shuts off as if a plug has been pulled, and for a moment there's nothing but the surf, the guitar strains, and the crack of the fire to fill the night. This comes from an overuse of the remote, I know, but there are times I attempt to rewind a scene or conversation until I remember, Oh, this is real life. I used to laugh about it, but I don't laugh anymore. Because I can't tell you how many times I've hit the rewind button since that morning almost a year ago. It doesn't work.

Right then I try to pause the scene I'm in, stopped at a close-up of that smile. But not too close. You don't want to miss the eyes.

"And it just got nicer." Sissy tightens the blanket around her shoulders, like a shawl. "Would you like a S'more?" She waits a ridiculously long moment before she offers him her hanger.

The smile engages fully and he shakes his head.

"You're not still on duty, are you? I mean, my goodness, that'd be more than thirteen hours in a single day." Her phony southern-belle accent is fully engaged. "They don't overwork you, do they, A.J.?"

"No, ma'am." He shakes his head again and studies our fire.

I know for a fact that Jaclyn wants to howl, because if there's anything Sissy hates, it's to be *ma'amed*. Her students—the ones who attempt to worm their way into her good graces—try it once, but only once. Then they learn to say Ms. Vanderpool, and spell it right too.

Sissy notices at the same time I do that A.J. isn't in uniform. "Oh, but I see you're off duty." In fact, he's in jeans and a flannel shirt with a turtle neck underneath. When he stands again I think Sissy just might get her wish about the right pair of jeans.

A.J. nods slowly and plays in the sand with the stick. I'm suddenly, uncomfortably, reminded of Jesus crouching in the dirt, writing, while the adulterous woman waits for a life-or-death verdict. The speculation is endless as to what he wrote. Many believe it was a statement of judgment against the men who, in my opinion, were guiltier than she, and hypocrites to boot. Maybe they're right, but I always thought it was something more tender, like the Old Testament verse he quoted somewhere in a red-letter passage, "I will have mercy, not sacrifice."

I always thought that. Till now. Now I'm pretty sure he's saying, "Stone her." But his indictment has nothing to do with the woman who stood where he knelt, with her tears and a stockpile of rocks littering the ground. Nothing at all. I think it has much more to do with the places my thoughts keep going, not one of them in regards to David.

"About your fire?" A.J. looks as if he doesn't want to deliver the rest of whatever it is he's come to say.

"Oh, don't tell me we need a license for that, too?"

"No, ma'am. But you see, we have fire pits, really nice ones up and down the beach, and you can only have a fire in the fire pits that the state provides."

"The state," Sissy says. "When did Big Brother get so finicky?"

A.J. looks as if he wants to laugh, not in a rude way, but as if he really is amused. I bet he's never had a bad day in his life, if that smile is any indication. Not one. I hope he never does.

Sissy pokes the hibachi with her hanger. "Are you telling me, then, I couldn't have a barbecue in this?"

"Well, ma'am—"

"Sissy."

"Excuse me?" A.J. looks a little startled.

"My name, it's Sissy."

"Ah. Yes, ma'am. Well, what I was about to say is anything you try to barbecue in this, right now, is likely to get a little overdone. But you could use charcoal. Without the driftwood."

That touch of insolence right there would earn him a whole day's worth of demerits in Sissy's classroom.

"Well, here's the thing, A.J. There may be fire pits up and down the beach, but there doesn't happen to be one here. And here is where we need it."

There's a brief but cordial standoff, then my sister bends down and fills her empty hot chocolate cup with sand. "We could put it out."

But A.J. holds up a hand. "You can let this burn out. But if you're planning a fire tomorrow night, you might want to use the pit just south of here. It's not far, really. And if you put your chairs there in the afternoon, folks will usually leave it for you. Enjoy the rest of your night, ladies."

He gives us his two-finger salute along with his famous smile, and heads up the beach toward the guitar music, with four pairs of eyes on his ... jeans.

About fifty feet out he turns, whips his dreadlocks back over his shoulders, and waves.

"Mmm," Sissy says. "That boy belongs somewhere visible."

Somewhere visible. Exactly what I said about the receptionist at I'm Just Sayin'. Not a likely pair, she and A.J., he with his dreadlocks, she with her poise, but both something special to look at. Standing in front of the receptionist's desk, as I am in my mind, I can see into Jeff Girard's office. When I get back inside the beach house I'll take my phone off

Jaclyn's charger, slip into the bathroom, and text him. God forbid that Sissy would catch me with a phone in my hands. I don't dare call. There's no such thing as privacy in that tin can of a trailer. But it doesn't matter. I don't want to talk to Jeff, I just want to get things arranged for tomorrow, to know it's all settled. It would have been so easy if everyone had just left me alone. Yes, I know, they want to help. But they're not. At all.

This toying Jeff has been doing with me began with a touch. Innocent on my part, not so for him, there's not a doubt in my mind. It was at our first meeting of our second go-round in negotiations for my Baby Talk line. He passed the draft of a contract across the table to me. When I reached out to take it, he slid his hand further down the paper until his fingertips touched mine. I'd have pulled away if I could, but in that split second it felt like someone had jump-started my flat-lined heart. I was fused to him, powerless to break the connection, even if I'd wanted to. But it felt excruciatingly good, compounded by the fact that the only thing I'd felt for months was dead. There was no mistaking the jolt I'd received. But it was seduction, pure and simple. And intentional. Jeff's eyes registered his score, then he released me.

I couldn't get out of there fast enough, couldn't still the erratic beat of my heart. I nearly tore up the contract on my way to the car, planned to all the way home, but that contract was about Kinsey, not Jeff Girard, and he wasn't going to cheat me out of it by what amounted to nothing more than a game to him. But there was no question I was playing with fire, and, oh, could I get burned, because having felt so intensely, I wanted to feel again. I wanted to look into eyes that weren't saturated with pain that I'd caused. Wanted eyes that didn't offer redemption that I could never, ever accept.

There was never an electric moment with David, never a heart-stopping, breath-taking encounter, not even in the beginning. Of course, we were young when we met, teenagers in a youth group at his father's church, but that only intensifies the lack. Because if there's ever a time when a girl is electrified by a guy, it's when she's a teenager. When she thinks true love is that roller-coaster feeling she gets when their eyes really connect for the first time, or when hand brushes hand, not quite by accident, or lips meet lips with a surprising intensity. It was never that way with David. Sure, he's nice to look at. Very nice, in fact. My beautiful Kinsey looks more like David than she does me, with the exception of our blond hair to his reddish brown, so he'd have to have looks, and he does. But that's not what drew me. What drew me was his kindness. He couldn't do an unkind thing to save his life. Or a selfish, mean or embarrassing thing. It wasn't in him.

Bottom line is that with David I felt safe. I felt here's a guy who doesn't say one thing and do another, who won't pressure me into behaving in a way I don't want to behave. But how things have changed. Because now, like I said, the thing I can't stand about David is his kindness. It would be so much simpler if he hated me.

"You have a message." Jac whispers the words and slips my phone into my hand. She's come from the beach house, where she's relieved her famously undersized bladder. "Thought it was mine," she says. "So who's J?"

My senses crackle as though a current has shot through me. I turn my eyes away, to the fire, the sea, anywhere else.

"Bree?"

"Hey now, no secrets." Sissy picks up her dog and brushes the sand off his paws, then settles him in the crook of her arm. His bulging eyes study me, and like always, he shivers.

Sissy's admonition is enough to break the spell. I could kiss her for it. But Jac is irritated. "Later," she says. And she means it.

"I'm going for a walk," I say, in a tone that excludes company. In search of the guitar. It's a Siren to my soul, that sound, but I'm already shipwrecked so I have nothing to lose.

Jac, Sissy and Ainsley tense, exchange looks, and just when Sissy is about to speak, I say, "I'll be back." I must be convincing, for they let me go without a word. I can't help feeling someone is trailing me, yet when I turn, no one's there.

The smell of wood smoke mingles with fog and sea, for the fog made its way ashore when we weren't paying attention. It turns the world into a misty, compact place, insulated with the sound of the surf, of indistinct voices, and of that guitar. I'm getting closer as I walk toward the distant beam of the lighthouse, for the voices are more distinct, and the guitar beckons more than ever. The blaze of a bonfire, safely corralled in a fire pit and muted by the fog, comes into view, then the forms of people sitting around it, some on blankets, some on chairs, one guy on a driftwood log—the guy who holds the music in his hands.

I stop, step back into the mist, and let the music ravage me. Some of the songs I recognize, others are new and mysterious. But they all have that sound that stays with you forever, in the deep places, emerging when you least expect them to, eluding point of origin. You know them, but you don't remember how.

It's a gift, this sound, that will soothe me on my way a day and a half from now.

"Hey." It's A.J., stepped away from the handful of fans surrounding the guitar god. "I hope your friend isn't too angry about the fire."

"Sissy's my stepmom. And she's over it. The fire, I mean."

"Ah, well, that's good."

Everything he says is wrapped in the promise of laughter. I'm not sure there's much he takes too seriously.

"You, um, you look familiar. You come here often?"

I might think this is a pick-up line, except, one, I'm at least eight years older than A.J. Okay, maybe twelve. And two, my face was plastered all over cable news for weeks after Kinsey disappeared, so, yes, I do look familiar to a good part of the informed world.

"Sissy owns the beach house," I say. "That's what she calls it, the beach house."

He laughs a little, and nods. He has these eyes that turn down on the outside, giving him a sleepy, seductive look, but the way he lifts those brows makes you think everything he sees is a discovery. I've said it before, but the irises are as clear and imposing as a glacier. You feel as though you could fall into them. I've never seen eyes quite like his.

I'd give anything to draw this face. The longing breaks free before I can harness it, and there's no stuffing it back inside. It's all I can do to keep from touching him, from tracing my finger along the contour of his mouth. It's not a sensual thing that drives this, but of course, who would believe that? And while it's true I'd love to draw him, *give anything* is a gross exaggeration, for I've nothing left to give. How easily we throw about our words and phrases without a thought to what they mean. Some things we learn too late.

"You know the guy with the guitar?" I move my thoughts to safer ground.

He turns back to his circle of friends. "That's James. My brother."

"Your brother. Wow. I was following the sound." I suddenly feel as though I have to explain.

"He gets that a lot."

And now I see a resemblance between the brothers, even from ten yards away. His hair is dark and shoulder length. No dreadlocks. But the difference about James, of course, is the hands, the magic he works with those fingers.

"You play too?"

"Taught him everything he knows." The smile tells me that isn't quite true. "But, yeah, I play. Just not when James plays."

I know exactly what he means. I never compete with Ainsley, the exquisite one.

He turns back toward the group, nods their way. "Want to sit?"

"Oh, no, I just—"

"Come on, have a beer."

"No. Really." I step back, glance out at the dark lines of the sea. "I'm, I'm just going to listen a while."

"Okay." I sense he doesn't want to leave, but at last he turns.

"Tell him it's wonderful, his music."

"I will."

"And don't compare." I don't know what makes me say this, but A.J. seems to take it under advisement. Then he makes his way back to his friends.

I retreat until all I can see is the fire through the mist, where I feel hidden and safe. I listen and finger the rough texture of the starfish in my pocket. The very next song is Cohen's "Hallelujah." Not a song you'd hear in my father-in-law's church, or in any church probably, but it holds me as surely as if I've been staked where I stand. James sings every verse, and though his voice is more texture, less polish, it's the most provoking sound I've ever heard. It's at that place on the circle where pain and pleasure converge, and you feel like you're dying, like death is the apex of it all.

I'm cold to the marrow of my bones, and damp, but it's not until I sense Ainsley at my side that I even consider going back. She finds my hand and takes it in her own.

"Bristol," she says. "You okay?"

I look right in her eyes and say yes. Though I'm not okay. Not even a little.

Thirteen

I've made it clear the moose is off the table. I don't want to talk after all. Not tonight, not tomorrow, not ever. If I make it to Sunday I won't have to. That is the goal.

Ainsley and Sissy are finally asleep. And Spike too. I can tell by their breathing, which is even, though out of sync. Jac, on the other hand, is in our tiny bedroom, waiting to talk. She hasn't said as much, but I know. I just don't plan to oblige her. I slip into the bathroom and turn on the shower as hot as I can stand it. Then turn it up some more. It's like standing in an upended casket, this crate of a shower. There's no room to shave your legs, barely room to bend down to wash your toes. But the water feels good. I lean against the cold fiberglass, wait for it to warm beneath my skin, and let the water cascade over me.

Inside my head I keep singing "Hallelujah." The chorus, over and over and over. I can only remember part of one of the verses, and I sing that too. About God above, and what I learned from love, and how to shoot someone who outdrew you. What a song. Lord in heaven, what a song.

When the water cools, I turn the knob up again, and repeat this until the lever is up as far as it will go and there's no more hot water to draw on. Then I have to move fast, rinsing the shampoo out of my hair in water that now makes me shiver. I can't remember the last time I stood as long as I wanted in a shower that stayed hot, with no one waiting to get in after me, no one needing my attention.

The tiny bath is full of steam as I stand dripping on the mat. I wipe the mirror with my hand, and though it fogs up almost instantly I observe my skin, still red from the heat of the water. I wipe the mirror again. I was right about the chili peppers. My diminutive breasts lie flat against my rib cage, their transient fullness—a sign of the life that had been within me—only a memory. An exaggerated one at that. My ribs are well-defined beneath my paling skin. I've lost a dozen pounds this past year, when I stood in need of gaining them to begin with. There's a confetti-sized mole just beneath the sternum, perfectly centered. I've never really noticed it before, but now it's like a neon Dot Number One in Connect the Dots. Moles should be random, not like this at all. This makes you want to grab a Magic Marker and get to work. All in all, there's nothing sensuous about the image I project.

I grin and shake my dripping head, because wouldn't Jeff be disappointed if he did get his way?

"Bree?"

There's a faint tap on the door that accompanies the whisper of my name. It's Jac, fresh out of patience.

I wrap a towel around me, tuck one end into the top, and open the door with as little noise as possible. It's warped and sticks badly, so it isn't easy to do. Jac nods toward our bedroom, and I follow. She slides the pocket door closed behind me with barely a sound, shutting us off from the adjacent bedroom, whose door stands wide open. And there we are, in a standoff.

"Who's J?"

Thankfully, she keeps her voice low. The last thing I want is for her to wake Sissy, but I don't think she wants my stepmother involved in this conversation any more than I do.

I could have used some of that valuable time I stood under the water to concoct a convincing lie. And now I wish I had. Boy, do I. Because when I tell her J is Jeff Girard and that he's coming here tomorrow, I can only imagine what she'll think. I've never given anyone a reason to question my fidelity to David, but I see how it looks, that I was supposed to come here alone, with plans for Jeff to stop by. But instead of working on a response to the question I knew was coming all I could think of was "Hallelujah." Even now it's all I can do to keep the song stuffed in a safe place inside my head as I rummage through my bag, pull out underwear, a T-shirt and sweat pants, and get myself dressed. Then I wrap the towel around my hair. I refuse to be rushed, and it shows, but all the while my mind races as I design answers for the interrogation that's begun.

I sit cross-legged on my narrow bed, facing the aisle that separates me from Jac, who's leaning against the rickety headboard. I settle myself and plop a pillow on my lap.

"You were saying?" I sound like a snot, I know. One more thing to apologize for in the letter that will accompany my Last Will and Testament.

Jaclyn crosses her arms and drills me with her eyes. "Who's J?"

I could kick myself for not reading the text message, which I fully intended to do when I got in the bathroom. But my phone is still in the pocket of my jeans, which are lying on the bathroom floor. I want to say, "Be right back," and go and read it so I know what kind of damage control to offer, because who knows what kind of seductive language he might have used. Instead, I have to fake it.

"J," I say. "Well, that could be anyone. It could be you."

"But it's not."

"Or it could be"—I search for another J name, as if I were playing that stupid name-our-imaginary-sister game, but nothing comes to mind. "A wrong number. That happens, you know."

"You're stalling, Bree. That's more telling than you realize."

"My mouth hurts," Kinsey says, pleading her cause before we even knew she was on her way down the stairs. There weren't many times Kinsey wasn't stalling when she'd get up at night, but there was one time in particular I remember. I remember because for once I got it right. "My mouth hurts," she says again. Tears streak both of her freshly-bathed cheeks.

"Show me where," I say, though I have a good idea. It's time for her molars to come in. Her nose has run all day and she's had a fever, too. She opens her mouth and points to her lower right gum. "Here," she says, a mumbled explanation. "And here." She points to the other side. Sure enough. Both sides of her bottom gums are swollen and fiery red.

I draw her onto my lap. She lays her head against my chest, even as she clutches Hippo, the turquoise, downy-soft animal she craves when she isn't quite herself. It's a death hold really, more than a clutch, and I know what she's thinking. 'I'm going to lose Hippo for this. I just know it.'

"It's okay, baby." I rock her and Hippo as we sit on the couch. "Could you get the Orajel," I say to David, "and the children's Tylenol?"

"Absolutely." He unreclines his way out of his chair, and rubs the top of Kinsey's head on his way to the kitchen.

"Hippo, too." Her voice has just the right level of pathos to thrum my heart. She holds Hippo out an inch or two for David to rub, then hugs him tightly again.

"One or two?" David says.

"One." Shouldn't he know this? Or at least he could read the label. I mean, what if I weren't here? What then? He'd call me, that's what. Or Ainsley or Sissy. Well, whatever.

At least he'd call.

It's not an angel on my shoulder telling me this, but rather a less-impy imp debating with the for-real imp on my other shoulder. There's nothing angelic about me these days. Not that there ever was.

When David comes back we administer the Orajel together, he encouraging Kinsey to open her mouth, and me rubbing on the relief with my pinky. Then he gives her the Tylenol, which she chews without prompting. She doesn't mind the dissolvable cherry tablet.

I rock her until she's asleep enough to lose her hold on her friend, then David takes her from me and carries her up to bed. I stand in the doorway and watch him ascend the stairs, and I have this urge to cry. Stupid, I say to myself. But that does nothing to alleviate the knot I can't swallow.

"Bristol, who's J?" Jac asks again.

"J is Jeff Girard, actually." I figure the truth may just be enough to throw her off. An eyebrow goes up and she holds me captive with her look. "Jeff Girard. From the card company."

"I'm Just Sayin'."

"I'm Just Sayin'. And why would Jeff Girard be texting you?"

"I sold the line. I told you."

"Yeah, and I'm happy for you. I wish it had happened ... before. I really do."

That's enough to break the hold she has on me. I look away.

"But why would he say, 'See you at 5.'? And why sign it J? Seems awfully familiar."

The room is small, but the wood paneling shrinks it even more, and dates this place as effectively as the lifeless shag carpet that runs throughout all but the kitchen and bathroom of the beach house. The lamp, small and impotent, which sits on the night table between the two beds, casts a pinkish glow from beneath its crooked shade. But it doesn't reach half far enough. At the moment I'm very glad. It's harder to lie with your eyes exposed.

Five? It says five? I expected him to pass through Half Moon Bay sometime in the morning. Now I really do wonder what he has up his sleeve. "I have to sign the contract. It happens that Jeff is passing through town on his way to ... somewhere. Carmel, I think."

"He's coming here?"

"You think I'd have him come here? Are you kidding?"

"Then where?"

I cross my arms even tighter than they were. "Jac, what is this? I don't like being interrogated."

"What's he like?"

"What?"

She waits, and I can tell this is one bone her bulldog self is not going to relinquish.

Jaclyn is a natural beauty, the quintessential California girl. Blond hair, just the right length, with just the right amount of sun streaking, made to look altogether natural. Perfect features and skin that glows. Your everyday cover girl. Personally, I've always loved the look of her collarbones. They're clavicles, I know, but collarbone sounds nicer. I mean, a clavicle could be anywhere. Weird, I know, how much I like them, but they're elegant, those Audrey Hepburn bones. And with just the right neckline, like the one she's wearing now, it's such a great look. I wish my neck and shoulders were half as attractive. I focus on them now, those bones, and at the hollow of her throat recessed between them. She's a raving beauty, Jaclyn is.

"He's your typical, boring executive." I lift my eyes to hers and hold them there, to add believability to the lie. "Though his office is nice."

Jac relaxes a bit with that last little detail that adds credibility, and I can breathe again.

"We're going to meet at the coffee kiosk up on the highway," I say as though it's already established. "Go with me and check him out for yourself."

"Really?" Her eyes narrow and her tone is suspicious.

"Sure."

"Bristol." She reaches for my hand, a symbolic move since she can't really touch it. "This is an excruciating time for you. For all of us, but mostly for you. I see you tottering on the brink, Bree, and I'm not going to let you fall."

I smile as if to say thanks. But what she doesn't see is the abyss, where I've already hit bottom.

————————

Fate, if there is such a thing, selected *What We Keep* to be the last novel I read. It's the story of a mother who deserts her husband and two daughters. I know, nothing like that ever happens in real life.

Right.

I could actually laugh at the irony here. It's the story of how the girls reconnect with their mother after an eternity of years. It's the one thing that gives me pause, that makes me want to dump my pills into the sea instead of down my throat. Not that I want to reconnect with Teri. That's not what I mean at all. But I'd wait an eternity of years to see my daughter again, that long and then some, the pain be damned, if not for the vision of Zachary Martin's mom that I just can't vanquish. Not to mention the accusation I know I'd find in Kinsey's eyes, were I to see them again, for me allowing her to be taken.

Kinsey has a dramatic personality. Like Sam. There's no end to the entertainment they provide. Like when Sam was being potty trained. Ainsley put him on the toilet on his Batman potty seat one afternoon and left him to his business. Thirty seconds later he calls out, "Mama! I need a book!" We laughed ourselves silly over that. And then when he said, "I need another one!" well, that pushed us right over the edge.

Eli, on the other hand, would sit wordlessly and push till his face was red as a pomegranate. Then he'd say, "Done," in a quiet little voice, and wait till you came to get him. Sweet, yes. Dramatic, no. He and Sam are identical, but I never had a moment's trouble telling them apart. Not from the minute they were born. Sam was the mischievous one; Eli the sweet. And that's how I think of him, Eli, the Sweet. And if you think being identical twins endeared Eli to Sam in a strong and mystical way, think again. I remember, the boys had just turned three. Eli, Mr. Uber-Passive, wanted nothing more than to be close to his brother, to play with his toys, to rub Sam's hair, because for him that strong and mystical bond existed in a huge way. Well, even at three, it drove Sam nuts. He'd hide out in a closet just to play with his Tonka truck all by himself, or slip under the bed to "read" his own book. Which broke poor Eli's heart. Ainsley said to Sam one day, "Sam, love, can't you try to be nice to Eli? Please?" Sam gets this look on his face, like he's a deep thinker, and says, "Hmm. Not yet." Then back in the closet he went.

Taking only personality into account, Kinsey is more like Sam's twin than Eli, but Ainsley thanks the Lord every day for her mellow guy. And so do I. The thing I love about Eli is that he takes time to hug. He melds to you and takes as much pleasure in affection as he gives. Not so with Sam and Kinsey. They haven't time to be bothered with all that. I can't recall a moment, ever, unless she was sick, that Kinsey didn't squirm within my embrace, ready to get on to the next thing. Her life is one big activity page from the minute her eyes open in the morning till they close at night. Then she sleeps as hard as she plays. Like Sissy, she can only be defined only in superlatives.

I'm reading again. Sipping tea and counting down the pages. A hundred and thirty to go. The beach house is quiet and dark, except for the wall sconce above where I sit in the eating nook. It sheds just enough light to read by. Jaclyn didn't resist when I told her goodnight and came out here to the parlor to read. I won't say she's asleep, but she's not being a pain.

I retrieved my phone, first thing—and picked up my clothes off the bathroom floor—and read the text message from Jeff. "See you at 5," is all it said, giving credence to my lie. I'll text him when the sun comes up to give him our meeting place. Surely he'll find it. I mean, how many coffee kiosks are there on the highway running through Half Moon Bay? And I'll take Jac with me as I promised. That will serve two purposes. One, it will allow me to get to the meeting in the first place; and two, it will keep me safe from whatever intentions Jeff may have. But I still have to figure out how I'm going to slip away from Jac, Ainsley and Sissy before Sunday morning. Sure, I could just swallow the pills while everyone sleeps, but not even I can be so cruel as to let them be the ones to find me. No, I have to get away from here, from them, and do this with as little trauma to them as possible.

I wonder what Ginny and Sharla will find after all these years when they reach their mother's house. And so I read. Elizabeth's book has nudged me into thinking about Teri. Sadly, I'm too tired to resist. I've spent only a wee amount of energy wondering about her over the years. She's a non-person, for no other reason than the fact that she's not even a memory to me. She's only that one photograph that hangs on my father's wall. He's left it there for Ainsley and me, all these years, though he needn't have bothered. But neither of us has the heart to scorn his thoughtfulness. And Sissy doesn't mind. As far as I know, she's never felt threatened by our mother's ghost.

But I've noticed of late a disturbing resemblance between Teri and me. You know the angles and planes in my physical build I was talking about? I see now where I get them. I see the shape of my nose, the curve of my chin. But that's not what I mean. There's this *leaving* look in her eyes I'd never noticed before. And I see it in mine.

I suppose she's a loose thread I'd like to follow to the end, now that it is the end. I might like to know if she found the life she was looking for. And if I've another sister somewhere, though that's highly unlikely. I mean, can you imagine? A Christine or a Cynthia after all this? No. I can't imagine that at all.

I'll admit I've searched a crowd a time or two for someone who looks like Teri. Not that she stayed in Walnut Creek, or even California. And not that I'd ever know if I found her. People change. In thirty-seven years they change a lot. She certainly wouldn't know me, not without my binky. I was a pacifier child. For way too long. A consolation prize of sorts, I suppose. But come to think of it, that didn't start till after Teri left, so the binky wouldn't be a clue for her after all.

And what would I say if I did find her? If she walked through the door right now, what would I say?

I find myself gripping my mug, though the tea is long gone. Because what I really want to know is, how could you do that? How could you choose to leave not one daughter, but two? How could you come to a place where you said to yourself, "This little person, bone of my bone and flesh of my flesh, doesn't mean enough to me to want to stay in her life"? Because this is what you'd have to say, to do what Teri did. Me? I'm on the other end of the spectrum. Because I would die for Kinsey. In fact, I plan to do just that.

Someone should bolt the door, because if Teri walked in now, what I'd say would be highly venomous. I set my mug on the table to keep from throwing it.

I've learned something about the etiquette of loss this past year. The do's and don'ts, if you will. Mostly the don'ts. Topping the list is visiting someone whose daughter has disappeared, spending an hour on their sofa, drinking their coffee, beholding the pain etched into every line of their faces, and not mentioning their child even once.

Kinsey had been gone ninety-two paralyzing days when Vern and Janine Price called to ask if they could come by. Vern had been a co-worker and friend of David's when they were both apprentice carpenters way back when. Vern and Janine left California a few years ago and went to one of the Dakotas or somewhere back there, but were in town for a niece or nephew's—maybe a cousin's—graduation. I found myself clenching my jaws so hard it hurt, when David said, sure, Vern, we'd love to see you guys.

What a lie that was.

I could hardly stand the sympathy anymore of people who came by to hold our hands and share their prayers. Grew painfully tired of filling in the long, silent gaps when they didn't know what to say. Of pretending to be buoyed when I was sinking into a pit I couldn't begin to crawl out of.

The Prices arrived thirty minutes after the phone call, and as we usually did, we ushered them into the living room, where photos of Kinsey stood on every table, hung on every wall, impossible to miss, and seated them on one sofa while we sat across the coffee table from them on another, and served them decaf. As was typical, the conversation began with the smallest of small talk, which usually evolved into The Subject. I braced myself for the inevitable outpouring of sympathy, but I needn't have bothered, because the subject of our missing daughter never came up. Not once.

Vern began by telling us of the incredible steal of a deal—who uses ridiculous phrases like that anymore?—he got on his house—not their house, his house—in South Dakota, or maybe North, in this endless, droning way he has, while Janine sat with her shoulders curled in and her eyes never rising above the level of my chest. At least she had the good graces to be embarrassed as he went on and on about the price of the quarter acre he bought to build this house on, and the ease with which he obtained the permits. Not at all like the red tape of California. And how inexpensively he built this monolith of a dwelling place, which includes a full walk-out basement, because everyone has basements in the Dakotas. He brought out a packet of photographs and passed them around one by grueling one, and never lacked for commentary.

From there he went on to talk about how he's practically retired—at forty-four, he says, with an exclamation point in his voice—because his house and everything he owns is paid for. Both cars, his riding mower, snow blower, big screen TV. And surround sound. You oughta hear his surround sound, he says. He can choose which projects he accepts now, and he only accepts the "sweet ones," and makes an obscene amount of money on those, he says. He shakes his head and laughs as he repeats *obscene.*

I think "obscene" as well, though it's not the only thing I think. But I don't shake my head. And I don't laugh. Instead I squeeze my fists until my nails dig bloody little grooves into the flesh of my palms.

I never knew a man who used so many words. Not in my whole life. And not one of them worth the breath it takes to utter them. Janine, on the other hand, offered a weak smile now and again, or made a sound inside her closed lips meant to say, I agree, I do. Isn't he brilliant?

And all I could think was, "Will you never leave? Because if you don't leave soon I fear I won't be able to keep this rage inside. I'm going to burst like a whacked piñata, and believe me, it won't be anything sweet that comes spilling out."

Ainsley held me—loosely, because of that smothered feeling I get these days—when I seethed out the story to her later that day. Then she said, "Oh, sweetie, some people don't know how to address tragedy, and so they skip over it and try to get to that normal place. It's wrong, I know, but they just don't know how."

And I said ... well, never mind what I said.

Fourteen

I wake in the morning of the three hundred sixty-fourth day, slumped over on the miniature sofa, my head resting on its brick of an arm, with one of Sissy's throws draped over me. I'm sure it was Ainsley who put it there. My sketch pad is there beside me, with nothing drawn. Inspiration doesn't exist for me anymore.

"Coffee?" Ainsley says, in that hopeful way she has. But of course she means decaf.

I sit up, and oh, the kink in my neck grabs hold. I moan loudly. "Tea."

Ainsley fills a mug with water and pops it in the microwave. "You can't have slept well."

She doesn't know the half of it.

Three minutes later Ainsley hands me a steaming mug of GoodEarth Original—and even that is decaf—then sits down on a corner of the dinette's padded bench. She watches me these days as though I'm as fragile as a chrysalis, afraid that if this thin shell that holds me together should break, there's no telling what would emerge. It certainly wouldn't be a butterfly.

"How about a muffin?" she asks.

I think for a moment, then say no thanks. There's an emptiness in the pit of my gut, all right, but it can't be touched by anything Ainsley, or anyone else, can offer.

I hear the shower running, hear Sissy singing some indeterminate song from behind a door the drab-gray color of sun-baked redwood. She isn't the least bit inhibited. Not Sissy.

Ainsley should have been the younger sister, should have been the B and me the A, since I'm the bossy one, the naysayer. She's the encourager, the one who wants to please. Me, not so much. I'm all too well acquainted with my *After* self, but it's hard to remember the *Before* version of me. The change, I know, is staggering. Whatever good parts I possessed are long gone.

"It's going to be another beautiful day, I can tell. The fog won't last any longer than it did yesterday. I wonder, should we try to save one of the fire pits like—" Ainsley stops and thinks a moment.

And I fill in the blank. "A.J."

"Right. A.J. Cute kid, isn't he?"

I nod. Yes, he's cute. And he's the brother of the guitar god.

"Though he's not really a kid. Quite a smile, huh?"

"You noticed, too?"

"Who wouldn't?"

Jaclyn emerges from our box of a bedroom, all put together. "We must be talking about the ranger."

"Oh, yeah." Ainsley pours Jaclyn a cup of coffee, and stirs in a helping of creamer.

I haven't told anyone about my conversation with A.J. last night. Or about how close I got to the music. I need that to be mine. But what I want to say is how stunning A.J. is up close, how honey smooth his skin is, how incredible his eyes. But I can't say that in a way that wouldn't sound wrong, so instead I repeat Ainsley's words, "Cute kid."

Jaclyn stops mid-sip, leans back from her mug. "Cute? Kid? Are you kidding me? He's gorgeous. And he's no kid."

Sissy selects just that moment to step from the bathroom, her hair wrapped up in a bleach-spotted, frayed-edge towel. She hasn't even begun her makeup yet. "Too bad he's too young for you—by a good decade."

"Thank you, Sassy, thank you very much. Although, as I recall, I did help to wipe the drool off your face as he walked away from our little clamming soiree yesterday."

She shrugs. "What can I say? I have eyes and I'm certainly not dead. But that's where it ends with me. I do not lust in my heart."

"Oh, really. What about the seventeen-year-old version of you?"

Sissy flashes that flirty smile she's so good at. "Now that's another story."

Ainsley takes advantage of the three seconds of silence that fill the beach house. "I have something for all of you." She reaches into a Target bag, one of those nice heavy plastic ones that doesn't tear with the least provocation, then hands each of us a gigantic Hershey's kiss wrapped in red foil, along with a card, each in a red envelope. "Happy Valentine's Day."

Jac and Sissy murmur their *you shouldn't haves* and so forth, but you can tell by their faces they're glad she did. Me? I think about the cards she undoubtedly bought for Grady and the boys, leaving them in places where they'd find them today, right on cue, and I think about the card I didn't buy for David, because what kind of a card could I find that could remotely navigate the tension between us, not to mention the fact that I'll be dead the next time he sees me? Maybe I should have designed one. The twisted humor of that thought almost makes me smile.

"We still don't call home," Sissy says, accepting her gift from Ainsley. "Our men can wait." She looks in Jac's direction, the only manless one among us, as far as Sissy knows, but stops just short of visual contact. She loves her rubs, Sissy does.

Jac presses her lips together and looks heavenward. She's counting. Already way past ten, I can tell. Sissy doesn't know about Daryn, or is it Loren? I never can remember. I'd tell her if I could summon the energy to come to Jac's defense. I hope Jaclyn knows that.

As I take the mound of chocolate from my sister I'm suddenly hit with another flashback. It was the day of Sam and Eli's ninth birthday, just over a year ago.

We meet at Pizza My Heart, our favorite pizza place, and by the time we arrive Ainsley has the pizzas and salad ordered, as well as pitchers of Pepsi, root beer, and Mountain Dew. The plates are stacked, the forks beside them, with little bowls of all the different salad dressings we like lined up in a row. That's Ainsley, the efficient one.

She's also ordered a pitcher of iced tea, which Dad and Sissy prefer over soda. Slices of lemon rim the pitcher. That too is how they like it, with lots of ice, no sugar. My taste buds come alive as I breathe in the strong scent of citrus, which reaches all the way to where I sit. It's a happy scent, lemon is. It surprises me to have such a thought. I make my way to the pitcher and drop a fat lemon wedge into my Pepsi.

Kinsey, who has just turned three, loves having another party so soon after her own. She loves the pizza, the balloons that decorate our tables, and the special table that holds the cake and the presents. She spends a lot of time circling that table, her shoulder pressed against the edge as she goes round and round it, taking note of the gifts and cards she can see, and the jar of rainbow-colored Skittles in the center to which the balloons are tied.

An hour later, with nothing but pizza crusts left on our plates, Ainsley lights the two 9-shaped candles, we sing the Happy Birthday song to Sam and Eli, and the best part of the evening, for them, is underway.

As Ainsley reaches for the first pair of gifts to distribute to her boys, Kinsey taps her on the thigh. "S'cuthe me, Auntie A. S'cuthe me." She leans her head back and looks up at Ainsley's face. Her little hands are together at her chest, and she picks at one of her thumb nails.

Ainsley squats down so she's eye level with Kinsey. "Yes, sweetheart?"

Kinsey leans toward her aunt, and with a look as serious as any I'd ever seen, she says, "Are any of those for me?"

Kinsey looks so vulnerable in that moment, her skin so fair you can see the veins running up from her jaw line. I reach for her, want to pull her onto my lap and wrap my arms around her. Want to explain that we each have our own special day, and that birthday presents are given to the ones whose special day it is. Like we had done for her just a couple of weeks before. That today is Sam and Eli's special day, and the presents are for them.

But before I can do that, Ainsley wraps Kinsey in a hug, and presses her cheek to Kinsey's. "Well, yes, sweetheart. One of them is for you." And she stands and retrieves a gift I hadn't noticed, one wrapped in paper that would gross out the boys if it were theirs.

Kinsey's smile is huge as she receives the gift. And then she says, "Nank you, Auntie A. Nank you very much."

And all I can think is, why hadn't I thought of that? When I was passing out all those gifts to Kinsey sixteen days ago, why hadn't I thought to do something like this for my nephews? Like Ainsley, the thoughtful one.

"Well, I have something too," Sissy says, rescuing me from the memory. Jac and I exchange looks that say all too clearly, *Well, aren't we the schmucks?* because I know I didn't bring anything for anyone, and it's pretty clear she didn't either. "Only it's not candy, and it's not a card."

Sissy doles out this dramatic look, with this cryptic smile, then she lifts her deeply purple, home-appliqued sweatshirt and pulls something out of the elastic waistband of her pants. She reaches for the glasses on top of her head—the ones with the electric pink frames to match the puffy flower petals on the sweatshirt—and separates the tickets, for that's what they appear to be, like a hand of playing cards.

What now? is my first thought. Are we going to that little theater after all?

"We are going, at ten o'clock this morning, whale watching. Just us and the skipper. Or captain. Whatever. I've already packed our lunch." She is pleased, Sissy is.

"Wow," Ainsley says, and from what I can tell, she means it.

Jac, on the other hand, is mentally searching for the Dramamine.

Me? I'm putting rocks in my pockets.

———————

Sissy has a past, the details of which I've always found amusing. It's related to one of those movie starlets from the forties and fifties, whose tiny waists were accentuated by their full breasts, which were funneled into bras as pointed as the torturous shoes Jaclyn wears when she dresses up, whose bedroom eyes and seductive lips were the sweet dreams of every mother's son, whose calendar pose was scandalous at one time, but a perfect G-rating these days. Sissy's BFF—her term, not mine—from the summer she turned ten right up till now, is the niece of said starlet. From the time she first met her friend—Ramona is her name—all the way through high school, Sissy spent two weeks each summer at the actress's family compound. Yes, compound. Down the road in Santa Barbara.

Well, the daughter of the actress—who by then was doing brassiere commercials on television in black and white, dreaming of the worlds she would conquer—was there with her boyfriend the summer she and Sissy and Ramona turned seventeen. They did all the summery things you'd expect, swimming, tanning, beach volleyball, but they also went on a hay ride, and played croquet as if they were part of the cast of The Great Gatsby. They even had a dance. On the last day of the compound getaway, with the signature send-off barbecue about to begin, no one could find Sissy. Or the boyfriend. Now the first time I heard this story—I was almost thirteen, and probably younger than I should have been for the content—I imagined the two of them secreted away under a willow tree, his arms around her waist, hers around his neck, making out like mad. You know how imaginative junior high girls can be. I could see them smothering their laughter on each other's shoulder while kids and grown-ups alike called and called their names. And I wondered, how are you going to get out of this one, with your simultaneous disappearance and your lips swollen and red, and maybe a hickey on your neck? Only

Sissy's generation called it a monkey bite. And isn't that strange? No matter, it's all the same.

But they weren't under a willow tree, or in the gazebo, or on the boat dock, or swimming in the lake. No, they weren't doing any of those things. They were in Mexico, getting married. Yes, married. Sissy and Ramona 's cousin's boyfriend. Married with his class ring, which he had to slip on her thumb to keep it from falling off, both of them in cutoffs and flip flops. And all before their senior year of high school.

When all this was discovered, both sets of horrified parents fought over—among plenty of other things—who would have the privilege of getting the marriage annulled, assuming it was a marriage, a valid one anyway. But of course that didn't take place till after the honeymoon, because no one knew till after the honeymoon. There were an anxious few weeks where everyone held their breath, but once they knew Sissy wasn't pregnant the annulment went through without a hitch, and senior year was all it should be.

Of course, the celebration came a long time before Sissy learned she'd never conceive, though it was by choice.

You'd think the elopement, brief though it was, would have been the end of the two BFFs. But no. It was too deliciously dramatic and Ramona didn't want to be left out, in spite of her cousin's extreme emotional suffering. Sissy Louise Parker was big man on campus among her peers that year, let me tell you. Even now she and Ramona laugh about it and pretend to forget the boyfriend's name. But I haven't forgotten. It was Preston Fisch. Sissy obviously didn't think it through, because could you imagine going through life with a name like Sissy Fisch? As a sixth grade teacher, no less? Dad likes to say he gave her a steak of a name when he married her. And I agree. Vanderpool's a great name. It has teeth. But Sissy likes to say, in return, that he didn't marry her, she married him.

And that's true. You know what they say about once burned, and Dad still smarted from Teri's defection.

I Googled the starlet's name one time, mostly to see if she really did have a daughter Sissy and Ramona's age, or if they made up the whole crazy story for their own amusement—and everyone else's. Well, they may have made it up, but there really is a cousin and a compound and all the other things they talk about, with not an iota of variance from their story, I might add, even after all these years.

Fifteen

I'm not sure what to call the vessel we hold tickets for as it rocks in its berth. Its name is *Coral Reef*, but that's not what I mean. It has a bow and a stern and a windshield, alright, but that's where the similarities end between this bucket and a boat. I've seen whale watching boats, and this isn't anywhere close to those. The captain wears an ancient Pink Floyd T-shirt with the sleeves torn out—torn, not cut—and sun-yellow shorts that expose way too much of his skinny, freckled thighs. He has a stubby, curly ponytail and fuzzy sideburns, but when he takes off his Florida Marlins cap in greeting, you see there's not much hair to cover his bony scalp. He makes up for it where he can, I guess.

The four of us send looks back and forth, and I know three of us consider turning back, but the one that matters outvotes us. Sissy takes a step forward.

"Ladies," the captain says, "welcome aboard." His smile gives me the creeps. He holds out a hand for Sissy and helps her step from the dock into the boat. His smile gets even creepier, his eyes more active as he takes Ainsley's hand, then Jac's. "Hel-lo," he says to each of them. As he reaches for my hand I spear him with a look that sends him back a step, then I grab one of the poles that holds up the canvas Bimini roof of this thing and step aboard by myself.

Captain Ahab slides his cap back on his head and nods my direction. "Well then." He clears his throat. "Name's Spinner." But of course it's not. It couldn't be.

"Nice to meet you." Sissy's voice takes on a tone meant to put the best face on all this, but the jury's still out when it comes to Jac and Ainsley. Me, I'm just glad I brought my book.

Spinner lifts the lid of the port—or is it the starboard?—side bench seat and pulls out life jackets for each of us, then four Nike seat cushions and passes them around. "Here we are. Just make yourselfs"—yes, that's really what he said—"comfortable, ladies, two on each side if you please, and we'll shove off." He points to Ainsley's chest. "If you need help with that vest, let me know." I don't know how, but we manage to get ourselves strapped in to the sun-bleached life vests without his stubby fingers fumbling around our upper bodies.

The seat cushions are all flat in the middle, and the thin plastic is cracked on mine. I turn it over then slip it under my rear as I take a seat. Spinner steps out onto the dock, unties the line that holds us there, then jumps back in. The boat rocks violently under his slight weight, and I grab for the pole again. He can't possibly be thinking about taking this boat out far enough to look for whales. I send that very message to Sissy with my eyes, who replies with that adventurous smile of hers.

Sissy has traded her purple sweatshirt and pants for beige capris, a boat-neck tee and canvas deck shoes. The electric pink glasses still work with this outfit. As always, she color coordinated when she packed. The glasses are fastened to a chain around her neck, as they usually are, but you think that stops her from losing them on a regular basis? Not on your life. Only now, instead of losing her glasses, she loses her glasses and the chain. I know. Don't ask. She clutches an oversized beach bag to her chest as we back out of the dock. It's ten o'clock, right on the button. A plume of gray smoke rises from the rear of the boat, choking us with diesel fumes. I bury my nose and mouth in the crook of my arm until the air clears. Just then I envy Jac her Dramamine, but I didn't take the one she offered because I plan to read, not sleep, the next three hours of this wasted trip. Because I'm pretty sure Spinner couldn't find a whale if it was leashed to his anchor.

We bounce from wave top to wave top, a jarring jolt that wracks my body with every crash landing. The padded seat between me and the hard bench might as well be a slab of marble for all the cushion it provides. And of course there's no way I can read, holding the pole as I am with one hand and the lip of the bench seat with the other as I try to mitigate the damage being done to my spine. I'm not alone in my endeavors. Jac, Ainsley and even Sissy have followed my lead.

The spray from the waves sends a steady stream of mist that baptizes us over and over. The part of me that's covered in jacket is warm enough, but the parts that are exposed—face, neck, shins, ears— are taking the brunt of this frigid sea bath, which is made exponentially worse by the relentless wind we create as we chop through the water. Sissy has slipped back into her sweatshirt, but I don't see how that can keep her warm.

My jaws are clenched to keep my teeth from slamming together. I've always said I want to die with the teeth God gave me. Now that the time is here I don't want to mess this up. Don't want to break one. Or ten. My jaws ache from the effort. Every muscle in me is taut as a guy wire as I stake myself in place against the reckless motion of this stupid boat.

Well, I've had enough. But I've barely tightened my grip on the pole in order to pull myself up, when Sissy, who misses nothing of what goes on around her, anticipates my impatience and beats me to the punch. She stands and staggers like a drunkard to where Spinner grips the wheel or helm or whatever it is, and knocks on his shoulder as if it's a door.

"Hey, now," he shouts over the wind, "you oughta be sitting down, ma'am."

Sissy tenses, then clutches his arm to steady herself, while his head swivels back and forth between Sissy and the direction he's driving.

"Ma'am," he says again.

"You need to slow this thing down," she yells, but the wind whips the words away before they reach their target." Spinner leans his ear toward her mouth, and she tries again. "Slow. Down!"

Spinner pulls back, gives Sissy a once over, not the undressing-you kind of once over, but the you-gotta-be-kidding-me kind.

"Now!" She lets go of his arm long enough to drive her right index finger into her left palm for emphasis. It's an exclamation point for dummies, a gesture Sissy's used forever. I've done it myself a time or two, now that I think about it, and so has Ainsley.

I've never been one to waste brain cells wondering how things might have been had Teri not climbed in her Beetle one day and driven off to who knows where. But from all I know about Teri, she and Sissy are as different as sugar and salt. And suddenly I wonder if and how that shaped my personality. If Teri had been my mentor instead of Sissy, would I be the same woman I am now? The same pathetic woman? Or might I have been another Ainsley? Wow. There's a thought that would have been worth a brain cell or two.

I'm not sure I even considered what my dad went through those days and days he waited to hear from Teri, or to hear bad news from some authority. Not even in light of all we've been through this past three hundred sixty four days. Never once did I say or even think, "Oh, Dad, you know better than anyone what we're going through. You've been here." And survived. I quickly dispose of that last, unwelcome thought. It goes without saying that fickle wives and vanishing daughters are two different things.

Still, Dad must have feared for Teri on so many levels. Then, when she called from a motel room in a location she refused to disclose as if she were an abuse victim or some such ridiculous thing, to say she couldn't do this anymore, she just couldn't do this, what must he have felt? There are men, and probably women too, who abuse their spouses without another soul knowing. They intimidate in such a way that their secret is kept, even from their children. That isn't my dad. And whatever he contributed to Teri's need to break away, he didn't deserve to be treated like a ruffian. She could have sat down with him face to face and told him anything, even goodbye, without fear.

The things he must have gone through, the suspicions of everyone he knew, when the problem simply put was that Teri didn't want to play the family game anymore. She might have stayed happily ever after if it had remained just her and Dad. If not for Ainsley and me.

Well, fine. We didn't need her. We still don't.

I'm right there with Ginny and Sharla, the girls in the novel lying idle at my side. They didn't need their mother either. They were as indifferent and unforgiving toward Marion as I am Teri—now that I'm forced to face the facts. If one can be indifferent and unforgiving toward the same individual. I say they can.

And yet, Ginny's on a plane to San Francisco, to see the mother who lives in Sausalito, after thirty-five silent years. Why, for heaven's sake? Eighty-two pages more and I'll know. Not that it matters. But I'll know.

It's been thirty-eight years for Ainsley and me. And now that I'm wondering, I wonder what Teri wonders. Did she ever think of us on our birthdays, for example, and wonder how we were changing? Did she think about our first periods and wonder if Dad had to bring home the mini-pads, and how high was the drama surrounding *that*? Did she think about the boys who would come into our lives, filling us with equal parts awe and confusion, or the friends who would betray us? Did she think of our graduations, our weddings, our babies? I sit back and expel a breath thinking of all the things she missed.

Which leads me to all the things I'll miss. But not because I got in a Volkswagen Beetle and left it all behind. But, really, is my sin any less?

Spinner pulls back on the throttle and the jarring falls to a blessed minimum. My teeth may survive this after all.

"We still got a ways to go," he shouts over the wind he creates, "if you want to chase the whales."

I turn my head his direction and level my eyes at him. "What are the chances? Really. Of finding the whales?"

"It's like I told her." He aims a lumpy-knuckled thumb in Sissy's direction. "Cain't guarantee. We do what we can."

"When's the last time you found the whales?"

"Well, Miss, we know the routes they take through here. All we can do is get there and hope it's a good day."

"How far away from the routes are we?" Ainsley asks.

"Thirty minutes."

"By your speed?" I say.

"Well, yeah."

"Tell you what, Spinner. Get us there in an hour, would you?" Sissy pats his arm and turns back to her Nike pad.

"An hour? We'll never get back on time if I do, not if you want me to crawl all the way back."

"Do you have another cruise this afternoon?"

Cruise? I can't believe Sissy uses the word so casually.

Spinner shakes his head. "Well, no."

"And we've plenty of time to get back before dark?"

He nods. "I guess."

"No, Spinner, don't guess. Either we can or we can't. Which is it?"

He shrugs. "I guess we can."

Sissy acknowledges with a condescending smile that's as close as she's going to get to a straight answer, and oh how she loves straight answers. "Well, then, let's see how far we get in an hour. At this speed. It'll be your job to get us there, and our job to hope. Doesn't that sound like teamwork?" Her forgery of an accent is so thick I can almost smell the magnolia blossoms over the brine and the diesel.

Spinner pulls off his cap, wipes his forehead on his arm, then tugs the cap back on. "I guess."

"Wonderful." Sissy nods her permission for Spinner to forge ahead. "And please, charge us for the overtime."

At that, a smile breaks his sun-baked face. "Yes, ma'am. And thank you."

I know Sissy is bristling at all the ma'ams falling out of his mouth, but she's magnanimous about it, I'll give her that.

At last, moving at a speed my body can tolerate, I pick up my book and begin to read. The wind is in my face, but it's no longer a gale. It's just the way I like it. Now I don't even mind the spray, which is greatly reduced since Spinner backed off the throttle.

I've read two-thirds of a paragraph when Sissy decides the noise has lessened enough that she must fill the relative quiet with small talk. I hate small talk. She's chattering on about some-thing, and at the same time prowling through her canvas bag, so I admit defeat and tuck the I'm Just Sayin' card back in the book. With a flourish Sissy pulls out bottles of water and passes them around. There's even one for Spinner. I didn't realize I was thirsty, but I twist off the lid on the still-cold bottle and drink a third of it and hope she has more in her bag for the return trip.

"And look what we have here."

She talks as though we're kindergartners and it's time for show and tell. But in light of the water, I'm willing to tolerate her childspeak and give her the benefit of the doubt. She doesn't disappoint. She pulls out something wrapped in foil and passes it my way. It doesn't take a full second to realize it's one of her famous homemade burritos, and it's still warm. I could have gone all day and not cared that I skipped breakfast, but now all of a sudden I'm ravenous. Because Sissy's burritos are renowned in our circle of family and friends. I know, I said she's not Julia Child, but I concede she has her specialties. All three of them.

I wait till everyone's served, including Spinner, who's suddenly Sissy's best friend. And I continue to wait while Sissy raises her own foil-wrapped burrito like an offering, lifts her face to the sky, and prays. I don't lift my face, and I don't pray. Once Sissy's through I peel back the foil and take my first bite.

Ainsley wraps an arm around Sissy's shoulder and presses her cheek to our stepmother's. "You thought of everything."

Well, of course she did. She had from Tuesday to Thursday to plan. Way more time than she needed. Because Sissy is nothing if not efficient. The slow-cooked chicken was probably already shredded and in the freezer, along with a dozen or two of the homemade tortillas she buys at the Mexican market across town. They're worth the drive, I'll say that much. And the refried beans and diced chilies were in her cupboard, I'll wager. So all she had to do was cook the rice and put it all together. The burritos had to have been in that breadbox of an oven, warming up while I slept this morning.

She's a meal planner, Sissy is. She spent most every Saturday afternoon while I was growing up preparing the basics for our weekday dinners, so all she had to do was slip this or that into the oven when she got home from school, while Ainsley or I made a salad. Sissy's big on salads, which are hard to mess up.

I take another bite. "This is good," I say. It's the best I can do.

"Delicious." Jaclyn says it as if she's surprised, which of course she's not. She's eaten way too many of these burritos at Sissy's table.

Sissy smiles and winks both eyes, one wink for each of us I guess.

Sixteen

$\mathcal{M}$y husband, when he was Davy, could make me laugh like no one. He did these great impersonations, not of anyone famous, but of people we knew. Like Sissy. How he could capture the essence of Ms. Vanderpool the sixth-grade teacher, having never been in her classroom, was a mystery. But he could do Ms. Vanderpool even better than Ms. Vanderpool. And Spike. He did this bulging-eyed impersonation of Spike—as the pimp of a dog, not the volleyball champ—that made me actually pee my pants once. Then when he'd finish he'd stand there with his head tilted to one side, reveling in my mirth. He loved to see me laugh, he'd say, more than anything. That's why he worked so hard on his routine, he'd say.

I see that tilted head, that crooked smile behind my closed eyelids, colored red by the sun that warms my face. I open my eyes and turn them to the glistening sea to erase the unwelcome image. He doesn't make me laugh anymore.

I'm sure a shrink would have a name for the way I transfer my guilt to David. Or try to. But no matter how I strive to heap the blame for losing Kinsey squarely on his shoulders, the residue left on my own is a weight I can no longer bear. Yes, I know, it was my carelessness, my immeasurable stupidity that left Kinsey in that car to be stolen away, but she shouldn't have been in that car in the first place. And that's what I can't absolve him from.

It was the biggest fight we'd had in our twelve years of marriage. Though he started the conversation as benignly as he could it didn't stay that way for long. Not when he said, "Bristol. Babe. I know this goes against what we planned, but, honey, it's time. You've got to find a job. Something with benefits. There's no way around it."

I studied him for a full minute, thinking surely not, and formulating a response that would keep this from escalating, but all I could think to say was, "You've got to be kidding."

He placed a ledger on the table and slid it in front of me. "We can't make it, Bree. There's not enough work right now. I've laid off Tim and Brad, and I can't keep myself busy. I'm even looking for home repair and remodels. I haven't done that in years."

"If the economy's hit bottom"—and it certainly had—"what makes you think I can find a job? Assuming I agree to look."

He took a slow breath then looked down at the ledger. "We don't have a choice."

I would count in my head to regain my composure, but numbers don't go nearly high enough to help me here. David had given up a good job to go into business for himself, just in time to ride the slippery slope all the way down when the bottom fell out. And now, I didn't care that we were tottering on the brink of another great depression. Didn't care that David's business was hurting, or that we were in danger of losing our home. I did care that he was proposing such a lifestyle change for our daughter.

"I waited eight years to have a baby, waited till I was thirty-five years old. After we got married, except for contributing to the down payment on this house, I put everything I earned into savings. As planned. So we'd have that to get us through the five years I'd be home with our preschooler. That was our agreement, that I'd be home with her those five years. Then I'd go back to work part time. That's what we said, David." His name did not sound kind coming off my tongue.

"I know, Bree, but—"

"But what? You used half that savings to expand your company, just as the economy was tanking. That's what. Well, wasn't that great timing." I held up a hand and worked to soften my voice. "I know, I know. You couldn't foresee what was coming, but that's not the point. The point is you coerced me into misusing half our savings, and now that we've used up most of the rest because everything's gone south, you want our daughter to pay for it."

"Misuse is a strong word, Bree."

"Well, what would you call it? Our personal savings was not for business investment. It never was."

He stared in one direction, while I stared in the other. Then he faced me and inched his hand toward mine. "I'm not asking Kinsey to pay for anything, Bree. I'm just saying we'll put her in preschool. The one at church. She'll be with kids she knows. She'll do fine."

My lips were pressed so tightly together it hurt. "I feel like we're having two separate conversations here. You are not hearing a word I say."

"I am, babe, but—"

"No. You're not. I didn't have a child to let someone else raise her."

"You're taking this way out of context. No one else is going to raise our daughter. I mean, really, how many women do you know who stay home with their preschoolers?"

"Not. Nearly. Enough."

He pushed back his chair and rubbed a hand through his hair. "I know how strongly you feel about this, Bristol, I know what we planned. But things have changed. We could lose this house." His voice took on a finality that infuriated me.

"Then we sell the house."

"In this economy? With the way property values have plummeted? Are you kidding? We won't even break even."

"Then we don't break even. We'll survive. David, I've done everything to economize in every way I can. Everything. If we can't afford to stay here, then we sell. Or short-sell. Whatever we have to do. We'll buy another house when I go back to work. After Kinsey is in school."

David paced the length of the kitchen. By the time he got back to where I sat his anger had waned. That's how it was with David. He seldom got angry, and never for long. "Look. Bristol. Our backs are against the wall. I—"

"David." I try not to sound as desperate as I feel. "Do you know what my earliest memory is? After Teri left?" He does, in fact, but I tell him anyway. "It's me crying as I watch my dad walk to his car to go to work as he leaves me and Ainsley at a babysitter's house. Day after day after freaking day. And crying with relief when he rings the doorbell to take us home again. I was cared for by women—and they were good women, all of them, Sissy included—but they had not one ounce of maternal feeling for me, David. Including Sissy. I don't want that for Kinsey."

"I wouldn't ask if there was any other way."

"Fine. You asked. I'm saying no. I'm not going to work until Kinsey's in school."

But, of course, I did. I found a good job in my field as a graphic artist. With benefits. I brought home more money than David most months, and made every mortgage payment on time. I dropped Kinsey off at preschool at 7:00 a.m. Monday through Friday, and picked her up at 5:30, unless David got there before I did. She spent ten and a half hours daily under someone else's care. Fifty-two and a half hours a week, for ten long months. She managed better than I did, I will say that.

My lips are pressed as tightly together now as they were then, my hands grip the book I haven't read a word of. I should have stuck to my guns. Should have, should have, should have. But I didn't.

"What does that mean?" I ask Sissy, raising my voice above the engine and the wind. "To stick to your guns?"

She gives me a quizzical glance. There's so much going on beneath the surface of her gray eyes, but she sends a smile my way. "It means to stay at your post and keep shooting, even under heavy fire."

Ah. Of course. That's where I went wrong. I should have kept shooting.

"Oh. Oh. Look!" Ainsley is on her feet and pointing at the water.

The reflection of the sun on the silvery waves hurts my eyes. I make a visor with my hand and squint until my eyes adjust to the brilliance. Then I see what she's pointing at.

"Whales?" Jaclyn, too, is on her feet. But she sees her error at the same instant the rest of us do.

"Dolphins!" Sissy says. "A whole school of them!"

"Pod," Spinner corrects. "Dolphins are mammals, you know, not fish."

Sissy turns an indignant face to the plebe who has dared to correct her. "Yes, well, mammals or not, *school* is certainly interchangeable with *pod*."

Of course, Sissy would know.

"Although," she concedes, "*pod* is the more common term."

And Spinner, who must be smarter than he looks, gives a conciliatory nod to the woman who has fed him so well today.

Sissy and Ainsley have joined Jac and me on the starboard side. Or maybe it's the port side. Who knows? Why don't they call them right and left and make it simple for idiots like me? But I relinquish such immaterial thoughts in light of the frenetic activity in the water on my side of the boat.

"Six at least." Ainsley's voice is rich with excitement. "But it's hard to count them!"

Their perfectly arced bodies breach the surface over and over, as if some unseen force beneath the sea is juggling dolphins. Their smiling faces come almost near enough to touch at times, as the water dances off the gleaming silver of their hides, and the sound they make is like laughter.

"They're bottlenose, of course," Spinner says. Maybe the most surprised among us, he's as excited as anyone aboard his boat.

Jac digs in her pocket for her phone. "Can you believe this? Can you?" She begins to snap photos with a fury that matches the dolphins' play.

Spinner holds up a finger as if to say *wait a sec*, then reaches beneath his dash and pulls out a big white bucket. "Lunch," he says with a smile. He reaches in and pulls out something disgusting, something with lots of legs. Or tentacles. "Squid. Their favorite. Here you go, ladies, there's plenty for everyone." He tosses one overboard, and the frenetic activity in the water increases exponentially. "Don't anyone be shy."

Naturally, Sissy leads the way. She tugs up the sleeve of her sweatshirt and reaches in as though she's mining carrots for a stew. And no surprise. Anyone who can mutilate a clam without so much as a gag, can toss a blob of squid to a hungry pod of dolphins.

Jaclyn goes next, then Ainsley. "Come on, Bree! Your turn." They both urge me on. My sister touches a hand to the small of my back. "You can do this."

"They're waiting," Jaclyn adds, with a push in her voice and an eyebrow hiked.

"Good Lord! They stink to high heaven!"

"Well, they're not for you, love." Sissy reaches past me and grabs another squid out of the bucket. "Let's see who can throw the farthest."

The farthest. As if it's a softball-tossing match. Lord, will I ever get out of the sixth grade in this woman's eyes?

She nudges me with an elbow. "Come on, love. LATSF."

I stop half way to the bucket. LATSF. LA ...TSF. *Launch a tasty squid, fast?* I toss a frown over my shoulder.

"Look at their smiling faces," she says. "Now, come on."

I use my thumb and index finger like pinchers, touching as little of the slimy thing as I can and still manage to grip it. Then I reach back, careful not to drip anything on myself. On Sissy's count of three I hurl the creature as far as I can. Which turns out not to be far at all. Because it splats against one of the aluminum poles that holds our Bimini lid up and bounces back at my feet, even squishier than it was before.

My audience laughs. Even Ainsley. And Spinner. And the dolphins. All of them laughing away. Well fine. I reach down, pick that puppy up, and send it sailing. It makes an arc against the crystal clear sky. Almost before it begins to descend, a sleek, silvery dolphin leaps and catches it midair, then does a cannon-ball. Right there in the middle of the Pacific Ocean, a cannonball. "You're welcome," I say under my breath. I reach over the edge of the boat and pour what's left of my bottled water over my hand. It's not enough to rinse the feel of the squid away, but it'll have to do. And while everyone laughs and claps, all I can think is, Kinsey would love this. The thought weakens my knees. I clutch the pole for support and lower myself to the cushionless pad.

"Mama?" I love how she says this. Not like a monotone baby doll's ma-ma, but like she's calling me to task. Come here and explain, that's what she says in that one, sparkling word. She's crouched down in jeans and purple-soled sneakers that light up when she walks. She never fails to stomp her feet when she wears them. Or smile. She loves these sneakers. Her bottom nearly touches the brick patio where she squats. "What do you suppose that is?" She points at a snail inching its way up the sliding glass door that stands between the patio and our kitchen. The creature is right at her eye level.

"That," I say, "is a snail."

"Snail?" She scrunches her nose when she says it. "Can I touch it?"

She's fearless, this three-year-old female version of Sam.

"Well, I wouldn't." That's what I start to say, but catch myself. "Sure, baby girl. Go ahead." I hold my breath and stifle a shiver as she reaches out and presses her little index finger against the amber shell. It has reddish-brown stripes in a pattern that's surprisingly pretty running the length of its fragile carapace. The snail stops the moment it's touched, pulls its slimy body into its shell, and hunkers down.

Kinsey presses again. "Why won't it go?"

Do I tell her it's because she's frightened the poor thing? No. Absolutely not. "It's resting. Like you do in the afternoon."

"Oh." She pulls back and watches. Waiting.

Just then, David comes through the doorway. "Hey there, ladies." He presses his lips against my forehead—as close as he dares to come to my lips these days—and bends down and scoops up Kinsey, who laughs and calls him Daddy, and holds tightly to his neck. "Ah, what's that?" And before I can stop him, he plucks the snail off the window and tosses it into the shrubs. Kinsey's eyes follow its path as the smile drops off her face. My heart sinks right along with it.

"Look! Look!" It's Ainsley again, calling me back from the place I'd much rather be. "What acrobats!"

She's right. The dolphins' movements aren't random, not at all. They're planned. Designed. I wonder which among them is the choreographer. Probably not my cannonballer. I can just see her instructor, clearing its throat, tapping its wand against a fin, calling back to attention the frolicsome one. The pod prankster.

The sun has broken through the clouds, and now that the boat is still, the blazing star sheds a blanket of warmth on us. Well, the boat is still except for the raucous way it totters on the waves, as if Neptune himself is rocking our cradle. Sissy tugs off her sweatshirt.

"Sissy." The concern in Ainsley's voice draws my attention. She reaches a hand toward our stepmother. "What happened?"

Sissy looks to the spot on her underarm that's garnered Ainsley's attention, and mine and Jac's, too, for that matter. "Oh, that?" It's a bruise the size of a grapefruit, all purple and puffy.

"And that." Ainsley points to the other arm, for there's another one just like it in almost the same spot.

"I got it, them, um ..." She's suddenly one of her students, explaining why her homework isn't turned in. "I fell. Off my pole."

Ainsley pulls back, the way she does when she's surprised. "Your pole? What, what kind of pole?"

"The, um, dancing kind?"

It's like we're instantly freeze dried, Ainsley, Jaclyn and me. Spinner too, except for the eyebrow that hikes up his forehead and disappears beneath the bill of his cap. His eyes lose their squint, and he turns them on Sissy.

We're in a vacuum. No sound, no boat, no dolphins, no sea. Just this crazy vision of Sissy. With a pole made for dancing. It's a vision I can't quite wrap my head around. And I wonder, *Does Dad know?* But the vacuum doesn't last long. It shatters in the laughter that erupts from Jaclyn. It bubbles up from her toes, this tsunami of mirth, and explodes out of her mouth. "Dancing? You were pole dancing?"

Splotches of red appear on Sissy's neck. Oddly, that's where her embarrassment shows. "Well, not *dancing* dancing. It's an exercise class."

"You pole dance for exercise? Whatever happened to Curves? Or Pilates?"

Sissy frowns and does her best to appear once again like the teacher in charge. "It's quite a workout, really."

"I bet. So how did you, you know"—Jac breaks into laughter again— "fall off your pole?"

"Oh, honestly, I don't know. And I wasn't even wearing high heels."

High heels?

Spinner's other eyebrow joins the first one, deep beneath the bill of his soiled Marlins cap. Judging by how wide his eyes spring open, those brows would be up to his hairline if he had one. I can tell by the way his open mouth turns upward that he's gained a new appreciation for Sissy that goes way beyond her burritos.

"That's what some of them wear," Sissy is saying. "That, and their hot pink sports bras and these booty shorts that don't begin to cover their cheeks, if you know what I mean. They're all skinny. And focused. I don't even know why they're there. The instructor, naturally, wears the highest heels, the tightest bra and the shortest shorts. And she has this rose tattoo on the small of her back that might look cute now, but when that thing begins to sag, she'll have thorns in places ... well, you get the idea."

"Oh, yeah," Jac says. "Ouch. And what do *you* wear?"

"Yoga pants. Floor length. And my Betty Boop T-shirt."

Sissy's a big fan of Betty Boop.

"And Spike? Does he go?"

"Spike?" Spinner can't seem to help himself.

"Now why on earth would I take Spike?"

Ainsley is laughing now, too, bent over at the waist, hands on knees, not able to suck in a breath. She just hacks out this laugh that takes me back to when we were kids. If, for example, she was about to get caught in tag, she'd just buckle and burst into laughter. So naturally, everyone always went for Ainsley in tag. Now, they just go for her, period. Ainsley, the joyful one. I never understood why she'd give in without a fight, but I loved it about her. Then, because it made life easy. Now, because it's a tiny strand that anchors me to sanity.

"Okay. Enough said." Sissy claps her hands in that attention-getting way she has. "Now that you've all had your fun, can we get back to feeding the dolphins?"

But they're gone, without a hint they were ever there. Like so many other things in my life. I sit back, stuff my hands in my pockets. And touch my starfish.

Seventeen

Enough said. My stomach pitches, but not from the movement of the boat as we head back to shore, but rather from a memory so real it's like one of those weird déjà vu moments that stops you in your tracks.

Kinsey reaches up and presses tangerine-tipped fingers to my lips. "Mama, no more words."

No more words? My first reaction is to laugh. Kinsey's way-beyond-three way of saying things always makes me laugh. But this isn't the time for laughter. I take her hand, soft as bath bubbles, and kiss those tangerine-tipped fingers that wouldn't come clean. The glittery polish on her tiny nails sparkles in the soft light cast by the Christmas tree lights woven in and out of the shelves and pictures that decorate her walls. Not your typical nite-lite, but Kinsey loves them.

"Baby girl," I say, "you know it's time for sleep. Daddy and I have kissed you night-night, we've said our prayers, you have your Manny tools"—at which point she tugs Philipe, the Phillips-head screwdriver out from beneath the covers and kisses it—"so, it's time to sleep. No getting up, okay?" She tugs Turner, the flathead screwdriver, out with the other hand and pretends the two little tools are having a conversation. "Okay, baby?" I wait for her nod, though it's slow in coming, then tuck both arms under the covers, kiss her nose, and give a little wave as I slip out of her room.

I hold my breath all the way downstairs, scoot into my favorite chair, folding one leg up as I always do, and shrug at David's unasked question. "We'll see."

It doesn't take long. I barely have time to retrieve my book from the arm of the chair and find my place on the page when I hear the familiar rub of pajama pants making their way down the stairs. I give David a look that says, "It's your turn, bud."

He blows out a breath. "How do we break her from this?"

I shrug again as she comes into the room, Philipe in one hand, Turner in the other. "It isn't working right," she says, serious as a little scientist.

"What isn't working?" David and I say it together. It has to be one of the screwdrivers.

"My bed. It isn't working."

This piques my curiosity. "How is it not working, Kinsey?" I mean, what's it supposed to do exactly?

She holds out her hand to me. "I show you."

I sigh, untuck my leg, and take her hand. Upstairs, she crawls onto her bed and lays sideways, her head hanging over one edge and her feet over the other. She gives me a look that says, See what I mean?

"Well, sweetie, you're supposed to lie this way." I turn her body, laying her head on the pillow, and pointing her feet toward the lower end of the bed.

"But I don't like this way."

And she doesn't. I know that. As a baby she always ended up crosswise in her crib with her head pressed snugly against the side bumper pad, no matter how I initially placed her. It was easy to see what had pressed against my uterine wall the last four months of my pregnancy. I never dared get far from a bathroom, and toward the end, it wasn't uncommon for me to walk from the bathroom to the kitchen, or some other place in my house, only to turn around and head right back to the bathroom. I thought I'd finally gotten Kinsey accustomed to lying the right way in her new little bed. Obviously, she's had a relapse.

"This is how Mommy and Daddy sleep," I say. "And Manny." What a stroke of genius, I decide, and mentally high-five myself for thinking of this. She gives me a suspicious look. "Really."

She sits up slowly, as if that will keep me from noticing, and lays her screwdrivers crosswise on the bed. She looks up into my eyes, a look on her face that might as well be saying, "Everyone knows this is the right way."

So much for genius. "And since you got up"—my impatience shows in my voice—"you have to give up one of your toys." I know, I'm breaching rules again, but I don't want to take everything away. I reach for Philipe.

"No!" She snags him before I have a chance to take him, her fingernail scratching a little white line onto my arm, and hands over the flathead. But her lip juts out and I know she's going to cry.

"Baby girl. I don't want to take your toys. But you have to go to sleep. And you have to sleep this way, otherwise you're right, it doesn't work." I press Turner back in her hand and tuck her arms under the covers again. "Okay?"

She rolls her head until her eyes are on the wall, as far from my eyes as the east from the west.

"Okay?"

She doesn't nod.

"Love you."

I step outside the room, and stand, waiting. I've not done this before, lain in wait this way. But waiting like this always activates my bladder and I need to pee. Weird, I know, but there it is. When Kinsey comes through the doorway, as I knew she would, she yelps in surprise and begins to cry. It makes me want to cry, too. Still, I hold out my hand. "Which one?" Reluctantly, she gives me Turner and I tuck her back in bed. "Now, Kinsey, look at me. If you get up again, you'll have to give me Philipe too. So, please, stay in bed."

I hear her cries all the way down the stairs.

They meld into the cry of the gulls overhead. Who'd have thought she'd be so right on when she said, "Mama, no more words"? That within a few weeks' time I'd not hear her voice for three hundred sixty four days, and counting? That she'd not hear mine, or David's, or the voices of any of the people she loves and who love her. It's all I can do to subdue the anger that maintains a constant boil just below the surface. I mean, really, could I not have let her lie crosswise on her bed if that's what she wanted? If that's how she found her own version of comfort? And if she wanted to plod down the stairs a thousand times a night, could I not have scooped her up in my arms every time, planting kisses wherever my lips would land, thankful, *thankful*, for one more chance to see her face, to hear her voice, to be one with my baby girl? Lord. I'd do it now. A thousand times I'd do it. Instead I sit here and wonder, whose voice does she hear today?

I grip the side of the boat and bite my lip to suppress the virulent moan that comes sharp as a birth pang, thankful for the noise of the wind in our ears, because I can't keep it all in. I swear, I can't stand the assaulting blows one more day. I'm done. So very done. I look out at the sea and block my face as if to block the sun, because if our eyes connect, all three of these women will see how very done—or more to the point, how very undone—I am.

There should be coaches for things like this. Lamaze for the grieving. Except, why work through the hellish pain when there's nothing to look forward to at the end of it? Why not just let it have its way?

My cell phone vibrates inside my pocket, tickling my thigh in an unpleasant way. Jeff Girard, I'm willing to bet. I want to pull the phone free to confirm or deny, but of course I don't. Because what if it is? I wait until the call has gone to voice mail, then ease my phone into the open, presumably to check the time. Three missed calls it tells me. I didn't intend to be out here so long. Didn't intend to be out here at all. If it is Jeff, he'll wonder why I haven't answered. Wonder, perhaps, if I've changed my mind about meeting him today. The thought brings a prick of panic, that he might scoot on down the highway with my contract unsigned, but I don't regret coming on this little excursion, and that surprises me. I mean really, how often do you have lunch with dolphins? And this, the next to last day of my life. I check the face of my phone once more, but all it tells me is the time. I return it, along with its secrets, to my pocket.

I feel a hand on my shoulder, then Jaclyn speaks into my ear. "I hate to admit it, but that was fun. I wonder what's next."

My one shoulder rises and falls. I haven't a clue. But whatever it is, it'll go on without me. For once we're ashore I have to make my getaway. I'm still not sure how I'll pull it off. I mean, I have my alibi, which I've already planted in Jaclyn's head. It's the getting away alone part that's mucking up the works, since they're intent on keeping me under a watchful eye. It would be so nice if these people napped. I look back at Jaclyn and draw her in with a look. She leans forward and turns her ear to me. "Thanks for being nice."

"To Sassy?" she says. "Well, why wouldn't I?" And she winks and laughs.

Not for the first time this weekend my conscience lectures me. These women are here because they care about me. How can I do this to them, leave them with the weight of guilt, the same kind of guilt I've carried for three hundred sixty four days, when they're so intent on keeping me under a watchful eye? How? It's not so hard when you're desperate, I reply to myself.

It should make my face burn that Jeff thinks I'm willing to sell myself, and for so small a price, but I'm beyond shame or any other emotion. It's remarkable to me how these things happen—if anything were to happen, which it's not. So unintentional. And effortless. I simply walked into Jeff's office with the hopes of selling a line of cards, my world still intact, and left without a sale, but with an invitation for so much more. And not a word spoken. I know too well the language of the eyes, have had more than one guy whisper obscenities with only his fluent irises to speak on his behalf. Well, let me tell you, Jeff Girard has mastered the art. I pretended I didn't speak the language eighteen months ago. Took my unpurchased Baby Talk line back home with me, my one last hope dissipating like the Pacific coast fog, joined the workforce and sacrificed my baby girl to daycare.

I know, that's life for millions of families, blah, blah, blah. But it wasn't my life. Or Kinsey's. Was never meant to be. And then, when it couldn't possibly matter anymore, I sell the same line, in the same office, the same invitation still on the table. I'm not foolish enough to think there's anything more to Jeff's interest in me than one man's thrill of conquest. One seductive man, who knows how to seduce so innocently. Take for example the smile. It could be offered to his priest, his mother, his handball partner. Perfectly innocent. Or the way his eyes nail you with their intensity. Such a look could be construed as earnest engagement of the professional kind. A superior could only wish for such focus in the workplace. But put them together, add a slight hike of the eyebrow for good measure, and you have Enticement.

In my defense, if there is a defense, a woman on her best day could barely resist the charm that exudes from Jeff Girard. Well. I haven't had a best day in nearly a year, but what Jeff doesn't know is that in this little game he's playing, he's the one being used. He's my resuscitator. Because, as anyone knows, you can't kill what isn't alive.

———————

Dirty puffs of diesel-laden smoke swirl around us as Spinner chugs the *Coral Reef* into dock, an ugly duckling of a boat amidst its fairer competitors. The fumes resurrect the headache that was never far from the surface, and sour my already unsettled stomach. Suddenly, all I want is to have my feet on firm ground and sweet air to breathe.

"Ugh." Ainsley covers her nose with the sleeve of her jacket.

"Breathe through your mouth," Sissy instructs. But I don't. I'd rather smell the diesel, or any other offensive odor, than draw it in over my taste buds. But neither is preferable, so like Ainsley I block my airways with one arm, as I stand with the other wrapped around the Bimini pole. I swear, I'll never look at another pole without thinking of Sissy in her yoga pants surrounded by booty shorts and rose tattoos. Not ever. Of course, *ever* is a much shorter proposition for me now than it once was.

Still.

With an agility you wouldn't expect from his bowed legs, Spinner bounds onto the dock and secures the boat to its mooring. This time when he offers his hand I take it. He's not a bad sort, I decide, though he still should be slapped for the way he allows his eyes to wander. He could take a lesson or two in subtlety from Jeff Girard.

Sissy, the last to disembark, presses a bill or two into Spinner's hand and thanks him for a perfect afternoon. "Dolphins are as good as whales," she says. "As good as." She nods, and as always, that settles it.

"Thankee, ladies." Spinner lifts the bill of his cap, then tugs it back down in one swift motion. He jumps back aboard the *Coral Reef* and sets to work stowing the life vests along with the good-for-nothing seat pads as we amble up the dock. Someone calls to him from another boat about catching a beer or two if he's done for the day, and he calls back with swell enthusiasm. His is an easy life, I find myself thinking. Then I wonder what right I have to assume such a thing.

"Coffee," Sissy says. She points to the restaurant that serves as one bookend to the weathered gray two-story building just ahead. "Sound good?"

"Yes, please," Ainsley says. A flotilla of clouds blocks the sun and she shivers. "I'm suddenly cold."

This could be my chance. Go ahead, I could say, I'll see you back at the beach house, and once there I could gather my things, slip away, and find some place to wait for morning, for my appointed hour. But, a) they won't leave me to myself, I'm sure of it. I bet they drew straws to determine their babysitting shifts; and b) coffee does sound good. It's not yet two-thirty. I have time. "Sure."

"Hot tea sounds good," Jaclyn says.

Sissy's smile oozes patience as she murmurs, "There's always one."

Well, I know with certainty that Jaclyn loves being that one, even without the smile she doesn't quite suppress.

The tablecloths are thick white cotton, the silverware nondescript. It's not the kind you'd ever select for a bridal registry. For that, you'd want something with roses on the tips of the handles, or a flourish of some kind. Like the silverware in my hutch back home, the silverware I rarely use. But though it's plain, it is heavy, and I like heavy tableware. As I line up my fork, knife and spoon, the bottom of the handles perfectly flush with the edge of the napkin, it occurs to me that I'll never help my daughter fill out a wedding registry. Or a registry for a baby shower. Or pick out a prom dress, or sign a permission slip for a senior trip to … somewhere. In fact, I begin to wonder about all the things I'm forgetting that I'll never do with Kinsey, and I force myself to unclench my jaws long enough to reply to our waiter that, yes, I'd like coffee too. The real thing.

But someone will do those things. That is my dying wish. That someone will do all the things I won't. Maybe it's a lot to expect that, under the circumstances, I'll have a dying wish. Just exactly how much does suicide negate? I sigh. There's so much I don't know.

I'm suddenly aware of three sets of eyes on me. One set green, one the very color of the sea out there, and one storm-cloud gray.

"Okay. What did I say?"

"Say? Nothing, love." Sissy reaches across the table and pats my hand. "I was just asking about dinner. We have reservations at Pasta Moon and the Miramar—"

"For the same night?"

"Oh, Puff, stay with me here."

"She always makes reservations for important dates at a minimum of two restaurants," Ainsley says. "We decide at the last minute what we're in the mood for and cancel the other reservation."

"Always," I say, in reply to Jac's unasked question. Really, she should know this by now.

"So. What are we in the mood for?"

"Pasta," Ainsley says, at exactly the same time Jac says, "Seafood."

So then, it's a standoff.

"Well, Bree, looks like you're the tie-breaker." Sissy looks at me over the rim of her coffee cup, her eyes crinkling at the edges. I can't help feel this is a setup. "Though you should know we can get seafood at both restaurants."

The Color of Sorrow Isn't Blue | 167

I could so easily upset Sissy's applecart by saying it doesn't matter to me, that I'm hoping to make my getaway under the cover of darkness. I nearly ask about the origin of the phrase *upset the applecart*, which I've no doubt Sissy would know, but I catch myself in time. For she'd surely wonder what applecart I might be planning to upset. That, I decide, she's better off not knowing. She'll find out soon enough. "You can get seafood at Pasta Moon?"

"Yes," she says. There's a superiority in her voice as she sends the most minuscule of glances toward Jac that says *any sophisticated person would know this.*

"Can you get pasta at the Miramar?"

Sissy sets her cup in its saucer and smooths the tablecloth on either side. The crinkles around her eyes are much finer than they were a moment ago. "I suppose."

"Then there hardly seems to be a tie to break. Just flip for it."

"Oh, well, I don't care either way." Ainsley's only too happy to acquiesce. "We can have pasta any time."

Jaclyn shrugs one shoulder. "I don't care either. Really. You know me. I'll eat anything."

"Ha," Sissy murmurs.

With narrowed eyes, Jaclyn rubs her lips together, then sips her tea.

"Well, I really should cancel one or the other," Sissy says, "considering it's Valentine's Day. Reservations are at a premium. Doesn't matter to me which one."

"What about here?" Ainsley says. "It's so close to the beach house, we could walk off our supper."

"But all those masts spoil the view."

"Oh," Ainsley says, "you're right."

Honestly. I drop my napkin on the table. "I say flip for it. I'm going to the restroom."

I wend my way to the back of the dining room and push open the door to the women's lounge. All three stalls are empty. I choose the farthest and lock myself in. I lean against the tile wall and pull my phone out of my pocket, but when I hear the lounge door open, I quickly tug out a seat cover and sit, in case it's Sissy or one of the others come to check up on me. But I don't recognize the shoe that shows under the stall divider beside me. I find that odd, that the woman, whoever she is, chose door number two. I would have taken the first stall and left the middle one empty, a buffer if you will. But that's just me. The shoe is flat, definitely sensible. Textured black, with a buckle meant purely for adornment across the toes, near where the toe cleavage normally shows, which Jaclyn hates but I rather like. There is no toe cleavage here. I'm guessing this shoe and the foot inside it belong to a woman Sissy's age at least. My chest touches my thighs as I study these shoes, then catch myself. What on earth am I doing?

"Oh." The tone of despair from beyond the partition is unmistakable. "Do you have any tee-pee on your side?"

"Excuse me?"

"Toilet paper? Do you have any? Both rolls are down to the cardboard over here."

"Oh, oh, sure." I pull a stream from my roll, then double it and pass it under the divider.

The hand that accepts my offering is that odd transparent white that comes with real age. There's a large ring on the middle finger, which seems far too heavy for its owner. "You're a dear."

The voice matches the transparent skin. I recall passing a pair of women on my way to the restroom, well-dressed, both with coiffed cotton for hair and splotches of pink on the sagging skin under their cheekbones, their eyebrows forming arches above their eyeglass frames in that peculiar shade of charcoal. They were like a set of earrings that match right down to the gleam.

"Is, is that enough?"

"Oh yes. And then some. You'd think at least one roll would have something on it, wouldn't you? If they'd done their job this morning, that is."

"You'd think."

"Lucky you chose the stall you did, with all that paper. Don't you hate getting caught alone in a restroom with nothing to use? What do you do in that event?"

Do? Is she really asking, like, for an answer, or is it merely a rhetorical question? Isn't there some sort of etiquette about talking between stalls in a public restroom? Especially with strangers?

"Hello? Oh, well, never mind. That is a bit probing." She gives a little chuckle, then flushes the toilet. "I'll have to warn my sister not to use the middle stall. And of course, I'll tell the maître d'."

I remain in my stall while she adjusts her clothing, steps out, and washes her hands with what must be painstaking care, then goes back to join her tablemate. Finally. In this odd moment in which I'm caught I try to picture Ainsley with cotton candy hair, sagging cheekbones and transparent skin. And me beside her, with my charcoal eyebrows. But the picture refuses to focus. Of course, in our case there's only one gleaming earring. Only one earring, period. Maybe that's what causes the disconnect.

The wallpaper on my phone is the most adorable photo of Kinsey, in a floppy hat the color of fruit punch, cocked over one ear, the color reflecting on her cheek, and a smile that verges on laughter. I can almost hear it, her laughter. And, lord, I could scream. I don't really know what keeps me from it. There's a trembling in my arms that tells me how close I am to losing it. I can't make it stop, no matter how hard I hug myself.

I check my three missed calls, prepared to send a quick text to Jeff. Because I really must get back. But the calls aren't from Jeff. They're from David. All three of them. I stare at his name and whisper a curse. What could he possibly want? That's the first thing that comes to mind. The second is that Jeff hasn't called because he's a confident man.

I hate them both.

I flip the phone shut. If David left messages I don't want to hear them. I stuff the phone back in my pocket, for there's no need to send a text to Jeff, who obviously has every assurance I'll meet him where and when I said I would. I wonder what he has planned in Carmel. Who'll be waiting for him, and what would she think of his little detour in Half Moon Bay? How could he go from one bed to another in the span of a few hours, and not feel the cheapness of it? Not that he will go from one bed to another. But he thinks he will, in his heart. And isn't that where the problem always springs from in the first place?

I pass the sisters on my way back to my table, and nod. I have no idea which one I've become quasi-acquainted with since I can't see their shoes from here. I'm already past the table when I think to check for the ring, but I don't look back. An active, low-toned conversation dies as I approach our table, and three faces turn a smile on me. I resume my seat, and see that my cup has been refilled. The coffee's nutty aroma rises on the steam that swirls from the cup, but I don't want any more. I know it's not what's brought on this trembling, but I don't need anything to add to it.

"Bristol? Love?" Sissy sits poised, phone in hand. "We should cancel one of the reservations. Some unlucky fellow without an ounce of foresight is clamoring out there for a place to take his sweetheart for dinner. It's in our power to make his day."

"And probably his night," Jaclyn adds.

It's a lot to ask, that I make a decision. Of any kind. "You know"—I touch the pressure points of this headache and push, hard—"who cares? Who. Cares."

There's a span of silence, then Ainsley touches my hand, still pressed against my temple. Little by little she gets her fingers around mine and brings my hand to her lips. I raise my eyes to hers, but there's too much feeling there and I have to look away.

"You decide." I aim my words in Sissy's direction. She slips the phone in her purse, and nods.

Jaclyn takes a twenty dollar bill from her wallet and lays it on the table. By all means, let's get me out of here before my craziness begins to seep out the cracks that are forming on the thin shell holding me together.

Eighteen

*T*he beach house is in sight before I say what I should have said right away. "I'm sorry, Sissy. That was uncalled for." The warmth of the sand resonates through the bottoms of my sandals. It feels so good I slip my feet out of them and dig my toes into the sunbaked beach.

"Oh, Bristol, I know that, love. No apology necessary."

"Yes it is. NEFBM," I say in an effort to please her, and make up for my rudeness. And we all say it together, for this is something we were constantly reminded of in Sissy's classroom: "No excuse for bad manners."

Sissy winks and gives me her best smile. "All's forgiven then."

"We know how difficult this is, Bree." Ainsley raises a hand to block the sun from her eyes and tilts her head in that sympathetic way she has.

"Which is why I wanted to be alone in the first place." That's not quite true, but it's true enough.

"And exactly why you shouldn't be." Sissy starts off again, the engineer of this little train wreck. "Not to ruin the moment, but my bladder is chiding me for not making a pit stop before we left the restaurant. And the sound of the surf isn't helping one little bit. I should have gone when you did, Bree. Besides," she calls over her shoulder, "don't you just love checking out women's lounges in fine restaurants?"

"Love?" Jaclyn gives me a look that says, *not so much.*

This is no secret to Ainsley and me, of course. We've known this about Sissy forever.

"You never know what you might find."

"You mean, besides a bathroom?"

"No, Puff. I mean in addition to a bathroom. Sometimes the accouterments are well worth the trip."

"Such as?"

"Oh, fine mirrors, heated towels, beaten copper sinks. I love beaten copper. Once, I saw the loveliest sconces. They made the place feel so elegant. Oh, wait, but that was in a museum." Sissy looks back at me again. "Did I miss much, love?"

"Not this time," I assure her.

"Good. And if you'll excuse me..." She leaves us twenty yards from the beach house and hurries inside. "Oh, Spike, hello!" I hear her say, and I know she's kissing the bridge of his nose, if he has such a thing.

Yuck.

"What is it about the sound of water that makes a bladder surge?" Ainsley says. "Remember when the twins were born? Oh my Lord."

"What happened?" Jac asks.

"I had to pee in the worst way. But everything was so swollen from delivering not one but two babies that I couldn't go. The nurse tried everything to help. Stuck my hands in warm water. Sat me on the john with the sink water running. All it did was increase the need, but, of course, did nothing for the swelling. Finally, they were going to insert a catheter, but at the last moment I managed to push out a little trickle. Oh, may I tell you how good that felt?"

Sissy steps onto the landing, with Spike on one arm. "Well, your body did yeoman's service that day, baby. No wonder you were swollen shut."

She sets Spike onto the sand. "Go on then, do your job." Which he does, squatting, then shakes his leg. I swear, he's such a dog.

"I had a catheter once," Jac says. "Made me very glad not to be a man. Not that it's harder to insert one in a guy, but all that ... *plumbing* hanging between my legs was so cumbersome."

Even Sissy laughs at that.

Of course, I remember the catheter. It was following Jac's hysterectomy, which was the year after mine. Hers was for a tumor, mine for acute endometriosis. Ainsley remembers too, judging by the sympathetic look she passes Jaclyn's way. My sister is the only one among us still able to procreate, though she'd die a thousand deaths should she find herself pregnant. Ainsley knows exactly how much she can juggle.

We'll never know if Sissy had been able to procreate in her younger years, because, as I said, she made it no secret when she married Dad she never meant to have kids. She was content with her students, thank you very much. Now that she's well through menopause, that puts an end to any debate. I think she felt her relationship with her students was like going straight to grandparenting. All the fun without all the fuss. She'd never have to deal with the terrible twos or the dreaded teen years. For a while, anyway. Ainsley and I were the surprise family she never counted on. But since she did the proposing and not my dad, she set her own trap.

Sissy tugs one of the Adirondack chairs into the sun and settles into it. "Tell me, is there a sound that begins to compare to that of the ocean?" She pulls in a deep breath and lets it out. Mindlessly, she pets Spike, who leapt onto her lap the moment she sat down.

"Kinsey's voice," I say. She has this alto tone, so unexpected when she speaks that people would say all the time, "I love to hear her talk!" Her voice breaks, the way mine does, but it sounds just right coming from Kinsey. I'd give anything to hear it right now. Anything. And everything. "Her voice," I say to Sissy, then draw a line with my eyes between her and the sea.

I sense more than see the glance that passes between them. Not one of them missed the fatalist flavor of my delivery.

"It is a sweet voice," Ainsley says.

Sissy reaches toward the other Adirondack chair. "Why don't you sit here for a while and read? It's such the perfect day." There's a deep spring of meaning to her words, a message she wants to impart. That all things do win out in the end. That the end is all that really matters. She disseminates this notion daily, with every opportunity she manages to hijack. Her accomplice in this is her Promise Box, which she draws from randomly every morning, 365 promises contained in Scripture. One for each day of the year, unless you count Leap Year. Apparently there's one day every now and again where God isn't looking, a twenty-four hour period without a promise to cover it. And wouldn't you know, my world got caught in the void.

Well, Sissy's message is grossly wasted on me. Nothing good—Nothing. Good—could ever come out of this. But I take the chair she offers, because I've learned to choose my battles, and I will win the one that's coming.

"I'll make you some tea," Jac says.

I give a nod of thanks. To Sissy I say, "The Pasta Moon for dinner. The Miramar for dessert." I'm Solomon, ready to cut the baby in half, which seems to suit everyone. Fine with me. If I have my way I won't be there to see the fallout.

"Wonderful," Sissy says.

And I open my book.

I ponder, not for the first time since starting this novel, what would entice me to fly across the country in search of Teri. Or to cross the street, for that matter. The answer is always the same. Absolutely nothing. Not sickness, not inheritance, not even if it were her deathbed wish. I'd as soon take a leap from the Golden Gate Bridge. Harsh? Well then, it must be the genes she contributed to the zygote that became me.

What would my sister think of the time I'm giving to thoughts of Teri just now? Ainsley, the forgiving one. It's not hard to imagine. In fact, I wouldn't be the least bit surprised if she came to me this minute and said, "You know, Teri is quite charming. We have mochas once a month." Not the least bit. I remember once in grammar school Ainsley came home with a card she'd made on white construction paper. A stick figure girl stood beneath a glittery rainbow, rough with wiggly strands of glue, an oversized sun beating down on the scene. Inside it said, Happy Birthday, Mother. Well, it wasn't Sissy's birthday—whose cards we gave never ever said *Mother*—but Ainsley seemed to think it was Teri's. I wondered for a minute how in the world she knew. Then I decided she didn't. She just wanted to make a card. She put it in a drawer underneath her day-of-the-week panties, and I never saw it again. Or another one like it. But she has this keepsake box, with one of those old-fashioned keys, that I'd love to browse through just once before I die.

The sun hangs suspended like a cosmic yo-yo in the west, and will soon dip behind the fog bank that's rolling in like thick meringue atop the horizon. My stomach begins to churn as I consider the thing I'm about to do. I replace the bookmark, less than a chapter from where I began reading nearly an hour ago, and push myself up from the chair. Quietly. For Sissy's napping, which is a godsend. Okay, that may be an overstatement under the circumstances, but it is fortuitous. I put a finger to my lips when Jac and Ainsley look my way. They're both stretched out on beach towels, taking in the last rays of the sun.

I skip the second step leading into the trailer. As long as I can remember, it's squeaked no matter where you place your foot. Sissy calls it her redneck alarm system. Which goes right along with the redneck beach house it's attached to.

I snag my purse on my way to the bedroom, and make quick work of transferring from one bag to the other the few things I'll need for my getaway: My book. And the pills. That's my Plan B. To take them somewhere else instead of here. It's the least I can do for Ainsley, Jac and Sissy. I slide open a zippered pocket and drop in the little prescription bottle.

I turn. And yelp. "What the—" I say in this breathless voice, as I press both hands to my heart.

Jac, in the doorway, gives me a studied look. "I know about the second step too," she says. "Why so jumpy?"

"Because you scared the crap out of me."

"Uh huh." She looks around as if she's missing something, which gives me hope that maybe she didn't see what I came in here to do, then looks at her watch. "Four-forty."

"Yeah. I was just going to change."

"Into?"

"Something else."

"Because?"

I run my hands down the front of me. "Crops and a T-shirt are a bit casual for business."

"Business." She looks at my purse as though with x-ray eyes. "This is business, right? Right?"

"Well, what else would it be?"

The thing is, every sneaky thing I ever did, I did with Jac. She knows all too well the sound of my lies.

She takes a step into the room. "You'd tell me, right? If this were something else?" Her voice is low, not quite a whisper.

"Something else? Like what?" I regret the question before it's out of my mouth, then decide to try the truth to throw her off track. "I mean, you act as if this is some secret rendezvous."

"You said it, not me."

I should have stuck with a lie.

I pull on my best pair of jeans and slip on an emerald silk blouse. The fabric is slinky, unforgiving. With practically a hundred mother-of-pearl buttons. I will my hands to stop quivering as I maneuver each button through its hole. This is taking way too long, but I have no better option. And speaking of options, I have none when it comes to shoes. It's either the sandals I have on, or my bare feet.

"You're meeting at the coffee kiosk on the highway, right?"

"Yes," I say. That should put her suspicions to rest. "How much can one do at a drive-up window?" I'd like to add how offended I am that she'd think me capable of what Jeff thinks I'm capable of, but I'm hardly trustworthy these days.

"Okay, good," she says. "Because I'd love a latte."

Surprise.

———————

She takes orders from everyone, including Sissy, who woke up when Jac all but bounced on the second step, with both feet, on her way out of the trailer. So, armed with a list, we plod through the sand on our way to the highway, me a half step in front, carrying on the most wicked conversation in my head with Jaclyn, my best friend in the whole world, about trust and won't everyone just leave me alone? I wonder what she'd do if I made a run for it, just took off and didn't look back. I probably would if there were any fog to hide in, but it's still holding its own offshore, and at the moment you can see all the way to Canada. If just once something would go my way.

We've reached the asphalt parking lot. It's easier to walk now than it was in the sand, but Jac's steps are slow, forcing me to slow down as well.

"Bree?"

I don't want to hear anything her tone of voice portends. I look away, at the pewter sea. The sun has dropped behind the fog bank. The world looks as gray as I feel. But there's beauty in the variegated shades of nature's gray. There's nothing beautiful about me at all. I brace myself for whatever Jac plans to say next.

"I know what Sassy said about not calling home this weekend, but why don't you? Call David, just connect for a few minutes."

My eyes stay on the horizon. "Why would I do that?"

Jac steps into my line of vision. "So he can hear your voice. So you can hear his. This is, well, hard doesn't begin to cover it. It's a terrible time for both of you. You should be together."

"Of everyone here you're the one I thought understood why that's the last thing in the world I want."

"Bristol, why?"

"Why?"

That's the best I can offer, the echo of her question. It's laden with the weight of desperation that fills every living cell of me. Sand has collected under the toes of my right foot. I shake it off and resume our march to the kiosk.

"Bristol."

The word is rich with frustration, but I keep walking.

My stomach does this flip flop thing when What a Grind comes into view. The asphalt parking lot that frames the little brown shack is empty. Empty except for one champagne-colored Lexus.

"Is that him?"

I shrug. "Probably." Of course.

"You don't know?"

"I've never been in his car, Jac."

Her eyes concede the point. "This'll just take a minute, right?"

"Why don't you order, while I ..." I nod toward the Lexus, and let that finish my sentence.

Jac fingers her list like it's the last thing she cares about. "What about you? What do you want?"

"Don't worry about me. Really."

She reaches out to me, more with her eyes than her hand. "But I do, Bree."

I look away, to Jeff's car. "I'm going to go take care of this."

"I'll get you a chai tea. Extra hot." That's what she says, but what she means is, *come back.* Come back is exactly what she means.

As I walk toward the driver's side of the car, Jeff leans over and opens the passenger door. I alter my course, but approach the open door as though it's the wall where my firing-squad will take aim. I don't want to mess this up. Just want to sign the contract and be on my way.

"Slide in," he says when I bend down to look into the car. I do, but I leave the door open. The aura of his masculinity is as strong here as it is in his office. He's cultivated this to perfection.

"Do you have the contract?" The question is ridiculous, I know, but I don't know what else to say.

Jeff taps the breast pocket of his sport coat. "I thought we'd have a drink first. Seal the deal, so to speak."

I'm pretty sure it's not the only deal he's thinking to seal, and for a moment I think I might panic. And then it occurs to me. This is my way out. My escape. It may cost me way more than I want to pay, but what choice do I have? Without a word I stretch the seatbelt across my body and snap it into the buckle at the thigh of my jeans, which, once again, are a sad contrast to Jeff's slacks and jacket.

Jeff looks over his shoulder, back toward the kiosk where Jac is intent on placing our order. "Want to tell your friend?" There's no mistaking the appreciation in the subtle upturn of his lips as he studies her.

Yes, I hate him. I really do.

Now that my moment of escape is here, when I realize I won't see Jac again, ever, I want to hug her, to carry something of her away with me. I want to go back to Ainsley, my sister, who breathed for me these past three hundred sixty four days when I couldn't, who held my place in line, so to speak, when I couldn't hold it myself, willing me to keep from falling off the edge of the world. I want to tell her an oceanful of things that only just now occur to me, to leave Ainsley, the good one, with something good to recall. I want to say thank you to Sissy. But, of course, I don't. I only shake my head and say, "No."

I close the door as softly as I can, and note with relief that the engine makes hardly a sound when Jeff turns the key in the ignition. I'm hoping to get away without a witness to my profound stupidity. But the crunch of tires on gravel catches Jac's attention. She turns and looks over her shoulder as Jeff backs out of the parking space. There's a split second between curiosity and awareness, not nearly long enough to close my eyes against the moment of understanding that reaches Jac's brain and slackens her jaw. It's the picture I take away as Jeff pulls onto the highway.

I bite my lip until it hurts, until Jeff reaches his arm behind the headrest of my seat. "You okay?"

I look straight ahead at the highway and wonder what he can possibly expect me to say to that.

Nineteen

I watch Jac's image grow smaller in the mirror outside my door until I lose her at a curve in the highway. Sitting there next to Jeff, with Norah Jones' jazzy voice crooning in the background, I feel like the canary that caught the cat. It begs the question, now what do I do with it?

"Sorry for the jeans," I say. It seems I'm always apologizing to him for the way I'm dressed. "I wasn't expecting to go anywhere."

He cuts me a look. "Hey, you look great. Really."

Uh huh.

He drives farther down the highway then turns onto a lane cut through a copse of cypress trees that winds its way to the beach. The fogbank hides the setting sun, but the sky just above it is awash in color. There are no other cars in the sand-coated asphalt parking lot, but a guy and girl amble hand-in-hand along the shoreline and disappear around a cove. Jeff turns off the engine, opens his door. "Let's take a walk."

A walk? What is this? A stroll along the beach as a prelude to what?

Jeff comes around the back of the car, slips his sport coat over my shoulders as I step out, and closes my door. The smooth scent of his cologne rises from the fabric, but is soon swallowed up by the stronger scent of the sea air. With a light touch on my back he leads me toward the water. A gritty layer of sand quickly settles between my feet and my sandals. I reach down and slip them off, purely for convenience, but the action broadcasts a sensual message I don't intend. Jeff's hand, which steadied me while I began my undressing, returns to the small of my back, only now it's on the inside of his sport coat.

We follow the course of the young couple, who have disappeared into the twilight, and stop behind the towering outcropping of rock that juts into the sea. We're misted by a fine spray from the breakers that crash against the rocks, but Jeff doesn't notice, or doesn't mind at any rate. "I like your hair down," he says.

"My—" I reach for a corkscrew curl. He's right. It's always been up, in what I consider my professional look, when I've been to his office. I say thank you, and wonder, what are we doing here on this beach? What is this mating dance all about? I know he thinks it's a done deal, and why shouldn't he? Though he'll be sorely disappointed once I have the contract signed.

Once we're past the rocks, out of the spray and protected by the cove, it's not quite so cool. I offer him his jacket, reach up to remove it, but he presses it to my shoulder. "You keep it. I'm fine."

We stand there then, in the moonlight, with the sounds of the sea all around us, held by each other's eyes. He moves in close, and I lean back. I'm not nearly as far gone as he thinks I am, not willing to sell myself for the sake of the deal, though I want the deal badly. I'm tempted to reach into the breast pocket of the jacket that's draped over my shoulders, pull out the contract, and have a signing party right here and now.

It only takes a moment for Jeff to realize it will indeed take a drink, maybe two, to loosen me up, and I sense he's not used to such labor-intensive women. It's an awkward moment, to say the least, and the one bizarre thought going through my mind is: there must be a lot of sand in his shoes. I almost speak it out loud, eyeing, as I am, his designer footwear. The leather alone probably cost as much as one of our mortgage payments.

I'm losing it. That's my next thought.

"Shall we ...?" He lets the sweep of his arm finish his sentence, and we turn back the way we came. If this is a test, I just failed part one.

Back at the car I give him his jacket and this time he takes it, folds it once lengthwise and lays it on the back seat, but only after he's opened my door and I'm back inside the car. He closes both doors and walks around the vehicle, then slips into the driver's seat. But instead of starting the car he leans back against the door and tilts his head in that way he has.

"I thought a walk might relax you. You seem ... not relaxed."

"I wasn't expecting any of this," I say, looking straight ahead. "I thought we were going to sign the contract, back there, and that would be that."

"Let's get that drink."

He leans toward me, his right hand settling again on the passenger seat headrest. I get the feeling that with the slightest enticement he would move in to kiss me. Evidently, he left his subtlety back at the office. I keep my face forward and thank God for cup holders.

He squares around and turns the key in the ignition. "I thought we'd go to the Miramar. Have a drink, then maybe a bite to eat. Would you—"

"No!" He's startled by my outburst, but not as startled as I am. "It's just— I don't— I'm not —" I turn and try to put on a business persona. "Jeff, let's keep this about the contract."

He studies me with the hint of a smile on his lips. "Certainly, Bristol, if that's what you'd like." That's what his mouth says, but his eyes say something altogether different.

This is the first time he's spoken my given name. Always before it was Ms. Taylor, all a show of business. I feel exposed at the sound of my name on his lips, at the smoothness of his voice when he says it. I turn and look out the side window, wishing, *wishing* the waves would wash over me and pull me out to sea. WTHAIDH? That's truly what I think in that moment, WTHAIDH. Wouldn't Sissy love it?

"We'll just go back to where I'm staying and take care of business."

"Where you're staying? I thought you were going to Carmel." My heart feels ready to leapfrog off my lily pad of a throat. I run an open hand down the front of my neck to settle it.

"I am," he says, "tomorrow."

The world outside the car has lost all color by the time Jeff turns onto the highway, heading north. I close my eyes and meld into the memory that settles over me, more real than the surreal moment in which I find myself.

"Mama. Where does it go?"

"Where does what go, baby?"

"All the color, when it's dark. Does it go night-night?"

"It does," I say, and think, What an observant thought for a three year old. Or anyone for that matter. Where does the color go? "It takes light to make color, Kinsey. The more light, the brighter the color."

"Why?"

Doesn't that start when they're four, I ask myself? The whys? Well, why should I think Kinsey won't be ahead of schedule in this, the way she's ahead in everything else? "Because ..." I don't want to give her a trite answer, but how do you explain this so that a three year old, even one as bright as Kinsey, can understand? "... that's how God made it. So that we have something to look forward to every morning."

She bunches up her favorite blanket by her face, its original lemon yellow stripes faded to a soft buttery hue with all the washings it's gone through. She's satisfied by my answer, though I'm not. Where does the color go? When every day seems more gray than not, and you never noticed the color fading away. When nothing—or almost nothing—is as it should be? I kiss my baby girl, breathe in and store away her scent as I always do, and think with the utmost satisfaction I'll always have this bright spot in my world.

Except I don't.

We've never talked about Kinsey, not once, Jeff and I. Not even when he first saw my Baby Talk cards—the simple line sketch that is Kinsey's profile. Not even when the disappearance of little McKinsey Taylor was the talk on all the talk shows, the top story on the cable news networks. He's never said her name in my presence. It tells me how aloof he is, because this omission is not in consideration of my feelings, I'm sure of that. It's just that how does any of this matter to the tiny universe of which he's the sun?

"It's for Kinsey," I say, "why any of this matters." There, I've crashed the hull of myself into that iceberg.

He's quiet for a ridiculous length of time, then, "Let's get that drink."

I look out my side window. That alone serves as my response.

"Your friend looked surprised." Jeff says this in the quiet space between tracks 5 and 6 of Norah's CD. The song titles revealed on his media screen are "Come Away With Me" and "Shoot the Moon." He cued them. I'm sure of it.

I wait for her mellow tone to provide background before I speak, something nice to buffer the sound of my voice. It breaks more than ever tonight. "I suppose she was." And so was I, I don't add.

"Who is she?" He thinks he's being nonchalant in the blasé way he speaks his words, but he's far more transparent than he imagines. Though in all fairness, it's hard for any man to be blasé about Jaclyn.

"Jackie Paper," I say.

There's just the slightest delay, then he turns with a smile. "Really?"

"Sort of."

Before I'd gotten to know him I might have offered Jeff her phone number. But now I'd die first. I look out my window again and chuckle softly at my private little joke.

I sit here thinking there's such a difference between David and Jeff, a level of sophistication that tilts deeply in Jeff's favor, that isn't quite as appealing as it was when I first met him; an arrogance that David couldn't begin to approach; a self-assurance that Jeff's all that and more. He thinks he's James Bond, minus the cuff links. So then, does that make me a Bond girl? I almost laugh out loud at the thought. Sophisticated he may be, but he has no clue how unattractive he is to me at this moment.

He turns at the next light and winds his way back toward a beachfront restaurant/lounge. The parking lot is packed. When we get inside there are a dozen or more couples waiting to be seated in the restaurant, but against all hope the hostess assures us there's seating available in the lounge. We follow her to a small table. Jeff holds my chair, then takes the seat next to, not across from, mine. I lean away just the slightest and keep my hands folded in my lap.

There's no time for conversation before our cocktail waitress comes to take our order. She's a stunning young woman in a little black dress cut low enough to display the butterfly tattoo over her heart. And me with my jeans. The streaked tresses dangling from her upswept hair shimmer in the soft light, and there's a tiny arrowed heart on one of her French-manicured nails. Acrylic, of course.

Don't think I don't miss the electrical charge that passes between them. It could power the entire Pacific coastline. In all fairness, the sparks fly more from her eyes than Jeff's. I'm sure to him this is completely commonplace. That's the thing about Jeff. He's a lightning rod. You might say he can't help it, until you remember he never diverts the charge. I can't help wonder if he'll slip her his business card before the night is through.

"What's your pleasure?" she asks, and it's all I can do not to laugh at the absurdity of the question. If I were really here with Jeff as a date I'd be more than offended. As it is, what do I care what happens between them?

Jeff's smile is charged with suggestion as he orders a drink I've never heard of.

"And you?" She manages to tear her eyes away long enough to look my direction.

I'm about to ask for coffee when Jeff says, "White wine for the lady."

She can't resist looking over her shoulder at Jeff, not once but twice as she walks toward the bar with our order. And he misses none of it.

Twenty

*J*eff returns his attention to me. "What do people call you? How do they shorten your name?"

"That seems to imply no one calls me Bristol."

"Do they?"

"Mostly no. But Bristol's good."

He considers that a moment, then gives me an alright-then-maybe-we'll-just-change-the-subject look.

I don't mean to offend him, but really, what does he expect here? Even if we were to go where he thinks we're going—which there isn't the remotest chance of—he wants to exchange pet names? But for the sake of civility I pick up the thread of his conversation and stitch away. "The name Jeff doesn't lend itself to nicknames. Is there something else people call you?"

"You mean that I can share?"

It's an old joke, and not funny, but I placate him with a smile.

And he moves on. "It depends on who it is. You're right, mostly it's

Jeff."

He leans back as the waitress returns with our order. She serves his drink, letting her hand touch his as it rests on the table, then she serves my wine. When she's gone, leaving the essence of an expensive perfume, he moves back in, even closer it seems to me.

I lean back a little more to compensate, but lock my eyes onto his. "Kinsey calls my sister Auntie A."

"Kinsey. Your daughter." He says this with just the right amount of feeling. Sometime during the last few minutes I've placed my hands on the table, intertwined as though it's my turn to pray. He covers them with his own hand, applies just the slightest pressure. It all seems very practiced. "And the A is for ...?"

"Ainsley."

"Is she younger, older?"

This seems ridiculously like an interview. "A before B."

"Ah. Ainsley and Bristol. Nice names."

"But hard to shorten."

He's right, of course, about nicknames. Who doesn't abbreviate the names of most everyone they know? We only extend them when we're angry. As David knows only too well.

"Do you have a sister? Or brother?"

"Nope. It's just me." It doesn't sound the least bit like a complaint.

I feel more off guard every moment I'm with Jeff, as though I'm inching away from the helm. It's an unpleasant feeling. "Kinsey has always been Kinsey," I say, "except when the search was launched. Then it was Little McKinsey Taylor."

The breath he draws is a little deeper than the ones before it. He waits an appropriate moment then picks up his glass and takes a drink.

I've yet to touch mine.

"Would you like to get dinner?" he asks.

"No. Thank you. I really need to get back before long."

There's not a bit of truth in that, for now that I'm away from my keepers I have no intention of going back. I have everything I need in my over-sized purse, including my book. The only thing left to be determined now is where I'll go for my last few hours.

"Are you sure I can't entice you? The steak and lobster is superb."

I could certainly do worse for a last supper, but all I want is to get down to business, then get away.

"So tell me, how did you get away?"

It's uncanny, how his words echo my thoughts, how he's practically read my mind, but I'm confused for a second. "You ... saw ..."

"No. I mean from home, especially on this particular weekend."

"Home." Painstakingly, I straighten the napkin that lies on my lap. "Well, I just said, 'I'm going away for the weekend.' Nothing else necessary."

"Yours must be"—he thinks a moment, shuffling around for the right word—"a contemporary marriage." Which is, of course, code for *open*.

"It's not. No." And I realize that he honestly thinks he's going to score with me. That I came to Half Moon Bay, leaving my husband at home on Valentine's weekend, for the sole purpose of sleeping with him. And why shouldn't he think that? I mean I'm here, right?

Every table within view is occupied by couples. There are cards, opened and not, lying on most every table. I'm ecstatic that Jeff didn't feel the need. A dozen roses, barely opened and blood red, adorn the table to my left. I'm close enough to enjoy the fragrance ... if they had one. But they may as well be plastic for all the perfume they emit, which is so true of most florist-shop roses. That could be me, those roses, since some have said I have a fair exterior, but it doesn't take long to realize I've nothing sweet to offer. The couple practically touch foreheads as they angle toward one another, his fingertips stroking hers in a deeply sensual way. He says something that elicits a demure smile, after which they collect their things and leave. I watch them and wonder, were they at each other's throats yesterday?

"Here's to this evening."

I turn to see Jeff with his glass raised to mine. I tap mine ever so lightly to his and take a tiny sip then place my glass on the table. "And what about you, Jeff? How did you slip away?"

"From?"

"You mean to say there's no one special in your life?"

He seems to measure his words, then says, "I live one day at a time. Right now I'm enjoying your company."

I smile, but what I really want to say is, "Then how is it you can't keep your eyes off the waitress—or her butterfly—whenever she walks by?" I would probably make his night if I excused myself to the restroom and didn't return. Chances are he wouldn't leave alone. In fact, if I had an omniscient eye from which to view this lounge I bet I could find any number of women whose eye continually strays in his direction. But in all fairness, Jeff is sublime in his appeal.

In a very surface way.

If I had to compare, I'd say it's the opposite with David—it *was* the opposite with David. His appeal was from the inside out. Nice looking, too, but in a safe way. I never thought I'd go for a preacher's kid, but there was something wholesome about him that I craved like sunshine.

My, how seasons change.

Jeff is good at conversation, which means I don't have to tax myself. A relief, since there's so little left to draw from. But there is one thing I want to know. The wine I'm not used to gives me the boldness to ask. "What are we doing here, Jeff? I could have signed the contract in the front seat of your car. Saved us both some time."

Jeff isn't the least bit put off by my question. He seems to weigh his answer, then ultimately comes out with the truth. "Ah, Bristol, more than anything I love a challenge."

It's the one thing he says that I believe.

I should have turned off my cell phone. It's vibrated almost non-stop in my pocket since I drove away with Jeff. I should do it now, but I can't bring myself to sever the connection that remains between me and my keepers. I suppose the debate between Miramar and Pasta Moon is now a moot point. I wonder what Jaclyn said when she got back to the beach house. How she explained losing me. How she explained Jeff. I hope Sissy isn't too hard on her. This wasn't Jac's fault, that's for sure. I'll request in my LW&T that Sissy let it go. Permanently. And speaking of wills, I so need to start on it. Not to mention I have a book to finish. I need these next twelve hours to be thirty-six or forty-eight hours long. Each.

My stomach somersaults when Jeff turns off the highway and into the garden-like parking lot of a bed and breakfast.

"Here we are," he says. "Ready to do business?"

I murmur something affirmative and don't give him the chance to open my door. For this is business. Whether he thinks so or not, it is.

I had no idea there was such a lovely place so near the beach house. The downstairs windows, and one or two upstairs, cast a golden glow over the front yard, which is also aglow with soft landscape lights that twinkle in the sea breeze, entwined as they are in the shrubbery. Even in the dark, this place could be a cover for *Coastal Living*. Probably has been.

Jeff takes my arm and leads me along a river-rock trail that takes us to the back of the B&B. There's a large bricked patio, dotted with tables for two discreetly partitioned with tall, wispy plants and plants that are sculpted, all growing out of enormous urns. Jeff continues to lead me to the far edge of the brick, beyond which is the beach and then the sea, the Earth's womb. The surf caresses the shore with a timeless rhythm I want to get lost in. I close my eyes, waiting for the spell to be cast.

A salty gust blows my hair back, whips it to the side, and in that moment lips touch my neck. I stiffen, lose my breath like an infant in the wind. Jeff, standing behind me, leans away in response, but his hands still hold my arms. He's testing the waters is what he's doing.

I turn, extricating my arms. "You asked if I'm ready to do business. I am."

He smiles, not the least bit embarrassed by my rebuff.

A piffle of sound, not quite tinkling and not quite clacking, draws my attention. I follow it with my eyes to a wind chime hanging from the spout of an old pump. The pump stands in the garden, as though sprouting from a tuft of sea grass, near the French doors that lead from the patio inside to a sitting room. The wind chime, placed there merely for decoration if you ask me, since it can by no means get the optimum wind movement in that location, consists, of all things, of a half dozen starfish. My hand finds its way to my pocket, which holds nothing but a cell phone. I know this, and still I reach in. The starfish that I'm fishing for lies at the bottom of the bag slung over my arm, but I swear I can feel it, that starfish, feel the coarsely bubbled surface of its four good arms, the ragged edge of the one broken. This too takes my breath away, this phantom thing that means ... what exactly?

Hope? A promise?

Nothing?

The phrase *don't kill the messenger* jumps to the front of the line of random thoughts sparring for first place in my head. But in this case, it is in fact the Messenger who needs to go. I know what he's up to, this wooing, know all the "Beloved" scriptures by heart. Well, he had his chance. Had three hundred sixty four days to meet my one and only demand, he who had the power to do so. And here I stand, enveloped in the breath of the sea, with empty hands, empty arms.

I shiver and gooseflesh rises on my skin.

"Let's get you inside," Jeff says. But he means so much more.

Twenty-One

We step from the patio into a parlor—a real one, and large—straight out of *Victorian Homes.* I shiver again in the warmth.

"Welcome," says a voice, smooth as liquid silk. It matches the face, and everything else, of the woman behind the check-in desk in the home's foyer. "Mr. Girard?" Thankfully, there's no presumptuous *and Mrs.?* But reservations, well, this tells me that Jeff's plans were more extensively thought out than I imagined. His expectations, I assume, are high.

Jeff confirms his identity with a smile and a nod as he steps toward the desk. I hold back and his arm falls away. "I'll just"—I let my eyes take in the room—"look around."

The clerk, or maybe the owner, gets this look as Jeff approaches, as if it's Christmas and he's the prettiest package under the tree. I bet he gets that everywhere. But I wonder if it doesn't wear thin, even for Jeff. No, probably not.

I move deeper into the parlor, toward a rosewood, glass-doored bookcase that stands floor to ceiling opposite the fireplace. It holds dozens of old volumes, but with no lock on the doors I doubt there are any first editions. I wouldn't mind curling up on that sofa in front of the fire with any one of them. Or better yet, with *What We Keep*. A couple of hours and I'd have it finished.

Besides the sofa, there are antique chairs grouped here and there, all leather and tacks, with bowlegged tables that don't match, but that fit all the same. The fire crackles and draws me, and gives off a perfume of smoke and wood that defines the season. I seldom have the pleasure of this since our house doesn't have a fireplace. Even Dad seldom builds a fire since he can heat the entire house with the push of a button. I move in closer and enjoy the warmth, but then there's a violent pop that sends me back a step. A flurry of sparks fly upward, and of all things, I think of that proverb from Job. About that very thing, sparks and trouble and life all bound up together.

"Bristol?" Jeff calls my name, maybe not for the first time.

The woman behind the counter keeps to her post, and it occurs to me how out of place she is in this place of vintage things. It's like moving through time as I step from the parlor to that check-in desk where she and Jeff wait. With one hand he reaches toward me, with the other he holds the key to his room.

My eyes stay on the woman until she finally turns away. "Let's go in by the fire. Looks like a great place to do business."

"We can have a fire upstairs," he says.

I glance at the briefcase in his hand, and know there isn't a doubt he's calling the shots.

"Enjoy your stay," the woman says, but her eyes don't quite include me, something I don't imagine Jeff notices.

I feel her gaze on my back until we make the turn on the first landing of the staircase. And I feel so Hester Prynne-ish, climbing these stairs without so much as a suitcase in my hand.

The suite is on the second floor. The hallway that leads to the room he had the presumption to procure is profoundly non-hotelish; the homey photographs on the walls, the lack of garish carpet meant to hide the traffic of dirty shoes, the absence of numbers on the doors. The key fob, not one of those plastic things you usually see, but a shell of some type, matches the color of the door, in our case a warm plum. That's how we know we've arrived.

Jeff turns the key and sweeps open the door, then moves aside for me to go in before him. A Tiffany lamp sheds its inviting light over the room, and I step inside. Under other circumstances I would be delighted with the upscale charm and the old-world feel of the room. More than delighted. Under other circumstances. Even I can tell the room is a treasure trove of antiques.

I've never felt so out of place. I avert my eyes from the room's centerpiece, but it's hard to avoid the four-poster bed, all done up in mounds of white satin, which starts that old Moody Blues song playing in my head, as surely as if a phonograph had been turned on. I know all the best songs of my dad's generation. The canopy is draped with lace that runs the length of each post and lies scalloped on the floor by each clawed foot of the bed.

I turn away, toward a small sitting area to my left. It horse-shoes a fireplace, as Jeff stated, that needs only a match to bring it to life. I move in and breathe deeply the lingering scent of wood smoke.

Jeff steps past me and opens the glass doors that lead to a balcony that overlooks the black expanse of the sea. That sound of waves washing ashore is the lullaby I will fall asleep to, in some yet-to-be-determined place, in the early morning hours, when my pills have done their job. That's why I'm here, in Half Moon Bay. For that lullaby. Jeff moves toward the fireplace, but then the breeze rushes in and ruffles the lace right down to the scallops and he reaches for the doors again.

"No," I say. "No. I like it."

He shrugs, then lights the fire.

While he's occupied I take further inventory of the room. This would be a lovely place to die in, if I planned on staying, which I don't. I'll take care of business, then my contract and I are leaving. I don't care how compelling Jeff tries to be.

Still, it is such a lovely place. But I imagine my dying here would devastate their business, especially if they had to declare to future guests not only a death, but a suicide. Or maybe they could capitalize on it and make me, the late Bristol Taylor, the resident ghost? I push away the thoughts and inform myself there will be no plan C.

The accouterments are perfect, right down to the crystal vase of rosebuds on the side table. I've never understood the hype about roses. They're too fragile, their life too brief, my least favorite flower to receive. But these roses draw me. Not the flowers, but the color. The pink.

Kinsey, not quite three, has a new Disney Princesses coloring book and, of all things, a box of Crayola markers. I'll have to watch the markers, which Auntie A should have known better than to buy. I can only imagine the damage to walls and carpet and clothing Kinsey could do with those markers. But how do you tell her no, you can't use these lovely new markers from Auntie A, you have to stick to the fat, round-tipped, paper-peeled crayons? I look away when the phone rings or some such thing, and when I turn back, Kinsey has painted her lips with the pink one, the way she's seen me do with lipstick. She's done a remarkably good job of it, for being not quite three. But with her heart of a mouth she looks like a little Geisha with her painted-on lips.

I try to hold on to this vision of my little girl, but as always, it morphs into that last glimpse of my sick little Kinsey nodding off in her car seat outside the school.

I die another death and put my face close to the flowers to take in their fragrance, for I concede, in surprise, that's one thing these roses have in their favor: they actually have a fragrance. Then I pull back, surprised again to see a small white envelope nestled in the baby's breath with my name written in gold calligraphy. I turn back to Jeff, who has succeeded in lighting the fire, but he's busy turning on the lamps that flank the sitting area.

I don't remove the little envelope. In fact, I step away and pretend not to have seen it. It occurs to me with more than a little regret that I should have gotten David a Valentine's Day card after all. To put with my will. To make it clear that, yes, there were good times too. And in that odd way my mind has begun to work of late I think of Teri, wonder if she left behind a card or a note. Not for Ainsley or me, but for Dad. To say, "Just so you know I loved you once. The smile in the photograph—that one of you and me at Yosemite—was real."

I might have thought up these questions at a more convenient time, when there was a way to get the answers, when the answers might have mattered. But no, I was busy not caring. Now, here at the end of it all, I see I'm more like Teri than I want to be, and that disturbs me. And, still, there's the matter of David's card. Maybe the gift shop downstairs has one. I turn my attention to Jeff, who's taken off his jacket and hung it neatly over a chair. Already I think if I had to deal with that jacket on a regular basis I'd do something psycho. With lawn shears. I bet Jeff's the type to line up his shoes, just so, and slide them under the edge of the bed till he's ready for them again. He looks as if he's about to say something, but I jump in ahead of him.

"Would you excuse me"—I hold up a finger—"for just one minute?"

"Of course." His eyes dart in the direction of the bathroom, which, judging by what I can see from here, would be a paradise of discovery for Sissy. But I don't move in the direction of the bathroom. I slip my purse back on my shoulder and head for the door.

"Bristol?" It's almost comical, that look of surprise. "It's not— You don't—" He spreads his hands to encompass the vase of flowers and me, and I think his point is *you don't have to reciprocate*. "Really."

"I'll only be a minute," I say, then I'm out the door.

By the time I reach the stair landing, "Fifty Ways to Leave Your Lover" plays in my head, Fred, and I decide I'm as cracked as an egg can be and still keep its insides inside.

The little gift shop isn't a shop at all, but rather a cubby hole between the parlor and the lobby, set apart by a revolving card rack on one side and a free-standing knickknack shelf on the other, displaying whales and seashells, Half Moon Bay types of wares. But no dolphins. No starfish.

The Valentines section of the revolving card rack is empty, save for three cards. The top one reads in a fancy script, "To the one I love ..." I don't bother to open it. The next one has a silhouetted couple walking hand-in-hand on the beach at sunset. Considering that Jeff was the last man I walked on a beach with, though not hand-in-hand, I decide that one's not appropriate either. I exhale a breath in the direction of my bangs and take the third card out of the rack. If I'm lucky it will be generic and vague, just right for a woman in my situation. I'm happy to find that's exactly what it is.

There's no cashier's station in the makeshift shop. I take the card to the desk and hesitate only a moment before I ring the bell. I really don't want to summon the clerk to my aid, not if it's the same woman who checked us in—and checked Jeff out—and probably ordered and delivered the flowers upstairs if the truth were known—but it's that or I make off without paying. And I don't want to add one more sin to my account, not at this late date. I barely have time to hope someone else will answer the bell, when the same woman steps through a doorway and up to the desk. Her smile is professionally warm, but there's a look on her face that says, You came here with a man as desirable as Jeff Girard without a Valentine's Day card? Or an overnight bag? What kind of idiot are you? The thought pops into her eyes the same moment it pops into my head: an Escort. That's what kind of idiot. Her smile freezes in place, and she hesitates before she finally rings up my purchase. I dig a five-dollar bill out of my wallet and pass it to her with my left hand, making my wedding set, with its chip of a diamond, as prominent as I can. But it's clearly not the type of ring Jeff Girard would buy his bride. She sees that as well as I do, judging by the arc of her brow. The day David slipped it on my finger he promised, among all his other promises, something grander on a future anniversary, to which I said no, I don't believe in upgrades. I'm rethinking that decision as the clerk counts back my change. She doesn't bother to thank me as she gives me the bag, which again I take with my left hand. But considering this telepathic discussion we've had, one mind to the other, I'm pretty sure I've only made matters worse. I'm glad for my jeans, though, for the first time tonight. They may be the one thing to dispel the misconception.

But then I think, what misconception?

Twenty-Two

I have to knock at the door because, of course, I don't have a key to get back in the room. No plum-colored shell to spare me this awkward moment. Jeff answers as though he really and truly doesn't know who to expect. Well, it's just me.

I slip by him, avoiding eye contact, pull my bag off my shoulder and hang it over the post of the chair that holds his jacket. David's card is tucked inside one of the zippered pockets of my purse. I feel Jeff's eyes searching it out, like the Eye of Sauron, but when I force myself to look past his chin and up to his eyes, his eyes dart to mine, all signs of curiosity erased. We stand there like freshmen on a blind date until he remembers himself. Then he motions to the little settee. Or love seat if you prefer. Which I don't. The fire has gotten off to a slow start and has yet to put off any warmth, but it pops and crackles as though it has something to boast about.

I realize as Jeff sits down beside me that he's found a source of music. I spot the CD player from which an instrumental version of some familiar love song is playing at just the right background volume. You have to give him an A for effort, I will say that. I imagine a man as practiced as Jeff has never had to deal with a situation like this, having to work so hard for what usually must come so easily.

I don't happen to care for instrumental versions of real songs, but of course Jeff has no way of knowing what I do and don't care for. But then, maybe the CD along with the player is compliments of the proprietors. If so, they've certainly thought of everything. But I'm pretty sure the champagne in the bucket on the table was Jeff's idea. He removes the bottle from its bed of ice, wraps a white towel around it like a pro, then twists out the cork. It makes this rich *thwump* of a sound and emits a frosty little cloud. I almost believe a genie could pop out, if it were a lamp instead of a bottle, if there were any part of my life that was charmed. If it were, I know exactly what I'd wish for ... the same thing I've been wishing for, for three hundred sixty-four days now. Jeff pours our champagne glasses two-thirds full, then turns the bottle just so to keep it from dripping, and slips the cork back in.

"Do you always go to such lengths for a contract signing?" I'm doing my best to keep him on point.

"To Baby Talk," he says, tapping his glass to mine.

The bubbles tickle my nose as I take a sip in time to Jeff's. The unfamiliar taste shakes up my taste buds. I can't say I particularly like the flavor, but the feeling in my mouth is amazing. I take another sip. This isn't the first champagne I've had in my life. It's the second. The first was on the occasion of the marriage of Jaclyn's father to his third bride at some little chapel in Vegas. Jac and I were fifteen, the bride halfway between that and Devlin Papier's age of thirty-seven, which I knew quite well considering the secret little crush I carried for him most of that year. The bride's name was Barbi or Bambi or some similar pseudonym she'd adopted the day she hit The Strip. Jac and I were highly disappointed when Barbi opted to trade her feathered headdress— reported to weigh thirty-five pounds if it weighed an ounce—for a fluff of lace headbanding her platinum hair on the day of the wedding. The rest of her costume, minus the sequins, she wore beneath her skin-tight mini wedding dress. If you get my drift. The marriage lasted about as long as it takes to obtain a Las Vegas annulment. Bride number four was a stewardess who worked the same flight Devlin piloted between Seattle and Denver. And number five was a law clerk moving her way up in the office of his divorce attorney. They're still together, he and that law clerk, who is now a top-notch partner in the same firm, but even Dev couldn't tell you everything contained in the pre-nup she authored and had him sign under the watchful eye of the senior partner.

Jaclyn's dad would fit his daughter into his schedule when he wasn't trying to wed or bed one woman or another. At least he had the decency to keep her away from the sordidness of it all. But it's no wonder she doesn't respect men. And the guys she's dated haven't helped the situation one little bit. You think they'd be falling all over themselves to win a woman like Jac, treating her like the prize she is. But they're fools, every one. I hope Loren or Kevin or whatever his name is becomes the exception. The irony is not lost on me that here I sit drinking champagne with a man who is not my husband, and me casting aspersions.

I discover as I tune back in that Jeff is studying me with a touch of humor in his eyes. "Where do you go," he asks, "on these little treks you take?"

"Here and there," I say. I've been caught red-handed, so why lie? I can't imagine what he's thinking of all this. Of me. When he could be here, or somewhere, with the hostess of the little black dress, or any number of appreciative women.

I set my glass on the table. "You have the contract?"

"We'll get there."

"In fullness of disclosure, I haven't completed the new cards you asked for. But I'm working on them." That's only a little lie, since I am working on them in my head. The reality is they won't be done, ever, but he doesn't need to know that now.

"No problem." He stands and reaches for my hand.

"What?" I say.

But he only motions me to him with his fingers.

I stand, move around the table, and he leads me to the space between the settee and the bed, where the doors are open to the starry night and the sea, and begins to sway back and forth to the beat of the music, with me in his arms. Unlike David, Jeff leads with his left hand, which throws me off. It's all wrong. Still, I do my best to follow as we turn in the smallest of circles. Which go in the wrong direction.

The song we're dancing to is "Try a Little Tenderness," and that makes my point exactly. Because what instrument can capture the emotion of Otis Redding when he sings out the lyrics from that deep place that harbors his soul?

"Relax," he whispers.

"This isn't why I'm here."

"Are you sure?" His breath tickles my ear.

The scent of his cologne is amazing. And what woman wouldn't appreciate the smooth skin of a face recently shaved, just for her comfort? For a moment, I'm tempted. It would be so good to feel something other than pain and regret, something halfway alive. But this is what I'm thinking: When I stand in David's arms my head fits perfectly beneath his chin. I can rest my cheek in the crook of his neck and feel the steady beat of his pulse. I used to love that, could tell so much by the rate of his pulse against my cheek. But Jeff's not quite so tall. The crown of my brow reaches just to his lips. I feel the vibration as he hums along to the music. He can't possibly know how much I hate that ... a dance partner humming to the music. It's so, I don't know, Cary Grant-ish.

I stop our movement and take a step back. "This isn't why I'm here." I'm as tense as a lifeline with no slack, and I'm the body connected to the other end. I'm lightheaded from the champagne. I wonder with some alarm what effect the alcohol will have on the pills I plan to take. You always hear that mixing alcohol with—

Are you kidding, I ask myself? I mean really, Bree, what does it matter? I think about that a moment, and almost laugh as I admit I'm right, what does it matter? In fact, I think of how much it can help, mixing pills with alcohol in this situation.

I know Jeff thinks he's irresistible, and to a thousand other women I'm sure he would be. He considers me for a moment, then says, "Okay."

He leads me back to the little sofa. "I brought you something."

My eyes shift to the vase of pink roses. "Yes, I—"

"Something else."

I sit back, trying to mask my frustration. The only thing I want is his signature on that contract, but I see I'm going to have to finesse it.

He steps to where his briefcase sits beside the chair on which hangs his jacket. He places the briefcase on the bed, snaps it open, reaches inside, then returns with a rectangular package wrapped in white and hands it to me. The bow is red, of course, and velvety. It's candy. Clearly. I hope it's See's, and I hope it's nuts and chews. Because now I don't have to worry about calories, and I don't have to share. I'll take them with me to wherever it is I'm going, and make myself sick with them. Unless they're cream filled. Oh, I hope they're not cream filled. I'm picturing a whole box of nuts and chews just for me.

"Thank you." I place the box on the table and wait.

The hint of disappointment flits across his face, then he goes back to where his jacket hangs and pulls out the contract. At last. He goes back to his jacket for his pen, returns to the table, and finally, *finally*, writes his name on the signature line.

His fingers are smooth and long, the nails manicured just so. You could do commercials with hands like Jeff's. David's hands are nothing like this. The ring finger on his right hand turns in at an odd angle below the large knuckle where he got it caught in an extension ladder a long time ago. He reset the break himself, duct taped the finger to his pinky, and kept working, which prevented it from healing the way it might have if a real live medical person had taken care of it. No, David's hands are not commercial hands. They pluck snails. And tie hair bows, though not well. That's what I think about as I watch Jeff write his signature. That and this: I can't see Jeff Girard setting his own bones then getting back to work.

I should stop comparing, but I can't help myself. That just shows how fickle I am when it comes to David. But in spite of the room, the flowers, the candy, the allure, I won't have reason to compare Jeff as a lover. David's the only guy I've ever known, intimately. We did everything the right way, waited till the honey-moon, partly because of me, mostly because of David. If I had to pick one word to define him, out of all the words available to me, I'd say he's upright. I know, it's not a modern term and there would be those who wouldn't understand what I mean by that. Perhaps even I don't. But that's the word association I have for David—now that I'm in a position to think with the munificent side of my brain. Now that I want to err on the side of fairness.

So we waited for the honeymoon.

And what a honeymoon.

I guess everyone feels that way, though. That there never was such love, such passion, never such a coalescence of body, soul and spirit. How idealistic we can be.

And yet it was that way for a while.

I thought for the longest time David and Jac would be the two to pair up, but that was nothing new. I always expected the guys to go for Jac. Every one, every time. But it was my number David asked for that night after the concert in the park most everyone in our youth group attended. And me he called the next day. I won't call it a whirlwind romance, that's not how David is. He's more—

All of a sudden I feel like a bug on the sharp end of a stick pin, as I become aware that Jeff is scrutinizing me with those green-flecked eyes. I don't know how long I've zoned out, but long enough. There's a smile in his eyes and on his lips, as if this really is a new one on him.

"Why did you come?"

It's not an accusation, but a real question. My shoulders curl forward and I look toward the open door and beyond, to the sound and the smell and the pull of the sea.

"You know what I saw in you the first time we met?"

I turn my head back to Jeff and my eyes eventually follow. *A sucker?* I want to say. Then I think, wait, *wait* the first time? That was Before. So I want to know what he saw.

"Determination. That you were going to make it, no matter what, whether I bought your cards or didn't. Now I see a different determination and I have to ask. Bristol, are you going to make it?"

When I fail to answer, he stands. He starts to say something, then offers a nod instead and reaches for his jacket.

"The room's taken care of if you'd like to stay. Enjoy your weekend. I mean that sincerely." He takes the plum seashell out of his pocket and tosses the key on the bed. "I am sorry about your daughter, Bristol. I hope you know that." His words are a weight that press the air from my lungs. They're not meant to be, I know that, but I'm caught off guard. And before I can recover, he's gone.

I don't know what to think at first as I sit there alone on the little sofa, with the bed and the sea and the anemic fire giving off a little smoke, but then I think okay. It's okay. This is exactly what I'd hoped for all weekend.

It's only right, I think, to at least wait till Jeff is downstairs and out the door before I slide my finger under the seam of the stark white paper and break open the candy. So I finish off the champagne left in my glass, pour another, and count to one hundred. Slowly. I imagine I hear tires on gravel as his Lexus pulls out of the driveway in the front of the house, but of course I don't. Not over the sound of the tumbling surf. I don't even hear the starfish chimes that hang on the pump handle right below the balcony. All I hear are the endless waves and the ghostly call of a night bird. When I'm sure Jeff's not going to rap on the pretty plum door, saying he's changed his mind, of course he's going to stay in the room he paid for, with or without me, I tear the tape away from one end of the package and slide out the contents.

I sit back, disappointed. It isn't nuts and chews. It isn't even cream filled. In fact, it isn't candy at all. I hold up the box that smells nothing like chocolate and everything like cardboard, and read the print on the thin side. A journal. He's given me a journal. I laugh at the irony, but it's more the champagne at work than anything else. I set the unopened box on the table and slip out of my sandals, relaxed for the first time all weekend. For the first time all year. Finally, something has gone right.

Twenty-Three

I tuck my feet underneath me and let the pieces of Plan A fall back into place. The location has changed, but everything else will go like clockwork with no one to disturb me as I complete my checklist. I'll leave a note telling the owner how sorry I am for the inconvenience I've caused, and suggest she use my ghost idea. *Yes, right here beyond the plum door, resides the ghost of Bristol Taylor. And not only in this room. If you listen you can hear her on a windless night agitating the starfish chimes on the patio below. This here is the starfish we found in her purse.*

Of course, it's now the new key fob.

It might work. There are those few odd souls who enjoy being haunted.

I breathe out a half laugh, purely artificial, and then this is the random thought that replaces the former one: if we can be guilty of sin by our thoughts, can we be absolved if we unthink them? If I forget about Jeff Girard and what might have happened here, what he anticipated would happen here, can I be forgiven? I can't say why this matters. But that's not true. I know exactly why it matters. That's a reality I can't unthink no matter how I try. And believe me, I try. I can't unthink his breath on my ear nor the tingling I felt that wasn't just from the champagne, any more than I can unthink the image of Kinsey's face I see through the car window, where I left her to be stolen away. They're two parts of a press that converge to condemn me. There is no escape.

This is the inducement I need to get me back on task.

I have a Last Will and Testament to write, not to mention letters of apology. I could have used the little note pad in the desk drawer. But now I have something better. I reach for the box that holds the journal filled with plenty of empty pages of paper, and lift off the lid.

Now I really can't breathe. Because etched into the burgundy leather is the profile image of Kinsey I sketched to create my Baby Talk cards. I might as well have found her body, I'm that stunned. I touch my fingertips to the outline as though it will disappear as thoroughly as she did if I'm not careful, and run my hand over the fine leather, soft as bunting. I don't let my eyes drift down to the image on the cover, at the simple lines that catch the whimsy of my baby girl.

"Oh, God." I say it aloud, oh, God. It's not a curse, for the first time in three hundred sixty four days it's not a curse. Nor is it a prayer. In my heart I know full well it's an indictment against the One who has the answer to my one and only question, and I can't unthink that either. *Why?* That's all I want to know, why. I tremble under the weight of it. Why?

Why?

Oh, God, why?

I'm as cold as I've ever been, but it's an emotional cold, not a physical one. There's a woven throw at the foot of the bed. I snatch it up and wrap it around my shoulders. A gust of wind propelled by the energy of the surf comes in through the open door and hits me like a slap. Like a rebuke. I gather the throw around me and shiver beneath its protection, standing on the spot where such a short time ago Jeff Girard danced me in circles. I turn in circles again, and wonder, what now?

It's 9:05, just over eleven hours to go. This is a real eleventh hour, of sorts. But there's no hope of salvation. I've debated this for some time now, whether to start the process at the exact time Kinsey was stolen from my life, or if I time it so that I take my last breath as close to that moment as possible, to 365 minus 0. I decide on the former, and hope once it's in motion it doesn't take long.

In reality I want to die the way my grandpa Vanderpool died. Just drop dead of a heart attack under a tree in the backyard with a glass of lemonade untouched, simple and painless, relatively speaking. That's how I'd like to go. I know, doesn't everyone? But we don't all get what we want, do we?

I'll keep the champagne on ice, ready for use in the morning, then I realize there's probably not an ice machine in the hallway, like your run-of-the-mill hotel. Well. I'll keep the bottle in the bucket as long as I can, then transfer it to the little fridge there in the corner. I want to swallow the pills with it, and I want it cold. Cold, the taste is tolerable.

The love songs are still playing. I locate the CD player and push the stop button. The only music I want to hear is the song of the sea. I was right to choose the coast for my last hours on Earth. The fire that Jeff started burns feebly. I use the poker to adjust the presto logs but only make things worse. I fish out a pen from my purse, grip the throw tighter around my shoulders, then take my seat at the end of the sofa. I open the journal and hold my pen poised over the page, but the lamplight is coming from the wrong direction. It casts a shadow on the paper, so I move to the other end of the sofa.

That's better. I smooth the pages of the journal though they don't need smoothing, and on the center of the top line on the first page I write LAST WILL AND TESTAMENT. Neatly, because my artistic nature has given me excellent penmanship. That and Ms. Vanderpool's endless penmanship exercises. Every other student not subject to her sixth grade class ended penmanship exercises in the fourth grade. But not us. I concede we did win more penmanship awards than any other students in the district, but what fun is that when you're standing in a sea of kids two years younger and six inches shorter than you?

I harness my wayward thoughts and smooth the pages again, then below the heading I write: I, Bristol Leigh Taylor, Being of Sound Mind—

That draws me up short. Sound mind? Considering what I'm about to do? Hmm. I can't very well draw a line through the words and I don't want to tear out a page from the journal to start over. That's how wills begin, I decide. Not everyone who executes a will is of sound mind, no matter what they say, right? I let it stand.

But then what? What does my sound mind tell me to do now? I Do Bequeath—

Bequeath. Does bequeath end with an e? I write it both ways on the palm of my hand and look at the words until neither seems correct. It doesn't really matter which way I spell it, I suppose. It's just that I want it right. Because what would Sissy say? Lord, how I've come to rely on spell check. I flip a mental coin and add an e to the end of the word. Only then does it look as wrong as it is. I could try to make the e look like a flourish, except it wouldn't go with the block letters.

Great.

Okay, so what do I have to bequeath? *What We Keep*, of course, which goes to Ainsley. Only I don't want to begin with something as trivial as a book. It's just that *What I Have Left* isn't much. What do I own that's of value to anyone—that isn't community property, anyway? Clothes? Maybe. I could say that Ainsley and Jac have their choice of any part of my wardrobe. I could dictate how the choosing should proceed, but if anyone can work it out, it's those two. I don't include Sissy because she is, in her own words, large boned. Nothing I have would fit her. Or match a single pair of her eyeglass frames. Polka dots and animal prints have never been my thing.

Thinking about Sissy's bones turns my thoughts to Teri once again. Because her bones, from what I can tell in the one photograph Dad holds onto for some arcane reason, are nothing like Sissy's, and everything like mine and Ainsley's. Not that I want to waste even one of my relatively few remaining minutes on Teri. But at the moment my mind is a gear, with its rack and pinion clacking along outside my control, at a pace not my own. All I can do is hang on for the ride known as free association.

The tooth in the gear known as Teri refuses to be skipped, especially as it relates to Kinsey, which has never happened before this very moment. But Kinsey's dimples came from somewhere, and I see in my mind very plainly they came from Teri. Not only that, but Sam and Eli's amazing smile was hers as well. I will say it was nice of her to share the better parts of her DNA, but that's all I'll say.

But oh the things I would say if she were sitting here with me right now. About how wrong she was to leave us with all the not knowing. About all the gaps we've inherited because of her One Big Decision. About how cheated I feel. Didn't she know we'd have questions, Ainsley and I, these daughters of hers? Questions not meant for a dad. Perspectives not in a dad's thought processes. He deserves a medal, our dad, for all the motherly things he did so bravely. Red-faced, but bravely.

It occurs to me I should call him, which is how this rack and pinion, free association thing works with me. To say goodbye. Only how do I keep it from sounding like goodbye? No. Best to say it all in a letter when I get that far.

I turn back to the will and tap my nails against my forehead. There's my charm bracelet, a favorite of Ainsley's, so that's easily settled. And my jewelry box was a gift from Jac so it should go back to her. But would she want it? Could anyone want anything from me? And what do I leave David besides a world of regret? This Will idea strikes me as the ultimate in vanity. Okay, so maybe I skip the will and go right to the letters. As soon as I write out my funeral instructions. Which has only one item. Bury me with Kinsey's blanket. Please.

Twenty-Four

I begin my letters with Ainsley, and write a cover sheet with her name in large letters to provide a modicum of privacy for what follows on the next page, as I will with each letter. There's so much to thank Ainsley for, I don't know where to start. She's been the best sister a girl could want, so I start with that and build up to what I most want to thank her for: keeping me sane these past three hundred sixty four days. Or at least functioning to some degree. And for giving up the job that was her one guilty pleasure to run the Find Kinsey headquarters. Those are the bookends of summation in all my sister has done for me, and I couldn't spread my arms wide enough to touch a fingertip to either one. She obviously wasn't old enough to mother me when Teri resigned the position, and yet she did, and did it well. Hers was the shoulder I cried on over all the silly girl things. And when events of a year ago tore open my heart and bled it dry, she massaged it through every subsequent beat to keep me going.

You'd think Ainsley would have been the one to want to stay home with her babies. That she'd have been the truly maternal one. But she was confoundedly eager to get back to work after the boys were weaned. It's not like her job was all that and more. No, she worked as a courier for a San Francisco law office and spent an inordinate amount of time on Bay Area freeways, and never complained. It paid well and offered benefits, but still. Only now do I suspect it was all about fear. Fear that she'd do what Teri did, and walk out on her boys one day if she didn't have a good reason to want to come home to them. It was hard having twins, that was the thing. And so unexpected. But Ainsley would never have done what Teri did. Not in a million years. Not Ainsley, the devoted one.

I turn the cover page to a clean sheet of paper and write *Dear Ainsley:* but nothing else comes. I decide it's because the lighting is all wrong. It's like a laboratory in here. I set the journal aside and turn off two or three of the lamps Jeff switched on, and heave a huge sigh as I begin to picture what was meant to happen in this room. God in heaven, what was I thinking, allowing him to bring me here?

I prod the fire with the poker once more, then take my seat and try again.

Don't feel guilty, Ainsley, for wanting it all. Because doesn't everyone? It's just that we define "all" in a trillion different ways. "All" for you means marriage, motherhood to your incredible boys, and working at a job you loved. I know I judged you for that, A, and I'm sorry. First, because it's not my place to tell you how to live your life. Second, because who am I to pass judgment on you? Of all people, me. Of all people, you. God, who am I? This line is offered heavenward, a genuine prayer. It won't be the last I pray before the night is through, coward, coward, coward that I am. *And to sacrifice that job to organize and run the Find Kinsey Foundation means everything.*

I hope she's able to get her job back if she asks for it. It's not like she left to move on to something better. Not like that at all.

I resist the urge for sentimentality throughout the remainder of the letter. That's never been me. I'm only tempted because it's Ainsley and I'd like to give her something to soothe her grieving soul as she reads this. And she will grieve. But I can't. It would seem a lie.

Jac's letter is next. It's much easier to write, because Jac's the one person I don't suck my stomach in for. You know? I'm just me, and she's good with that.

You're furious as you read this, I begin. *And even more furious because you can't throw this letter across the room, not with it being in the Kinsey journal. But you want to, right? Of course I'm right. Does anyone know you the way I know you, and vice versa? That makes you the most angry, because you're telling yourself you should have seen it coming. Trust me when I say I went to great lengths to hide this from* you *most of all. I did that by continuing to be the same old hateful me. Ha. Ha.* ☺ *If I'd turned suddenly sweet you'd have seen right through that. The thing is, you weren't supposed to be near enough to get a blast of the immediate fallout. At least I managed to put a little distance between us, here at the end.*

Regarding Jeff, do what you want with this: Whatever you might think happened, didn't. I don't tell her how close I came, though. *And here's one more thing to add to your anger: I need you to be the strong one now. Please.* I add a few remember-whens for nostalgia's sake, in a weak effort to deflect some of the sting.

It's despicable, what I'm doing. I know it is. I'm counting on their virtue to blur the lines between judgment and pity in the hopes they'll find some middle ground in their final assessment of the life and times of Bristol Taylor. A pathetic story, for sure.

My phone vibrates yet again in my pocket, their desperation pinging off some tower, reaching across the air waves to tug on my conscience. I owe them that, and so I let it vibrate instead of turning it off. When at last it stops I check my calls and see that the inbox is full. That's the message they'll get, unable to leave one more of their own. Maybe now they'll stop trying to reach me. The calls are all from Jaclyn and Ainsley, with one notable exception. David called thirty minutes ago. I drop my head to my chest and rub at the knots in my shoulders as if it would actually help. I slip the phone back in my pocket and return to my letters.

Sissy is next, but I have a hard time finding traction this time, not sure where to start. I know it's because of the hazy nature of our relationship. I think of her as Dad's wife, not as Stepmother, because that's the relationship she cultivated from the beginning, and it was fine with me. She was Sissy, the quirky aunt all families seem to have. Except when she was Ms. Vanderpool, the teacher you wanted to hate, but couldn't. Not that she was hands off in our upbringing, I don't mean that. She had no problem in the discipline department. It's just that she preferred there be a step or two between us. The maternal gene was all but missing from Sissy's DNA.

As it clearly was with Teri. Or maybe hers died an early death. Who knows? Is that even possible? Whatever. The real shame is that a daughter abandoned by her mother can't, of her own volition, sever that eternal cord, that connection that's simply too deep inside to reach, which I'm forced to admit is my own untenable case. Try though I do, I can't exorcize the knowledge of her, can't de-Teri-fy my memory bank. There have been times in my life when I've gone months without a thought of Teri. But against my will she's elbowed herself into the time frame of every one of these past three hundred sixty four days. Completely in the context of contrast, mind you. She deserting her child, me having my child stolen. She never looking back, me never looking forward. Always a contrast.

Until now. For she and I both may have daughters who feel abandoned, who'd sever the cord in a heartbeat because of it. I mean, what does Kinsey think about what's happened? That I left her in that car to be stolen away? That I, like Teri, don't care to see her face ever again? Lord. Oh, Lord. This is one of the numberless phantom thoughts that have come out of nowhere this past year to strike with all the hellish torment they possess. I refuse to nurture it and grip even tighter the pen in my hand, as I wait for the initial pang to pass. Then I banish the thought to that place deep inside my inner self, where all the other painful thoughts are compressed into one heinous mass. Still, the damage is done. And the trouble is, I've long overloaded the system. My guess is that my inner self is about to hurl that horrid mass. All I need is eleven more hours.

I harness my thoughts with a tight rein and turn them back to Sissy, but I don't write until I'm sure I can keep the quaver out of the pen. She's not a hugger, Sissy isn't. Not even with Kinsey and the boys. Even in that relationship she's Sissy. Not Nana or Mimi, or God forbid, Grandma. But Sissy. The letter I write to her is mostly a thank you note. *Thank you for the things you taught me*, like always to use trash bag liners in the bathroom wastebasket and never to put a preposition at the end of a sentence. But there's more Sissy tried to teach. Like how to recognize the important above the pressing. How to laugh at one's self.

How to love your husband.

"I'm going to marry Eli when I get big." Like all of Kinsey's declarations, this one comes out of nowhere, while she and I sit on the kitchen floor painting our toenails a bright nectarine. I put an old towel underneath us and let Kinsey handle the little brush all on her own. She loves this.

"Really?" I ask.

She nods, one definitive nod. Her ponytail swishes with the motion. She's so sure of herself, this amazing three year old. So positively opinionated. Everything about her is such a delight. But I can't help wonder why she'd choose one twin over the other, and so I ask. "Why Eli, baby girl? Why not Sam?"

"Mama." This is Kinsey's lecture voice. It accompanies a roll of the eyes. "Because. Sam is my friend."

I laughed at the time and probably said something like, "Well, there you are." But I don't laugh now. I don't think, "Well, there you are." I think instead, "That's it." Husbands aren't friends. They're adversaries. Opposing thumbs. His black to my white. No. No. In my case, his white to my black. Definitely the white. To my black.

The transition from lover to adversary is deceitfully subtle. Like lying under an April sun. It burns away your defenses and all the while you're thinking, *This feels so good*. And then, there you are, sunburnt, with every nerve exposed. Suddenly, everything's a trigger. And you wonder, how did we get here?

But since I'm being honest I concede that I'm the problem. Those are my exposed nerves, not David's. David is ... David is steady, and that rankles as much as anything. See? There's just no appeasing me.

I have more thank yous to say, this time to Dad, beginning with his stability. He could have gone off the deep end when Teri left, turned to the bottle and made our life a cliché, or dropped Ainsley and me off with a babysitter never to return. Instead he married Sissy. It could have been worse.

But he'll want more than thank yous, and he deserves more. If you think of all the really good TV dads you've ever known rolled into one man, that's Marty Vanderpool. They don't come any better. And here I am, his one sure failure. I do apologize for that. Sorry, sorry, sorry. My life is one sorry mess. But I love him and I say so, and swallow the stone in my throat. If I thought for one minute it's what bottled up the ocean of tears that lies stagnant inside me, thick as sludge, I'd physically rip it out and let the torrent begin, but there's no hope of release. I will die with the suffocating weight of my tears and my guilt. And that still won't be enough to pay for the damage I've done.

The thing I love—well, love may be too strong a word in my present state of mind. The thing I appreciate about Ainsley, Jaclyn and Sissy collectively is that they aren't obsessed with fixing this. As if it could be fixed. They aren't compelled to put a good face on the situation, or to blather on about the will of God. I should add a collective note to thank them. Because we've all known people who have to provide an answer to every question. They must solve every problem. It makes me crazy, people like that. Commiseration. That's all you want sometimes, you know? But I can't forget they're obsessed with getting me through this week-end, so forget the note of thanks. And while I'm on the subject, the thing I can't stand about David is his kindness. It would be so much simpler if he hated me.

How I wish this past year were a dress rehearsal. That I could say to the Great Director, wherever He is, "Oh, wow, did I ever mess up that scene! I'll get it right this time. I promise."

And if I don't, somebody bring in the understudy. Please.

But there are no second tries. No understudies.

"Mama!"

"What? Kinsey, what?" I've pinched her skin in the safety seat buckle, I just know it. But no.

"I forgot my truck!'

"Your truck? That's all this is about?" I'm so relieved I scold her. I can't help it. "You scared me, Kinsey. Don't sound like that unless you're hurt." I actually wag my finger at her. It's one of those things I swore I'd never do. One of the many things. "Next time say, 'Excuse me, Mama, but I forgot my toy.' "

"Truck." She looks at the headrest in front of her, her lips pressed tightly together. God help her, so much like me.

"Okay, truck."

I was going to Ainsley's to make plans for our New Year's Eve party— not having a clue, of course, that it would be the year from hell we'd be ringing in—and Kinsey wanted to play with Sam and Eli. Hence the truck. It was sweet the way they didn't mind spending time with their baby cousin. And a girl, to boot.

I lean in and kiss the pout on her lips. "Which one? I'll get it."

"The red one."

Well, that certainly clears it up.

I left Kinsey strapped into her car seat and hurried back into the house to dig through her bucket of miniature automobiles. I had the car keys in my hand. Still, I'm horrified, in hindsight, to realize I'd developed such a dangerous habit for the sake of convenience.

I'm back in less than a minute and drop the truck into her waiting hand. She gives it a studied look, as if I've passed her a pile of poop, then turns those eyes on me. Her face says everything I need to know. She hands the truck back and says, "Um, Mama, try again."

Try again? From a three year old? Are you serious? Yes. And it takes two more tries after that one before I get it right. Of course, I laugh about it with Ainsley—out of Kinsey's hearing—and she confirms how much Kinsey is like me, and inside it makes me proud.

I can't breathe. I'm at that place of panic before my lungs finally open enough to receive the oxygen I madly try to gulp. It's like that whenever these true-to-life flashbacks occur. My heart beats hard and fast. As I wait for my breathing to become regular again, I think what a wasted opportunity, this inability to breathe. I could have ended it right then. But I know better. No one has ever killed herself by holding her breath. Even if you passed out, reflex would take over and that would be that. Sadly, all the easy ways are lost to us.

My fingertips are white where I grip the pen. I ease up, but in no time I'm gripping again. Lately, even when I sleep my hands make fists, so that I have to pry my aching fingers open when I wake from a sleep that doesn't refresh or restore. There was a time when I was at ease with myself, when I nestled my baby girl on my stomach, or held her high at arm's length while she kicked and cooed. But I can't remember how it felt. I'm a spring wound tight. So tight.

You can't draw with fists. It takes a light touch. And I've lost mine. Just ask David.

His is the next letter I write. I've left it for last, and it begins not with a thank you, but with a worthless apology. I'm sorry. It's so flat, the look of those two words, so one dimensional, especially in light of what I'm sorry for. And yes, Sissy would make me restructure that last thought. I add one more apology for the flatness, and say if I could scoop out the repentance in my heart and hold it in my hands for him to see, it would fill the universe and everything beyond, and maybe then he would know the bitter weight I'm buried beneath, and forgive. But of course I can't scoop it out, and I say that too. And as for forgiveness, he granted that long ago. Don't think I don't know that if the tables were turned, if he'd been the one to lose Kinsey, I would wield my unforgiveness like a club. I would slay him with it. Every day, for the rest of my life. It's enough that I blame him, in that convoluted way I have of thinking. If he hadn't ... I wouldn't have ...

I read the paragraph back to myself and drop the pen in disgust. This is a pathetic document, made all the more pathetic by the way it's bound together, with everything private exposed. A notepad would have been so much better, with pages I could tear off and fold. Well. It is what it is.

What more do I say to him? The list of things I could apologize for is endless. If I could go all the way back to that concert in the park and not give him my number, and save us from this loss that's too wide to navigate, too deep to resurface from, I'd do it in a flash.

But that would mean No Kinsey. That's what I'd trade for? Really? If that doesn't say how unfair life is, nothing does.

Twenty-Five

A ghost of a sound floats in through the open door, a sound not part of the sea. I set the journal aside and clutch the throw tightly at my throat as I unfold my legs, stand and move toward the balcony. But as I lean over the rail toward the beach, I hear only the waves in their ageless cycle of tumbling to and pulling away from the shore. I'm trying too hard, like straining to see in the dark. I force myself to relax, to focus on nothing at all, especially the sound. And there it is, still a ghost, but I hear it. Guitar. Riding on waves of another sort, though broken. Intermittent or not, there's no mistaking the sound of my guitar god. I wish I could raise a hand and silence the surf long enough to make out the melody, because if I got it in my head the surf wouldn't make a difference and I could follow along. But I can't hear it well enough to string the notes together into something I recognize.

Still, the sound draws me.

It can't be far, the place from which it emanates. I lean out over the rail and look to my left, as if I had a chance of seeing the campfire, and decide I need to hear his music one last time, up close. Need to see his hands work their magic.

"Don't think I don't know what you're up to," I say to the sky. It shimmers with diamond light, but it's not the sky I'm speaking to.

I step back inside, find my sandals, wishing for boots, and tuck the journal into my purse. My eyes land fortuitously on the ice bucket. I snatch up the bottle of champagne and stuff it in as well, glad I brought the biggest purse I have. I have no jacket and so I take two twenties out of my wallet and drop them on the bed where the throw should be. That should cover the cost of my makeshift shawl, in case I don't make it back, because I don't know if and when they lock the doors here. I know that means I'd better devise Plan B after all, and that just ticks me off. But I have to go. Have to follow the sound.

I feel like a kid sneaking out of the house as I tiptoe down the stairs. It's quiet below, and there's only a very soft light coming from the registration desk. Still, I hold my breath on the landing and listen a full minute before craning my neck around the corner. The desk seems to have been put to bed for the night, but a man sits on the sofa in the parlor, facing the fire, his back to me. He's sipping a drink, amber liquid in a tumbler, no ice. I think his night isn't going as planned. And then I think, that could be Jeff sitting there. I wonder in that instant what he's done to compensate himself, and immediately a butterfly tattoo flitters across my mind.

It's likely the man with the drink will see me if I use the patio door, but it's the closest route to my destination. And besides, what's he going to say? Get upstairs to your room? Get a grip.

I see in the reflection of the large picture window that I startle him when I open the door. I turn to murmur an apology, and catch a fleeting glance of expectation in his eyes, but then he turns back to the fire, back to his drink, before the words are out of my mouth.

It's cold outside with the wind coming off the sea. I'd give my soul for a pair of socks and a sweatshirt, which is all it's worth these days. But ten hours from now I'll be past feeling, so bring it on, I say to the elements.

I stand on the edge of the patio and listen, straining to hear the music over the wind and the waves. A sorrow builds from deep within at its absence, but then, in a moment of relative still, there it is. I follow as though it's the Pied Piper himself that draws me, and am surprised to find I was closer to the campfire—and the beach house—than I would have imagined.

Like before, I hang back in the shadows, and position myself to see the face of the man with the guitar. Only tonight, there are three. James is in the middle. He puts his guitar pick between his teeth and adjusts two or three of the tuning keys, as do the other two players. They nod at one another when their pitch is just right, then James gives a final nod and the music begins, soft and beautiful. They play a long introduction in perfect unison, then James begins to sing. I've heard the song before, but I've been out of touch these past three hundred sixty four days. I don't know one song from another. But one thing I do know, he's into it, his music, James is. And it's not for an audience he plays. I know a little the feeling, from when I used to draw, not for commercial reasons, but for me.

The music builds, and it is so good it hurts. Way deep inside. *Freefalling*, that's what the song is. Could it be more perfect, this parting gift from my guitar god? The other two don't sing, but they play exactly what James plays. Their hands move together, the ones that strum and the ones that make the chords, and it's amazing to watch. I can't take my eyes off their hands as the three play as one, the synchronized swimmers of the guitar world.

"Hey."

I startle at the sound of the voice, even though it's a mere split second before I know it's A.J.

"Hey." I avoid his eyes, though I can't tell you why. I'm past feeling the shame I should feel.

"Been out here long?" he asks.

I clutch the throw tighter about my shoulders and shake my head.

"Want to move to the fire?"

I shake my head again and fix my eyes on the trio's hands. As nice as A.J.'s voice is I want to shush him, want to hear every last note. He must read my thoughts because he doesn't say another word till the song ends.

"Do it again."

I thought I only whispered the words to myself, but A.J. asks, "The song?"

I look at him, surprised. Then, "Yeah."

"James," he calls to his brother. "Encore."

James strains to see through the darkness, locates us, and nods. Then he counts to four and the trio is at it again.

When the song is over for the second time I say, "He should be on tour."

A.J. leans toward me and laughs, like I've made a joke. Typical brother, I think. "No really. He's that good. He should be on tour."

Evidently it's quite a good joke, because A.J. laughs again. Then he cocks his head and studies me. "Our last name is Mikelson."

Okay. So. "Mikelson," I repeat. His hair, I see, is tied back with a pair of dreadlocks. My own hair would never hold that way, tied back with two strands of hair, not even if they were braided. There must be something to those locks.

"Right." A.J. waits, that amazing smile a bright spot in a very dark night. "Mikelson," he says again.

When I give nothing in return, he turns and points to a house on the bluff, the west-facing walls nothing but windows pouring forth buttery-yellow light. "See that place up there?"

I follow his hand with my eyes, and nod. "Yeah?"

"There are two platinum albums on the wall of the recording studio, there on the north end of the house."

"Platinum albums?" I'm not getting his drift.

"Right." A.J. nods.

"James Mikelson," I say. And then, oh! "James Mikelson! Your brother is James Mikelson? The James Mikelson?"

A.J. laughs again. "I get that a lot."

Well, no wonder, is all I can think. No wonder I'm drawn to the music. When he sings *Freefalling* he's not just covering someone. He *is* the someone.

"You sure you don't want to move closer to the fire?"

He obviously sees that I'm shivering, but no, I don't want to move into the circle of friends singing along with James Mikelson as if it were no big deal.

"They can't know he's here," I say, *they* being the hordes of fans who'd be swarming the beach if they had a clue.

"We do our best to keep it quiet when he's home. But the neighbors are cool."

A.J.'s hands are shoved into the front pockets of his jeans, forcing his shoulders up into an "aw shucks" kind of look. It fits him, that look. He seems like an "aw shucks" kind of guy.

"So what do the initials stand for?"

"Initials?"

"A.J. What do they stand for?"

He looks away and gives a little laugh that makes his Adam's apple bob, then looks back and gives me a look that says, *you asked for it.* "Andrew Jackson."

"Really. He gets James and you get Andrew Jackson?"

"Don't forget the talent, he gets that too. Hardly seems fair, huh?" He never loses the smile.

"It could be worse. Trust me." In another life I might tell him about our name game.

"Yeah? Like ...?"

Alright, just one. "It could be ... Angelina Jolie."

"You got me there." He frowns for just a second. "Do I look like an Angelina Jolie?"

I shake my head. "No." Not. At. All.

"That's a relief. I mean, not that she's not beautiful, it's just that *I* don't want to look like her, you know?" He laughs, then shifts from one foot to the other, and casts a glance down the dark shoreline in the direction of the beach house. "They were looking for you. Earlier."

I blow out a breath and nod. "I know."

"Don't mean to pry. It's just, they care. A lot."

"I know that too."

He looks over my shoulder for a moment, out toward the sea. "This has to be an awful time for you." The look he turns back to me says he knows exactly who I am, exactly what's going on here. So, he figured it out.

I feel betrayed, like he's held out on me. It's unrealistic, how I feel, but what does that matter? I can't hold back the sigh, though I doubt he hears it. "It is what it is."

"And it sucks."

"Yeah." My heart feels like a stone in my chest. A year in hell takes its toll.

I stand where I am, listening to the music of the guitar god brother of A.J. until I can no longer feel my toes. In fact, I'm way past feeling them. Everything in me wants to head back to the B&B, to close myself in behind the plum door for the duration, but my numb feet have other ideas.

"I'll see you," I say, though I know it's a lie.

A.J. gives a parting nod. "'Night."

I wait for a second or two, hoping to see that smile one last time, but his face has taken on a serious expression, and I know it's time for me to get away. "'Night." A wave of dread washes over me as I move south down the Pacific coastline. The one direction I don't want to go.

Twenty-Six

I'm met with three pairs of astonished eyes when I walk through the door of the beach house.

"Bree!" Ainsley is on me in an instant, wrapping me in arms that are stronger than they look.

"Oh, darlin'," Sissy says, "we've been scared half to death."

Jac's the only one who doesn't speak. Instead she spears me with a look I feel all the way to my spine.

"Where did you go?" Ainsley's eyes probe mine. "Are you okay?"

I shrug out of her embrace as politely as I can, which isn't polite at all as it turns out. I'm so cold it hurts, and I'm shivering like Spike when he finds himself in a room with just me.

"Would you like a nice hot chai tea?" Jaclyn says. "Oh, wait, that's right, it's cold now. And dumped. But I thought I'd ask."

I shoot her a look she can't possibly misinterpret. "Is the water hot?" I ask of anyone but her. I wet a finger, reach across the narrow space between me and the stove, and dab at the tea kettle.

"Yes," Sissy says. "Here. Let me help you."

"I can do it."

The tea bags are in a jar there on the counter. I reach in and grab one, not at all particular about the flavor. Then I fill a mug with hot water and dunk the bag. The essence that's released is pepperminty. Not my favorite at all, but it's hot. I clutch the mug with both hands and hold it close to my face.

"Are you hungry? I can fix you some soup or something."

Sissy is already in motion when I say to her, "No, I'm not, no."

"Where have you been?" Ainsley asks again. "Are you sure you're okay?"

An odd follow-up question, considering I never answered the first one, and certainly not in the affirmative. But I answer now. "I'm fine." My eyes lock on to Jaclyn's and I wonder how much she told them of what she thinks she knows. Her eyes are glaring. Beyond angry. But she gives nothing away. I can't blame her for her suspicions.

I should be humble considering what I've put them through, but I'm more contentious than ever, and toward Jaclyn no less. "I had a contract to sign."

"A contract."

"Yes." My voice is sharp and barbed. We might as well be throwing darts at one another. Or knives.

"And now it's done," Sissy says. Jac's obviously filled them in on details of the sale. "And you're back home." She heaves a stage-worthy sigh and lifts her glasses from her nose and sticks them into her hair where they get lost in the brassy spikes. "NHNF."

No harm, no foul.

"Oh, good grief," Jaclyn says.

"Leave her alone." I lift the mug to my lips and take a sip of tea.

"Leave her alone? Is that what you said? You of all people? Leave *her* alone?"

"Yes!" I slam my mug onto the counter, splashing hot tea on my hand in the process. I yelp and swear. Really swear.

"Oh, that's classic." Jac crosses her arms. "Is that the best you can do?"

"You want my best? I'll give you my best!" And I do. I throw out every swear word I know, including the ones in Spanish and French, a beaded string of profanity, and when I get to the end I start all over again. I grab a plate out of the dish drainer and slam it on the edge of the sink for emphasis. It sends shockwaves through my hand, but doesn't so much as crack. I hit it harder. Then I pummel the sink with it.

"What the—"

"Melmac," Sissy says as she takes the plate out of my hand. "It doesn't break, love."

"Well that's just plain stupid!"

"I'll say," Jaclyn mutters.

Sissy rolls her eyes, but only at Jac, not at me.

"Well, it is," Jaclyn defends. "How do you ever get new dishes if they don't break?"

"That's the whole point, Puff, dishes that don't break. You're supposed to choose your pattern carefully, so you don't get tired of them."

Jac looks at her dumbly. "Pattern? They're white. Just white. Unless you count the scorch mark on this piece here."

"The white"—Sissy's accent thicker than ever—"reminds me of magnolias."

"Magnolias? If that isn't the most—"

"Stop. Stop!" I grab another plate out of the drainer and continue to beat the sink. When that doesn't work I move to the table. I'm determined, and dare anyone to stop me.

"Bree, honey, don't. Come on." My sister steps close, then backs up again.

"Let her rant," Jaclyn says, not a drop of compassion in her voice.

"Well, aren't you some friend."

Jac lifts her bony shoulders in a shrug of indifference that feeds the fire in me. Her arms are still crossed, and she leans against the wall in that cocky stance we resorted to in junior high when a rival girl walked by.

I turn to Sissy and slam the plate against the table so hard it flies out of my hand. It lands on the soft, worn linoleum and, in a surreally-delayed reaction, splits in two. Spurred by success, I kick both pieces out of my way and reach for another plate.

Jaclyn steps to my side of the aisle and opens the cupboard. One by one she hands me the plates and the saucers as I whack and scream and curse.

"Oh, Lord." Sissy looks as if she might break in two herself. But her little prayer—for that's what it is—infuriates me.

"Lord? *Lord*? What does he have to do with this? What does he have to do with anything? Not much in your lives that I can see. You call yourselves Christians but look at you!" My voice breaks from all the screaming, but still I scream. "Sassy! Puff! What's with that? You were her teacher, for God's sake. And you," I say to Jac, "you're only happy when you're inciting her! Christians? Really?"

They both look as if I'd slapped them, which is deeply satisfying at the moment, but Jaclyn quickly recovers herself and resumes her casual stance. I reach into the open cupboard for a Melmac cup and rear back my arm.

"I wouldn't if I were you," she says, her voice cool as can be, but she's breathing hard, her nostrils flaring with each intake of air. Her chest rises and falls beneath her sweater.

Much as I hate to, I heed her advice. Those cups would zing my hand for sure. Jac pushes closed the cupboard before I can grab something ceramic.

"Who gave you your first cigarette?" Sissy says.

"My first— That's it? That's why you hate her? We were stupid kids, for crying out loud."

"I don't hate her," Sissy says, though her body language says something else entirely. "Christians don't hate."

Jac pushes away from the wall, her arms not crossed nearly so casually now. Now her fingers grip her arms. "It was one cigarette," she says. "We were both too sick to ever try another one."

"But it was you who gave it to her, now wasn't it?"

"And how do you know that?"

"I know far more than you think I do, *Puff*."

Jac's eyes narrow. "That's what the D was all about, isn't it?"

"The D?"

"Don't act like you don't know. It kept me off student council, that D. And honor roll."

"Oh." Sissy cocks her head and raises an eyebrow. "*That* D. You earned it, of course."

"Not if you'd been more objective in your grading, I wouldn't have."

"Well." Sissy studies her fingernails. "That's the nature of essay tests, isn't it? And while we're on the subject"—Sissy thrusts an arm in my direction —"who helped her remove the screen on her window so she could crawl out in the middle of the night? She could have been hurt ... or *hurt*."

"For heaven's sake, Sissy, we were fourteen!" The words croak out of my mouth. "If it hadn't been Jac it would have been somebody else. That's what we do when we're fourteen." I can't help but glance at my sister. "Unless you're Ainsley." This is not an accusation and she sees that. Ainsley, the honorable one.

"At least now I get it," Jaclyn says. "The D. The stupid nickname."

"Do you?"

Ainsley takes a step closer to ground zero. "Everyone, please. Please, stop."

"And he certainly has nothing to do with my life." I push my voice to the max as I get back on topic. "If he's even up there, he has a habit of looking away at the very worst moment! If he's everything he claims to be, why? Why? Why! Why! Why! Why!" I can't stop the invectives that erupt from that deep hollow. "WHY?!"

I breathe like a boxer at the end of round ten as my rantings bounce off the beach house walls. In the vibrating silence that follows, a little knock sounds at the door.

We stop in mid-action, as if suddenly freeze-dried. Sissy, who's standing the closest, cracks open the door. Then sniffs and smiles.

"'Evening, ladies."

Twenty-Seven

A.J. pokes his head around the door, his dreadlocks swinging with the movement, and takes us all in with his eyes. He reaches down and retrieves one half of the broken plate. "Things okay here?"

Everything about him is apologetic, from the way his eyebrows lift to the puckered smile.

"Okay?" Behind her glasses, Sissy's eyes are rimmed in red, and puddles of tears threaten to spill with every blink. "Why yes, yes they are. Just fine."

I stand there trembling and panting.

"I think it's fine, *now*," Ainsley says. I can't look at her face, but I hear the tears in her voice. She clears her throat in an unsuccessful attempt to swallow them. "Fine."

"Don't they ever let you off? It's, my goodness, nearly eleven," Sissy says.

"Oh, no, ma'am, I'm not working." A.J. pulls on the front of his civilian shirt for emphasis.

"So this is not an official call?"

He casts me a look before he answers. "No, ma'am. I just happened to be nearby."

"Well, how nice. Could we offer you some tea?"

He chuckles and says no thank you.

"Well then ..."

"Well then. If you need anything"—A.J. points over his shoulder with a thumb—"I'll be out here a while."

"We'll keep that in mind," Sissy says, though she has no idea what he's talking about. "Good night, now."

"'Night."

He sends a final glance my way, then pulls the door shut as he backs down the steps. The second one creaks beneath his weight.

We stand there in the aftermath of A.J.'s visit, like characters waiting for the director to call "Action!" so we can get at it again.

I should not have come back here. I should have stayed behind the purple door, counting down the hours as I disbursed my earthly belongings, and sped through the paragraphs toward that last page of that last book on my last day. What on earth was I thinking?

I thrust my arms into a warm jacket, then snatch up my bag and sling it over my shoulder. "I'm going for a walk. Do not follow me." I look at no one as I make my exit, just shut the door firmly behind me and trip down the steps. I will do this now, this thing I came to do, and forget about the symbolism of time. Dead is dead, and that's all that matters.

I start in the direction opposite the music, the bon fire, the circle of friends, and slip into a misty charcoal world. The sea is to my right. I'm heading south. Boy, am I. I feel on my face the spray of the waves that pound the shore, and taste the salt on my lips. I smell it in the fog. My heart swells and abates with each assault and retreat of the surf, as though the waves in their aggression stand in proxy for me. I don't know if it soothes or incites, but I do know it moves me. I walk a mile or more and encounter nothing living, save the sea and that same lone bird that haunts the night with its plaintive call.

I stop at a rock that will serve as an adequate resting place and sit down, facing the water. There's another thing or two I'd write in the journal—every scathing bit of it to Jac—if I had even a little light, but the fog and the clouds hide whatever milky glow the moon might cast. I guess I've said all I will say. I'll certainly have less to regret.

I gave up on my sandals almost the minute I left the beach house, tugged them off and hurled them into the waves. Now I sit barefoot atop the rock, its coarse surface sharp and wet beneath my feet. The wind blows straight into my face, and I can hardly be still for the shivering. But I'm grateful for the intensity of the elements as they deliver some of the last sensations I will ever feel. There will be stillness enough to come.

I tug my cell phone out of my pocket. Kinsey's face lights up the moment I touch the key pad. It's my favorite photo of her, this wallpaper on my phone. Wallpaper. Who comes up with these terms? I go to Messages, then Inbox. A stream of unopened text messages appear. I erase them one by one until I get to the messages I've saved and re-saved for up to a year and a half. The first one I open is from Ainsley. She sent it to my phone one Sunday morning from the Sunday school class for three-year-olds she taught at church, to where I sat beside David in the sanctuary, listening to his father talk about the God whose goodness I was more than beginning to doubt. It was one of those Sunday mornings I forgot to turn my ringer off, no surprise there, and right in the middle of the sermon Etta James began to sing "At Last." I couldn't hit the button fast enough to silence the song, any more than I could stop the fire that ignited my cheeks and caused my scalp to sweat. David tensed beside me, one of the few folks around who didn't snicker.

I forgot about the text message until I went to get Kinsey from her class.

A dozen kids romp, wrestle or cling to Ainsley, waiting for a mommy or daddy to come for them. I sit down on one of the kiddie chairs and scoop Kinsey into my arms. Her hair smells like fruit, her body like sweat from an hour and a half of running, chasing, climbing, jumping, romping, wrestling but never clinging. Even with Auntie A, Kinsey doesn't cling.

When it's just the three of us left, Ainsley tugs on one of Kinsey's ears and laughs. "Can you believe this little monkey?"

"What?" I ask.

"The text I sent."

"You mean the one the whole church heard arrive?"

"Ah. Sorry."

"Nah, it was my fault. Forgot to silence my phone."

"So read it."

This is what it says: "Okay, so the lesson today is on "Let the little children come to Me." I read the story then ask the kids if they want to pray to invite Jesus into their hearts, and of course they all do. We bow our heads and I lead them in a simple prayer. 'Dear Jesus,' which they all say out loud after me, 'please come into my heart,' which again they all repeat. And before I can say anything else, Kinsey's little voice says, '... but later, Jesus, 'cause right now I want to play with Daniel's new yellow Tonka truck really bad. Okay?'

Ainsley's laughing the whole time I'm reading. "Can you believe this stinker? You are too cute for your own good, Little Miss."

And Ainsley's right. She is.

I go back to my Inbox and scroll down to voicemail. I hesitate for only a moment before I hit Select. I enter my password when prompted and hold the phone to my ear, then listen to the message. Kinsey's voice is a stab to my heart. And a balm.

"Mama. Mama? Are you there?"

I hear David's voice in the background telling her to go ahead and talk, Mama can hear her. It's easier than explaining voicemail to a three year old.

"Mama, you need to tell Daddy the words. Call us back. 'Kay?"

And so I do. She and David are on the way home from preschool, because he got off work before me. Again. And a short day for him means a short paycheck for us. But it's one less hour that Kinsey won't be in daycare. There's a laugh in David's voice when he answers. I'm not sure which makes me angrier: the daycare, the abbreviated day, or the laughter.

"What's up?" There's nothing remotely close to humor in my voice.

"I'll let her tell you."

There's a rustle as David passes his phone to the backseat, then Kinsey says, "Mama?"

"Yes, baby."

"Tell Daddy the words."

"To what, baby girl?"

"E-i-e-i-o."

"Well, Kinsey, Daddy knows the words to E-i-e-i-o. I've heard him sing it." Or try.

"No, he doesn't." Kinsey's voice is adamant. "He says there's a donkey."

And in the background I hear a laughing David begin to sing. "Old MacDonald had a farm, e-i-e-i-o. And on that farm he had a donkey, e-i-e-i-o. With a hee-haw here and a hee-haw there, here a hee, there a haw, everywhere a hee-haw. Old MacDonald had a farm, e-i-e-i-o."

I fail to find the humor, but David continues to laugh while Kinsey says over and over, "No, Daddy, you messed it up."

When I finally get Kinsey's attention again, I ask her, "How did Daddy mess it up?"

"Because, Mama, there's no donkey."

"Well, how do you know?"

And without missing a beat she says, "Because I went to that farm a long time ago and there's no donkey. Just pumpkins."

And David is laughing again.

My bottom lip is caught between my teeth. I'm biting so hard I know there must be blood.

There's one more recorded message, the first one Kinsey ever left on my phone. I can't describe how decimated I feel as I listen to it now. She's two years and five months old, and David is prompting her.

"Mama." She says my name in that sing-song way I relish. "Happy—" She leaves off her message, and I hear her whisper to David, "What, Daddy?" Then she's speaking to me again, following David's prompts. "Happy birthday, Mama. I. Love. You." Her words are spoken like any two year old, boof, and wuv, and oo. I can hardly breathe for the pain. On his sixtieth birthday my dad jokingly said birthdays are nothing more than reminders of all you've lost, beginning with youth, and it only goes downhill from there. Well, we didn't know how much we would lose, and how quickly. There's no fixing this brokenness.

I root around in the cavern of my purse until I feel the prescription bottle there on the bottom. The cap covers the plastic cylinder, but just barely, it's stuffed so full. I take that bottle and the bottle of champagne out of the bag, then toss the bag to the ground. My plan is to take a few pills at a time, and wait for them to enter my bloodstream before I take another dose, thereby reducing the danger of vomiting them up. It could take a while, and that's fine.

But I do wish I had my book. And a light to read by.

I hate things left undone.

Twenty-Eight

*I*t's quiet where I sit, if you don't take into consideration the endless song of the sea, which is among the best of all sounds if you ask me, that crash of the waves and then the inverted whoosh as it recedes. It's colossal, that sound. How small it makes a body feel. And vulnerable.

I'm fairly familiar with the biblical view of life after death, and therefore have a fairly good handle on my fate. But if I could rewrite the end of the story this is how it would be: I'd fill my bloodstream with the blessed drugs I hold in my hand, then when I could no longer keep upright, I'd lay down in the sand, still warm from the day, and with my arm for a pillow I'd fall asleep to that thunderous lullaby, and because it's the last sound I hear, it's the one sound I'd hear forevermore.

But then, if I could rewrite the story I'd be home with my baby girl in her strawberry dress with flowers in her hair.

The pill bottle has grown warm in my grip, a surprise since I'm so very cold. I balance the champagne on the rock, squeeze it between my knees, and pop the top off the pills. There are more than a hundred white tablets. If I take ten every ten minutes or so, it will take an hour and forty minutes to get to the bottom. I could cut that in half by taking twenty. But twenty at a time would certainly be too many. I'd throw up more than I keep down. So I compromise and settle on fifteen. At fifteen, I could finish the bottle in just over an hour. But would I still be coherent by the time I had, say, forty-five or sixty in my system? Probably not. So this is what I'll do. I'll take fifteen every ten minutes until I feel myself going, then I'll take what's left in one final dose.

I draw in a resolving breath, tug the cork out of the champagne, and count out fifteen tablets as they pour into the palm of my hand. I vacuum every last one into my mouth and swallow them all with a large gulp of the flattened drink. The pills feel like tacks in my throat. I take another long swig to dislodge them, and swallow again and again as they make their rugged way down my esophagus. Next time, I'll do them in thirds, five, five and five.

I don't feel anything for several minutes, then I get this incredible rush to my head as though I'm dropping like an anvil through space. Whoa. Man. Somehow I keep my balance, and then the feeling fades and all I am is lightheaded. My stomach tightens as though it might revolt, but that too passes, and I'm left with a sense of euphoria, which for me means I feel none of the anguish that has dogged me for three hundred sixty-four and a half days. None of it. I feel like I'm in neutral for the first time in ages. And ages and ages.

My first ten minutes have passed, I'm sure of it, but this feels too good to interfere with. I'm going to sit here like this for a while and just enjoy it. I'll make up for it later with a larger dose and fewer minutes between. But I want to revel in this while I can.

I wish I had a backrest.

I find a small fissure in the rocks just the right size for the bottle and tuck it in the cranny, and slip the pills into my jacket pocket. The lid fits snugly now.

We took Kinsey to the beach just once. When David was still Dave. We laid out a great big sheet with pink and gray stripes, and stuck an umbrella in the sand at the head of it. I slathered Kinsey in sunblock and kept a floppy hat on her head. She's good about hats, Kinsey is, unlike most little ones. That hat was the color of raspberries, and had a big white butterfly on the side, in stitching you could feel. It matched her little bathing suit, right down to the butterfly.

It was a perfect beach day, warm enough to enjoy the water, and a surf that was slow and tropical. Kinsey wasn't sure about the waves at first. She'd grip David's fingers in her little hands and climb up his legs like a crab when she'd see them tumbling in. But he'd wade out little by little until her feet were submerged, then her knees, and soon she was up to her waist, loving every minute.

I remember peeling off her bathing suit and standing her under the shower there at the beach. She was covered in a fine white sand that I smoothed away with my hand, careful to clean the most delicate places, under her arms, the creases of her legs. We had a two hour drive home and I didn't want it to chafe. I wrapped her in a beach towel and carried her to the car, dressing her in the cargo area of our SUV. The one that was stolen with Kinsey inside. She slept a peaceful sleep, and barely stirred when I tucked her in bed, just clutched her blanket and turned on her side.

That's the scene that comes to mind when I think of serenity, Kinsey finding the edge of her blanket and turning on her side as she settles into sleep. Though I haven't thought of serenity in a good long while.

My hand is working at my side, my fingers rubbing my palm, as though that fine white sand was still on my skin. My senses are so heightened at the moment. I know it's the drugs. I close my eyes and continue to rub. And then I snap to and reach down for my bag. The movement throws me off balance and I half slide, half hop off the rock. In the process I twist my foot and I say, "Ouch!" but then I realize it doesn't hurt. And so I chuckle as I rummage through the bag until I find the starfish. My boomerang starfish. Its coarse skin is not so very different from the phantom feel of the sand. Just enlarged. My fingers seek the broken place, the place I like the best. The place I rub and rub and rub.

I'm tempted to stay on the ground since I'll end up here anyway, but

I'm not ready to abandon my perch. So I climb up the rock and resettle myself. A wave crashes ashore, sending a frothy spray my way. I should be freezing but there's a warmth in my belly now that spreads out to my limbs, even my bare feet. I could stay here atop this rock forever, a modern-day Niobe, tears flowing from the stone that is me. But I'm maintaining a precarious balance. On so many levels.

It's time for the next round of pills. Past time actually. I retrieve the plastic bottle from my pocket and pop the lid off with my thumb. The wind catches it and, before I can stop it, sends it sailing like a tiny white Frisbee. Already, my reflexes have slowed considerably.

My eyes don't focus quite as they should as I tip the bottle and tap out five pills, but I can see well enough to count the tablets in my hand. I reconsider and make it ten, to make up for lost time. As before, I suck them into my mouth and swallow them with a good swig of champagne. Well, not good, not anymore, but it gets the job done. I lean my head back for a minute. It's heavier than it should be, and loose, like a Pez dispenser on its last leg. That makes me laugh, a Pez dispenser that is my head, on its last leg.

My face feels numb where my hand touches it, as I lift five more pills to my mouth to make it fifteen. I'm about to suck them up when something slaps my hand away. No, not something. Someone. And she's screaming.

"What are you doing? Bree! What are you doing?"

For a moment I'm too stunned to grasp what's happening, but when Jaclyn snatches the pill bottle out of my hand, I'm Bilbo Baggins wanting the ring back.

"That's mine!" I scream. I grab for the bottle and fall off the rock in earnest this time.

"How many did you take? How many?"

"Give them back!" I demand, but Jaclyn hurls the contents at the approaching wave. "No! No!" I curse her, drop to my knees and sift through the water in search of the pills as though I could scoop them up like jacks on the sidewalk, as if they hadn't already dissolved in the salt and the sea.

Jaclyn shakes me by the shoulders. "How many did you take, Bree? Tell me!"

"Go to hell!" I claw at my pocket, hoping some fell out of the bottle, but there are none. How many *did* I take? How many? Enough? Let it be enough, God. Please. Please.

"I found her," Jac is saying.

I look around, confused, before I see the phone in her hand. I grab for it, but she turns away, and, off balance, I fall on my shoulder. I'm screaming again, at her, at the world. And I can't stop.

Twenty-Nine

I have no voice, yet I continue to scream and pound the sand with my fists. I'm screaming still when Ainsley and Sissy drop breathless onto the sand beside me. "Baby, baby," Sissy soothes. "Shh. Shh." She and Ainsley and I are a tangle of arms. Ainsley is crying. My cheek finds her shoulder, and it feels like blessed heaven as I rest my head against it. I continue to pant as rasps escape my raw and burning throat.

"No, no, no, no, no." It's all I can say, over and over, no.

I don't know how long we stay in our knotted huddle, but when I clutch my stomach and groan, Sissy and Ainsley pull away and give me room. One of them holds my hair, while on hands and knees I hang my head and vomit. I don't stop until it seems that if I heave one more time I really will throw up my guts. There's nothing else left.

My throat is on fire and my head pounds. I feel my pulse with every painful throb. When at last I sit back on my heels someone puts a bottle of water in my hand. I rinse, spit, and gulp until the bottle is empty. Then I toss it away and reach for another, and mercifully it's there. I drink it all, but more slowly this time, and cover my vomit with sand.

Little by little I regain what's left of myself. I can't imagine what's shoring me up.

"What in God's name happened?" Sissy demands of Jac.

"This." She thrusts the empty pill bottle toward Sissy, and I look away.

There are no human sounds for the space of an age, then Ainsley kneels beside me again and rocks me in her arms. Ainsley, the compassionate one. "Bree, oh Bree." Her voice is a soft whisper. "Should we call an ambulance?" she asks Sissy.

"Bristol. Love, look at me. Come on, now, look at me."

Ainsley pulls back and gives me room to comply. But I don't want to comply. I want to—

"Bristol."

"What!"

"How many did you take?" Sissy's holding the bottle now, squinting as she tries to read the label in the dark.

I shake my head and look away.

"How many did you see her take?"

"A handful," Jaclyn says. "But I don't think it was the first."

"Bristol—"

"How many did you take?" Jac is far more demanding than Sissy. "How many?"

"I'm calling," Ainsley says.

"No!" I reach toward her. "No. I didn't— Only a few. Not enough to— I'm fine. I'm fine."

Ainsley doesn't believe me, I can tell by her face. She looks to Sissy for direction.

"With what she threw up there can't be much left in her system. Let's wait a few minutes."

"Should I call Grady?"

"No!" I grab for her phone, but Ainsley's reflexes are a thousand times faster than mine at the moment.

Sissy looks at the bottle again, pulls her glasses down onto her nose, not that it helps. "Let's hold off. At the slightest change we'll call 911." She kneels in the sand in front of me. "You've not been taking your meds, love. For how long?"

"I have. Just not all the time." My words are slurred, and every one's an effort.

"Then you've been saving up for quite a while."

Yes, but not on purpose. It was just a dumb-luck decision.

"Why?" Jaclyn, fierce as I've ever seen her, is standing over me. "Why would you do this?"

"Oh, Puff, honestly. We can do this later."

"No. We can't. Look at me, Bree. Look at me. We're all here trying to get you through this. Doesn't that count for anything? Apparently not, because what do you do? You sneak off like a schoolgirl and do who knows what, with who knows who, while we're sitting here frantic. Frantic!"

"Frantic?" I stand, but too quickly, and just barely keep my footing as the world spins and tilts. "You think I don't know about frantic? Do you know what tomorrow is, *Puff*?" It infuriates me that I don't have more voice to throw at her. "Do you even care?"

"Care? Are you kidding? Why do you think I'm here?"

"Did I ask you to be here? Did I? I did, in fact, make it clear I do not want you here. I made it clear I want to be by myself!"

"Of course you do." Jaclyn snatches the bottle out of Sissy's hand. "And won't this just solve everything?"

"It may not solve everything, but it will end everything."

"For whom?"

"For me!"

"You. Is this all about you now, Bree?"

"Good Lord, girl, leave her alone!"

"Is it?"

"Who else would it be about?" I curse her and slam a fist to my chest.

"Oh, I don't know. Us, maybe? Or David?" Her sarcasm is sharp as a coral reef.

"David? Don't even go there."

"What, he hasn't lost enough already? He's got to lose you too?"

"Like he cares."

Sissy takes a step that places her between Jac and me and holds her arms out like a barricade. "That's enough."

But apparently it isn't, because Jac stands on her tiptoes and looks over Sissy's shoulder. "You think he doesn't care? You think he's not dying a slow death two times over as tomorrow morning approaches, wondering if you're coming back? What makes you so special, Bristol? What gives you the right to do this?" She shoves the prescription bottle in my face.

"Because! It was my fault! And I don't want to be here!"

"Please. Jaclyn. Stop this." Ainsley is sobbing now.

"I don't want to be here!"

"So you swallow a bottle of pills and float off to la-la land for the rest of forever? Is that what you think? Because there are consequences, Bristol. Did you think about that?"

"I don't care about consequences."

"Today you don't. Right now you don't. But you will. This isn't all there is, you know."

"I hate you." I turn and walk away.

"I don't care," Jaclyn calls. "Hate me all you want, but you can't do this!"

"Oh yeah?" I know the words are swallowed up in the wind. They would be even if I had a voice left. "Watch me."

What I need is to run into the waves, with rocks in my pockets and a strong undertow. What I need is to be left alone. But I know without looking back, they're following close behind. There's no getting away this time. I've blown my best chance to do this, and the realization hits me like a tidal wave.

I stop and turn on them. "Go away! All of you, go away!"

"We're going to get through this, Bree." There are tears in Ainsley's voice, but she's all solidarity again. This is making me crazy.

"I want to be alone. And you needn't worry because"—I throw up a hand—"I have nothing left to take."

"We're not leaving you," Sissy says, the period on the end of the discussion.

I stomp off, but they're right behind me. When I stop, they stop. "Do you at least understand? Can you see my side in this?"

"We do," Sissy says, but there's no give.

I have nowhere to go. Nowhere at all.

Thirty

"Wait. My purse." I turn to retrace my steps, but Ainsley stops me.

"I have it," she says, and I see it is indeed draped over her shoulder.

I reach in my pocket and feel for the starfish, because if it's not there I'm going back for sure. But it is there. I turn it in my hand until my finger slips into the notch where the missing arm should be, then I hold on for dear life.

It doesn't escape my notice that this odd sort of lifeline is, itself, dead. Newly dead. As of two days ago, three at the most. And still I cling to it.

Another wave of nausea hits me. I drop onto the nearest rock and hold my throbbing head in my hands. I should be on my way to feeling nothing right about now. Instead I feel like my head's caught beneath a boulder. I silently curse Jac for her interference. And then, out loud, because I'm that angry.

Sissy and Ainsley are at my side in a moment. "What is it, baby?"

"Are you gonna be sick again, Bree?"

"Here, love, here's some water. Drink."

But before I can reach for the bottle I'm dry heaving again. My insides feel like a grinder as they work to expel the drug from my system. I sit with my head between my knees, Ainsley holding my hair, and feel as undone as a body can feel. My groans are involuntary. And humiliating. When at last the bout has passed, Sissy offers the water again. I wipe my mouth on my sleeve, and drink.

"Just tell me why."

I have very little voice. Ainsley leans in. "What's that, Bree?"

"Why?" I throw my head back and send a wimpy scream to the heavens. But the empty sound bounces back, repelled by the ceiling of fog. Like my prayers the past three hundred sixty four days, slammed right back down onto my head. "If you were God, would you do this? Would you hide her from me?" Ainsley's shoulders slump in compassion, and I turn to Sissy. "Would you?"

"Oh, love."

Jaclyn stands at a distance, her stance as rigid as her face. Her eyes don't shift from mine and it infuriates me, this hard act of hers.

"And don't tell me God is making a tapestry of my life, and that I can only see it from below where it's messy. That when I see the big picture from the other side I'll finally get it. Don't tell me that. Because it's crap."

"Look out there, love, at that immeasurable horizon. It's not even a blip on the radar of the big picture. The entire universe is not even the span of his hand."

"And that's supposed to make me feel better?"

"It tells us we're not alone. That there's something—Someone—so much bigger than we are, looking out for us."

"Yeah, well, they lock people up for believing in aliens. And as for looking out for us, right. He's done a bang-up job."

"I don't pretend to have the answer to this. But his promises are for the very worst of times, or what's the point?"

"His promises?" I count them off on my fingers as I recite. "Like not leaving or forsaking? Like asking and receiving? You think I haven't asked? That I haven't begged? Groveled? You think I believe any of that now? Where in God's name was he when someone drove off with my daughter?!"

"God doesn't have a blind spot, baby."

Like the Eye of Sauron, I think, for the second time tonight. It gives me pause for a moment, but just a moment. "Then he's indifferent, and that's worse." I scoop up a handful of sand and throw it at the sky. "Far! Worse! Do you hear me up there? Every phone call, every doorbell, for a solid year, I've begged it's news about Kinsey. Begged. Every time. Every freakin' time! And the one who could help, *the only one*, does nothing!" I beat at the sand, throw it again, and beat some more. I can barely lift my arms, and still I beat.

"Bree, honey. Stop. Please stop." Ainsley pulls me up into her arms.

"I can't do this, not one more day. Ainsley, I can't. It's like when I had Kinsey, when I'd push and push and nothing would happen. And I'd think, if I cooperate with what that stupid nurse is telling me to do, even though it hurts so bad, I'll finally get through this. Only I didn't. And this is the same, Ainsley. I keep bearing down against this pain, but it doesn't stop. It won't let me be through. There's no getting to the other side. I'll die if I don't get this out. All this"—I clutch my hands to my chest—"feeling. It's killing me."

"Then let it go, Bristol. Don't keep holding it in."

"I don't know how. I'm drowning in all this pain inside me. I can't live like this anymore. Ainsley, help me. Help me end this."

She steps back and holds my face between her hands. "I can't do that. You know I can't do that."

"Help! Me!" I look up to the dark heaven and blaspheme as I've never blasphemed, daring God to strike me down. Begging him to. "I don't know what you want from me! What did I do wrong? Was I not a good enough mother? Not perfect enough for you? Huh? You have to take my daughter the way you took my mother? Okay fine, now me! I want out!"

I drop to my knees. The pain presses in from every side until I can hardly breathe. The despair is overwhelming because I know without a doubt God won't strike me down. He won't deliver me from this living hell. Not tonight. Not ever. "Lord." The word is just a whisper, but it's rife with defeat. "If I'd known Kinsey would be ours for such a little while, I'd have loved her better. I'd have done it right, every minute of every day. I swear I'd have..."

And something breaks inside me, as though my bones, all turned to glass, have shattered. The pain is white hot, and for the first time since this nightmare began, tears sting my eyes and spill over my lids, a trickle at first, but then it's as if someone has opened wide the tap. Finally. Oh, God, finally.

I cry so long and hard my tears make pools where I kneel in the sand. My head feels as though it could burst. If I could take it off for a while, I would. Instead, I press against my temples and dare not let go. That pressure is all that's holding me together. I know it.

My keepers keep their distance—for fear of stanching the tears that are flowing at last, I'm sure. But I feel their eyes on my pathetic self, feel the collective breath-holding going on around me. And of all the things to come to mind it's the scripture that says, "you are wretched, pitiful, naked." That's just how I feel, wallowing here in the sand.

At last, I sit back on my heels and work to steady my breathing, while my bruised ribs protest with every intake of air.

I am so undone.

Jac is the first to take a step in my direction. "Feel better?" Her voice rings with a familiar compassion, and in that moment I get it. She was the midwife, helping me push out the afterbirth of the pain I'd conceived and finally delivered.

I nod, but that nod is a lie. For though I feel empty at last, I do not feel better. Not better at all. Only different.

Thirty-One

*L*et's get her back to the beach house," Sissy says. "She's cold and wet and— Where are your shoes?"

I shrug and nod toward the waves, and realize that Sissy's right. I'm shivering like crazy from the inside out. But it's not all about the cold.

"Get into something dry," she says, the minute we arrive back at the trailer. "I'll find you some socks." She lights the fire under the tea kettle and I could cheer.

I drop onto the bed, barely able to hold up my head. The throbbing is worse than ever. I wilt onto the pillow and curl my legs up tight. I have no idea what time it is, but all I want is to close my eyes and never move again. Not ever. I'm sinking into blessed nothingness when someone shakes me by the foot.

"Hey. We need you out here." It's Jaclyn. The midwife has disappeared, the D.I. is back.

"Go away."

"Here's a sweatshirt—hope you don't mind fabric paint. Ah,

magnolias. Cute—and matching sweat pants. Lucky you."

"Go away."

"I'm pretty sure the socks are your dad's. Want help with this?"

"I want you to Go. Away."

"So you said." Jaclyn rolls me over, unbuttons my jeans and begins tugging from the bottom of both legs.

"What the— Are you nuts? Quit it!"

"Tea's ready," Sissy calls from the kitchen.

"Tea's ready," Jac repeats. She drops my wet jeans on the floor and holds up the socks. "You or me?"

I swipe them out of her hand and shove my feet into them. And yes, they are my dad's. Black. And calf length. Then she hands me Sissy's sweat pants. "I am not wearing those."

Jaclyn drops them onto the bed beside me and points to my blouse. "Can you handle the buttons?" She nails me with a look, and I swear, I think she thinks I'm not the only one who's handled these buttons since I dressed myself this afternoon. My face burns in spite of my innocence, if you can call it that, as I snatch up the sweatshirt. I tug it over my head and thrust my arms into the sleeves, but that's where I draw the line. I rummage through my suitcase, which is lying on the floor where I left it a few hours ago, for a pair of flannel sleep pants.

Jac tosses out a chuckle. "Well, one thing's for sure. You won't step foot outside the front door in that get-up."

I mutter something nasty, tug the bedspread off the bed, drape it over my shoulders, and follow her back to the kitchen.

Sissy hands me a mug. "Here we are."

I let the warmth of it soak into my hands, while the steam dampens my face. I breathe in the citrus. "Thank you." I say it grudgingly.

Sissy pulls out the chair between her and Ainsley. "Sit," she says, while Jac squeezes into the chair across the table from me.

This is it, the Inquisition.

I sip my tea, thinking how nice it would be if I could shrink my way out of here, like Alice in her alternate universe. But, with all eyes on me, I feel like the bigger-than-life Alice, stuck here in a universe that's just as twisted.

"Talk to us, Bristol." Ainsley reaches over to touch my arm. "We knew this would be a difficult weekend, and that's why we're here. But we didn't expect this."

Ainsley nails me just like Jac, and I have to look away.

"You know we love you."

My eyes sting, and what I fear is that now that the stopper is gone I won't be able to manage the spillover from that fathomless well inside me. But I refuse to sit here and blubber. I've exposed myself far too much already. By sheer will, I force back the tears. "Then show it."

"Bristol. Love." Sissy sets her mug on the table in that annoying sixth-grade-teacher way she has of doing things. "We're getting through this. All of us. No exceptions."

"I can't." I don't rant or whine, just let the words speak for themselves.

"As your sister pointed out, that's why we're here. To help you."

"And then what? We come back and do it all over again next year? And the year after that, and the year after that? You need to get this, all of you. I can't do it." I thump my finger on the table with each word for emphasis.

"You can't give up, Bree." Unlike me, Ainsley doesn't fight her tears. She just blots the stream with a napkin and dabs at the table for the ones she misses.

"We all gave up a long time ago."

"No. No one's given up." She nods toward Jac and Sissy. "They haven't. I haven't. It's why I go to the headquarters day after day, because that might be the day someone calls. Someone who's seen her picture and calls, Bree. We've all seen on the news those incredible stories of recovery. That could be Kinsey. That could be us."

"And if it is? What do I say to my daughter? How do I explain that my stupidity"—I slap the table to effect the full force of the word—"led to whatever horror she's had to live through? How do I do that? No. The best thing is for me not to be here."

"That's selfish," Jaclyn says.

My eyes narrow, but before I can snap out a response Ainsley cuts in. Ainsley, the mediator. "I know you feel the guilt of this—"

"Yes. I do."

"—but this wasn't your fault. We've all done what you did. Well, maybe not Jac, but"—Ainsley makes a motion that encompasses the rest of us—"I have, we have. You think, it's just for half a minute. What could possibly go wrong? And then, this."

She's trying hard, I know she is, but I'm not buying it. Not for a moment.

"I know you think you want to die." Ainsley creeps up on the word, says it in a whisper, and her eyes fill up again. "I know you think you can't get through this. I know that."

"The truth is," Sissy says, "there will be days you go through all seven of the five stages of grief before breakfast. And days you'll want to decorate Trump Towers just so you don't have to think about it. One is as right as the other, love."

Jac studies Sissy in the odd moment that follows. "All seven of the five stages?"

Sissy gives a stiff shrug. "Conflicting theories. The point is, you do what it takes to get through."

"Listen to you." I'm crazy with frustration. "You talk as if there's an endpoint. Well, barring some unexpected miracle—and I don't believe in miracles, unexpected or otherwise—there is no endpoint. We're stuck in this limbo for*ever*."

Jaclyn leans in toward the table. "Bristol, I know you don't want to hear this, but here it is anyway. Sometimes God says no. Sometimes there's no happy ending. I don't know why. And I hate it. But there it is. And all we can do is believe in his purpose and play by his rules."

"His rules? Are you kidding me? Well, let me tell you, this girl doesn't want to play anymore!"

"I know." She reaches for my hand, but I turn away and cling to my cup. "I know."

"You do, huh? You with your idyllic life? What do you know, Jac? What do you think you know?"

"For one thing, that you're not going to shake me, no matter how snotty you act. And for another, that God doesn't have to prove his love. He already did."

"I don't want to hear from him or about him, so save your sermons. I'm done. I'm. Done."

"Bristol." Ainsley waits till I shift my eyes to hers. I finally do, but everything is still so out of focus. "We seldom know what God is up to. His ways—"

"I know all the verses. I've heard them a million times this past year. I just want her back, Ainsley. I want my baby girl back. That's all I'll ever ask for again. I swear. You pray, Ainsley. You. Please. He'll listen to you."

I watch her head fall to her hand, watch as tears hit the table in silent little splashes. "I haven't stopped praying, Bree. I'd do anything to find her. Anything." She looks up again. "But until we do"—she falters, then catches herself—"until we do, we have to know that God has not lost sight of her. No matter what. I'm sorry, I am. But there's no better answer."

"No better answer," Sissy echoes.

A humiliating squeak escapes my throat, and now it's my tears hitting the table, but I have none of the dignity of Ainsley. "It wasn't even two minutes. Not two minutes." It's all I can do to catch a breath, and once I do, to let it out again. I see myself bursting, an overfilled balloon, and wish with all my heart I could do just that, just break apart and drift away. Lord. There's no end to the way I see myself dying.

Thirty-Two

Sissy fills another kettle of water for tea, then turns down the burner when the whistle blows, and refills our cups. This is our third kettleful. We're mostly out of words, though we haven't resolved much, and we're exhausted. Completely. And still we sit and drink our tea, while Spike snores from his bed beneath the built-in desk, so called, and passes gas from time to time. I hate that dog. The effects of the drugs I took are wearing off, and I'm finally able to focus again. The clock above the sink says 3:28.

"I didn't sleep with him." My words intrude on the silence, but my timing is bad, as Sissy has just lifted her cup of Constant Comment, and, thanks to me, misses her mouth completely. Her odd whoop, as the steaming tea spills down her front, ends with a "What?!"

"But I might have, so I'm as guilty as if I did."

"Who?"

"That's how it works, right?"

"Love, what are you talking about?"

Jac gives me a cool look that says, *You said it, not me.*

Well, great. She might have let me know she hadn't told them.

Sissy takes the towel Ainsley offers, but does nothing with it for the moment. "Who, who didn't you sleep with?"

The clock tick tick ticks in the ensuing silence, and when I don't answer, Jac does. "Jeff Girard. Mr. I'm Just Sayin'."

Yes. If only I could shrink away.

"You might have? Why?" You can tell from Ainsley's voice she hardly believes it.

Why? I run my finger round and round the rim of my cup. That's not a question I thought I'd have to answer, so I don't know what to say.

"Bree?"

I shrug, knowing full well that will not suffice. "I didn't. Wasn't going to, no matter what he thought. But if I had it was because I wanted to feel something besides ... what I feel."

Ainsley lets out an anguished breath. "We haven't helped you nearly enough. Not nearly enough."

"You've tried. Believe me, I know that. But God forbid, if this were Sam or Eli, you'd understand. I walk around with a knife in my heart. That's how it feels, Ainsley, like a knife in my heart, and I can't stand it anymore."

"Not a day passes that I don't think about what I'd do if it were one of my boys. Not a day. I don't know how to console you, because I don't know how I'd be consoled. But don't leave us, Bree. Please. Please don't leave us."

A knot of emotion closes my throat. I silently curse my stupidity, because right this minute I could be in the plum room, making my way to the end of *What We Keep*, Plan A or Plan B still intact. Or is it Plan C? I can't keep it straight at the moment, but what does it matter, because now there is no plan. No plan at all. But I still want out. As much as ever.

"How did this come about?" Sissy asks. "This thing with mister ... him. I mean, you weren't really ... not really ...?"

"Does it matter? I might just as well have."

"Well, there's certainly less to confess in the preferred scenario."

"I don't want to talk about it anymore. I just wanted you to know I didn't." I turn my eyes to Jac across the table from me and send a look that says, *Thank you very much*. She responds with a prolonged blink and a shift of her gaze.

"We should get some sleep." I have no intention of going to bed, but I would like to be done with this inquest.

My wardens confer without words, then Sissy shakes her head. "We're fine," she says, though her eyes are hooded with heavy lids, her spunk all but gone.

"Why don't you go on to bed," Ainsley says to her. "You have to drive tomorrow. Today. Later. We'll sit up, Jac and I. We're good."

"No one needs to sit up. I'm not a two-year-old."

Jac bites back a response that I can all but guess. She clasps her hands behind her head and winks at me. "I'd never sleep after all this tea."

I roll my eyes. "It's decaffeinated, you know that."

"And you know how inadequate my bladder is. I'd be up a dozen times before dawn."

Okay. She has a point. Not that I'm one bit happy about it. I turn to Ainsley. "There's no need for both of you to babysit. You go on and get some sleep. I won't leave and I promise not to cut my wrists or hang myself from the rafters. Oh wait, there aren't any rafters in this beach house, are there?"

"She's right," Jaclyn says to Ainsley, ignoring my sarcasm, "that you should go on to bed. But don't worry. I'm wide awake." The last two words she says directly to me.

It takes another minute or two to persuade them, but eventually they both get up from the table. Sissy puts her cup in the sink then lifts Spike out of his bed. When he growls at her she swats his nose. "Don't be mean to Mama. It's time for night-night."

His underbite is more pronounced than ever as he cocks his head at her, his bubble eyes darting about uncertainly. If he could speak I know exactly what he'd say: "You woke me up to tell me it's time to go to sleep, you crazy woman?" Okay, the crazy woman part is strictly mine, I admit, but he'd think it too if it weren't for all the treats she plies him with. I'll just bet you.

Ainsley hugs me and whispers, "I love you."

"You too," I say. Because I do. More than anyone now, I love my sister.

"See you in a while."

There's a tense silence between Jac and me as we sit here at the table. I'm by far the more uncomfortable one. "This is ridiculous."

"Oh, I completely agree."

"Do not start in on me."

She nods toward our bedroom. "Let's go where we can talk."

I follow, not because I want to but because I know as well as she that we're going to talk. Might as well make it as private as possible.

Jac closes the door behind us then sits cross-legged on her bed. "So, what made you change your mind about Jeff Girard?" She says his name with much derision.

"What makes you think I did?"

"Because I believe you. You're not nearly as far gone as you think you are."

"Really? Well, what if I tell you he was the one to leave?"

Which is true. What I don't say is that he left because I made it abundantly clear he was wasting his time on me.

"I'd say maybe he's not as big a chump as I took him for, but he is a chump all the same."

"He didn't take advantage of me, if that's what you mean. We had a drink and— I just wanted the stupid contract."

"Did you get it?"

"I got his signature. He didn't get mine."

"Why not?"

"We just didn't get that far."

"That far? It should have been the first and only thing you did. What made him drive off with you? I'll tell you what. You think he didn't know opportunity when he saw it? Think he didn't know your state of mind? Your circumstances? That, my friend, is taking advantage."

"He asked about you. At the coffee shack as we were driving away."

She stares at me long and hard. "And you didn't hit him with your shoe or something? How despicable is that, that two-timing—? I take back what I said. He's a bigger chump than I thought."

"He gave me something."

"I'll just bet."

"No, really, I want you to see this." I slide off the bed. "It's in my bag."

She quickly unfolds herself and moves to the door, holding her hand up like a stop sign. "I'll get it."

"Oh, good grief."

"Uh-huh. Be right back."

Be right back. I sit down again, hug my knees and rest my forehead on the peaks they form. My stomach swirls like an eddy as the memory comes into focus. It's summertime. We're at Ainsley and Grady's house for a barbecue and a swim, David, Kinsey and I. She's not quite two and a half.

She comes in from the back yard in her bathing suit and water wings. She already has the funniest tan lines. "Mama?"

"Yes, love?" I surprise myself by how much I sound like Sissy. I surprise Ainsley too, by the look she gives.

"Be right back."

"Oh yeah?" My sister and I chuckle as we stand in the kitchen slicing fixin's for the burgers. She says the cutest things, in the cutest voice. But when Kinsey heads for the front entrance, I quickly put down my knife and follow her. "Where are you going?"

"Be right back," she says again, shaking a finger for emphasis, only it's three fingers because she can't yet do just one. Her apple green flip flops squeak on Ainsley's polished wood floor. They're adorable, those flip flops, with the big white daisies, and the straps that go behind the heels to help keep them on. It's my mission to find a bathing suit to match before the summer ends.

When Kinsey gets to the front door she stands on tiptoe and reaches for the knob. Thanks to David she's in the eighty percentile for height for her age. She reaches the knob with ease.

"Kinsey, honey, where are you going?"

"Be right back," she says yet again. It's suddenly not so funny, but I'm curious as can be, so I follow her outside. She walks right past our Explorer and marches down the sidewalk.

"What on earth . . .?" Ainsley says behind me.

"Kinsey." I step in front of her and kneel down so that we're eye to eye. "Where are you going?"

"I forgot my squirt gun."

"Your what?"

"My squirt gun."

She says it three times before I finally decipher her words. "Your squirt gun?"

"Uh-huh." She nods and tries to step around me.

"At home?"

"Uh-huh."

"Oh, baby." I scoop her up in my arms. "You can't walk home. It's too far, and you don't know the way."

"But I forgot my squirt gun."

And then Ainsley gets it. "The boys. They have these super soakers for the pool."

And I get this clutch in my stomach. Because, Lord, what if I hadn't been there to stop her?

"Bree? You okay?"

I look up at Jaclyn where she stands with my bag.

"You don't look okay."

I mean to form a caustic comeback, but in that moment it occurs to me for the first time ever that Kinsey has these flashbacks too, she must, these memories she's not equipped to analyze, and I let go a keening sound I can't hold back. "God, oh God, oh God."

Jac is on her knees beside the bed, with her arms around me. "What? What? Bristol, it's okay. It's okay. Let it out. All of it. Let it go."

And I'm Alice, shrinking. Shrinking.

Thirty-Three

I wake with a start and snap to a sitting position. My head feels like
the winning ball in a rugby match. I groan and press my fingers to
my temples. Tenderly. It takes a few moments, but when I realize for
sure where I am, I look across the narrow space between the beds, and
there's Jac, leaning against the headboard with a pillow behind her back.

"'Morning," she says, and turns the page of a book. No, not a book.
My journal. My *journal?*

"What are you doing with that?" It hurts to move, but I span the gap
in a flash and snatch it out of her hands.

"Hey, I just— Isn't that what you wanted me to see?"

"The cover. I wanted you to see the cover."

"Which is"—she tears up, swallows, and clears her throat—"lovely.
Really lovely. A nice gift, no matter what his intentions were."

"You shouldn't have read it."

"Okay, maybe not, but since you won't let any of us inside your head,
we have to do sneaky, unscrupulous things to find out what you're

thinking." She nods toward the journal. "You were really planning to ... do that? Kill yourself?"

"'Til you came along and messed everything up, yes."

She shivers in an odd kind of slow motion then nods at the journal. "Well, you're right, I'd have been furious if you'd pulled it off. And you're also right, I should have seen it coming. Or at least anticipated. So what now, where do we go from here? How do we keep you—"

"Wait, wait! What time is it?" I pray the grayness that bleeds through the corduroy curtains means it's early, not just foggy.

Jac makes an I-don't-know gesture. The pain in my head intensifies with every step as I hurry into the kitchen. "Please," I whisper, "let it be before." I'm so relieved I could cry when I see the clock over the sink. It's 7:49. Twenty-five minutes to go.

"Well, good morning," Sissy says as she comes into the kitchen. She opens the front door and lets Spike out to do his thing. "I'll put on some coffee. Sound good? Oh, hey, what's this?" She stoops down to get a better look at what I'm holding in my hand.

"It's a journal."

Then Ainsley is there, looking over my shoulder. "Let me see," she says, and I show her. "Oh, Bristol, how precious. Where did you get this?"

"It was a gift."

"From Mr. You-Know-Who," Jaclyn says, coming into the kitchen. "And actually, it's her last will and testament."

Sissy's eyes grow big as she steals a look at Ainsley. I grip the journal even tighter, but what I'd really like is to whack it up against Jaclyn's head. "Thank you very much."

"Sorry," she says, without sounding the least bit sorry, "but we've just learned the hard way that secrets aren't safe."

"May I?" Sissy holds out her hands. "I'd just like to see the cover."

I hand it over with a good deal of reticence—I don't trust anyone right now—but Sissy doesn't try to open it. She runs a light finger over the outline of my baby girl's profile.

Ainsley's right beside her. "What a thoughtful gift."

"Yes, indeed, he's quite the gift giver." Jaclyn doesn't even try to squelch her sarcasm.

"He is in this case," Sissy says, and that serves to settle it.

"Could we have that coffee?" I ask. "I want to"—I glance at the clock again—"walk on the beach."

It's Ainsley who answers. "Certainly." She says it in such a way that the other two get it almost at once, and the three of them become an assembly line. Ainsley measures coffee into the filter, while Sissy fills the carafe with water and pours it into the tank. Jaclyn gets the Styrofoam cups, and spoons Coffee-mate into each one, then adds a packet of Splenda to Sissy's. Spike's on his leash and we're out the door with three minutes to spare.

It's too much to think they'll let me go alone, though there's nothing more I want at the moment. The morning is indeed gray, but there's a promise of better things to come should the thin veil of fog dissipate. For now, the grayness suits me fine. Barefooted and with my capris rolled up, I step ankle-deep into the surf and begin to walk along the shoreline. It takes only moments for my bare feet to become numb enough that I can ignore the temperature of the water. The incoming waves roll ashore and soon my legs are wet to the knees.

There are harbor seals out on the rocks, heard but not seen. The urgency of their barks doesn't match their laid-back life, I've always thought. Really, it should be so simple. You hang out at the beach, eating, mating, and bearing young. Okay, and dodging killer whales and great white sharks on occasion. But if they want urgent, I can give them urgent.

The others stay well back from the waves, content to keep abreast of me, but dry. They don't impose on my thoughts by spewing worthless words no matter how well intentioned, but instead give me the space I need, and for that I'm grateful. My phone is in my hand, the one closest to the sea. I keep my eye on the time. At 8:14, I stop and view the numbers for a full minute with a sick kind of resignation, while the scene from a year ago plays in living color in my head. I see Kinsey in the backseat of my car, eyes closed, her head resting on her left shoulder, her cheeks hot with fever. Trusting me to take care of her. There are no signs in the heavens to declare that the moment has arrived, that it's now officially a year since I last saw my baby girl, a solid year that feels like forever. But the weight of it is crushing. I can hardly breathe as the last fleck of hope seeps out of my soul.

"Lord," I breathe. "God."

I curse that I'm alive, that all my plans have failed. It's karma for my one great sin, if you believe in that. Me, I don't believe in anything, because there's nothing left to—

"Hey."

I look over my shoulder, surprised, as Ainsley steps into the waves and takes my hand. She's barefoot and smiling. She doesn't flinch as the water hits her ankles, nor when the next wave soaks the lower half of her jeans. She stands and holds onto me, my lifeline. And then Jac and Sissy are there in the water beside us, and we're all connected. We totter as the sand shifts beneath our feet with the strength of the outgoing surf, but we hold, and suddenly Sissy begins to pray. Her prayer is what my prayer would be if I could summon the faith to think it would matter. It's simple, her prayer. "Help, Lord. Please."

I don't feel the least bit changed as Jac and Sissy and Ainsley murmur their amens—though I begin to think I want to—but I do feel tethered to this world in a way I haven't felt for an interminable year. Dangling over the edge, for sure, but tethered. Whether that proves to be regrettable or not remains to be seen.

I turn back to the sea, and draw into my soul as much as I can handle of the potency of its life, wishing I had a vastly larger reservoir. Wishing I could stay forever in this time and place. But wishing has never gotten me anywhere.

"I'm ready to go," I say with next to no conviction.

Sissy studies me for a moment as if to discern my meaning, then nods. "Okay then. Let's pack up." She tugs on Spike's leash three times before he gets his nose out of the sand, then heads back to the beach house. Ainsley follows her lead, but Jac holds back and I hesitate, look to see what she's doing.

When they've put a dozen yards between us, Jac looks me in the eye. "You're ready to go? You're sure?"

"I'm not sure about anything. But I have some things to face. I just want to get to it."

"What are your plans about David?"

I look out to sea, count seven gulls in the mist, all fishing for breakfast. "I have no idea."

"Will you tell him? About the pills? About Girard?"

"What do you think he'd say, about Jeff?"

Now she counts the gulls, watches one dive and come up empty. "I know David loves you."

I take a small step forward, swishing my feet in the foam. "I can't remember how that feels, to love and be loved."

Jac takes my hand the way Ainsley did. "Your feelings have been focused elsewhere, and understandably. But, Bristol—" She's still holding my hand, and waits for me to look at her. "Your feelings will fail you. You hear me? They'll fail you every time. It's a decision, to love. And let me ask you this: do you want a man who makes you tingle in all the right places? Or a man who's walked every mile of this nightmare with you, who knows and shares your pain, who sees it as something precious and holds it close?"

She's still wrong about Jeff. He has his appeal, I'll give you that, but I never desired him, not for a moment.

And about the other half of the equation. I have the unmistakable feeling she's not just talking about David.

Up ahead, Sissy turns back to us and calls, "You girls coming?"

"Yes, ma'am," Jaclyn says, just like in sixth grade. Our eyes connect, and we smile.

Thirty-Four

We're loading up the Land Rover when A.J. happens by, though *happens* is probably a stretch. I think he wanted to see if we all had survived the night.

"Here, let me help you with that."

Sissy hands over a suitcase without objection. "Just put it by the back of the truck, if you will, so we can load them in order."

"Sure thing." He carries four more bags and a box full of empty casserole dishes to the Land Rover. Then he heaves the bags and the box one by one into the back of the vehicle under Sissy's careful watch, placing them just where she tells him to.

"It was a pleasure, ladies." He smiles that unforgettable smile, then his eyes settle on me. He hands me a plastic case and I know he didn't happen by at all. "Thought you might like this. It's a jam session. Can't get it in stores."

It's a CD of the guitar god, of course. I could cry all over again with the sweetness of his gift. "Thank you," I say, though I don't have much voice left after last night. "Really. Thank you." My keepers are surprised by the exchange, I can tell, but I don't explain.

A.J. nods, gives us that easy salute of his, and says goodbye to each of the others. "See ya next time."

"Next time," Sissy agrees.

We're on the road by eleven. Traffic's much lighter than it will be this evening, with lovers heading home from their Valentines' getaways, some with spouses, some to spouses. It makes me queasy to think I might have fallen into the second camp, and in fact avoided it mostly because Jeff isn't nearly the taker I took him for.

"What a fun weekend," Sissy says. She's met with total silence, but if she notices, she doesn't let on. "We should do this more often. All of us."

All of us? Granted, the "all" was weak. Still, it's something of a start. Maybe.

"I want to know something," I say all of a sudden, though even a second ago I hadn't planned to ask this. "Has Dad ever heard from Teri? Ever? In all these years?"

Sissy gets this pinched expression on her face. "Well ..." I can't believe the "caught" look I see in her profile. "Actually." My stomach clinches as I watch her lips form the word, "Yes."

"Yes? *Yes?*"

"What? *What?*" Ainsley, who's sitting behind Sissy, scoots to the middle of the backseat and leans forward to try to get a look at her.

"Several years ago." Sissy's suddenly committed to keeping her eyes dead ahead on the highway. She licks her lips then rubs them together to dry them. "She was—well, getting married again, and ... needed to know if she and your dad were divorced."

"Divorced." There's an unmistakable trace of disappointment in Ainsley's voice. "And were they?"

"Well, Marty and I had been married for some time, so I certainly hope so. And desertion is strong grounds." Sissy's laugh sounds hollow in the cavernous Land Rover. "Of course they were. Though"—she bites her upper lip, and looks exactly like Spike—"I've never actually seen the papers."

"And you didn't think we'd want to know this?" I wave my hand back and forth between Ainsley and me.

"That I haven't seen the papers?"

I blow my bangs out of my eyes. I hate when she toys with me. "You know what I mean."

Sissy hesitates as long as she can. "No." Her earrings rattle as she shakes her head. "We didn't think you'd want to know."

"Well then, didn't you think we *should* know?"

"Only if you asked. That was what your dad decided."

"Well, I just asked."

"And she just answered." We all look at Jaclyn, each as surprised as the other that she's defending Sissy. "Well"—her voice falters—"she did."

I turn back to my stepmom. "And Teri's not called about— Not once this whole year?"

Both hands are on the steering wheel, but she's twirling her wedding set with her thumb. Like crazy. She gives me a sideways glance, which, had I blinked I'd have missed.

"Sissy?" Ainsley and I say it together.

And the twirling gets faster.

"Actually—"

"That's the second time in two minutes you've said that in just the same way. Explain."

"Well, love, as you might imagine, under the circumstances, Teri was ... interviewed after Kinsey was taken. I guess it's standard procedure in this type of case when a family member is estranged."

That's something I didn't once consider, though I should have. "She's not," I say with all the irritation I can muster. "A family member."

"Technically—"

"Not."

Ainsley sits back with a little thud and blows out a breath. I can't tell if she agrees with me or not, but she doesn't argue. "Did she ask about us?" There's a hopeful tone to her voice.

"Is there a C?" I ask, with a cutting edge to mine.

"She spoke to your dad, of course, not me," Sissy says to Ainsley, ignoring me altogether, "but I'm sure she did. I'm sure."

I turn and stare at the landscape whizzing by the passenger window until my eyes refuse to focus.

No one talks for several miles. Then from the backseat Ainsley says in a little voice, "Constance."

And Sissy says, "Drucilla."

And Jaclyn says, "Eowyn.

I groan. No, no, no, no. "No!"

"But, oh dear, that brings us to F again with you-know-who." Sissy's tone is playful as she nods in my direction, as if the Teri-moment has passed. Well, I can tell you it hasn't.

But before I can get us back on target, Jaclyn taps on the back of Sissy's seat. "Did I ever tell you about my aunt Constance? Oh, she's funny. And beautiful. Really beautiful."

"There are obviously good genes in your family," Ainsley says. Ainsley, the stunning one. But her voice sounds a bit hollow.

Jaclyn pats her knee. "You're sweet. Anyway, she was married to this guy. Jock."

"Jock?" Sissy shoots a look over her shoulder. "Are you serious?"

"Well, actually it's Jacque. He's from Quebec. But since the divorce Connie's dropped the French connection."

"Speaking of divorce," I say.

Jac ignores me. They all do. "And what a looker. But therein lay the problem."

"Ah." Sissy says this as if she completely understands. "One of those."

"Couldn't keep his hands—among other things—to himself."

I straighten up and listen more closely, because I know this is a difficult subject for Jac. The one guy she would have married had the same wandering body parts. I say, with a devious tone, there's a solution for such things, but then I take an introspective moment and wonder what of myself I would have to excise after this weekend. I decide to be quiet for a while.

"So they split, and all in all it was amicable. The guy was a cheating scumbag, but he wasn't otherwise bad, if that makes sense."

"Amicable. Wow," Sissy says.

"Except ..." Jac draws out the suspense until we're all wanting more—even me, and I already know the story. "Except, they both wanted the 1960, candy apple red, convertible Corvette, which they bought together. And what a lesson there is in *that*. He wanted it so he could pick up chicks; she wanted it so he couldn't. But he made off with it before she had the chance, and took both sets of keys. She found out he was living in an apartment in Van Nuys, so she—and I wish you could hear her tell this, you'd wet your pants laughing—talked my mother into going with her to get the car back. So there they are," Jaclyn says, as if it's happening before her eyes, "at this apartment complex in the middle of the night, and they find the Corvette, straddling two lanes in the parking stall—Jock was ridiculously anal about scratches, though I guess you can't blame him—only Connie doesn't have the keys. So she calls this guy she used to know, before Jock, and he tells her how to get into the car. And it works like magic. She pops the lock, but once inside she still doesn't find her keys. So she calls this guy back and he tells her step by step how to hot-wire the thing."

Sissy snaps the rearview mirror to the right so she can see Jaclyn's eyes. "Your aunt is a carjacker?"

I already have my vanity mirror open so I can watch her tell the story.

"I swear, I'm not making this up. And it gets better. She's bent under the dash, with her phone squished between her shoulder and her ear so she can hear the instructions. My mom's on lookout. And wouldn't you know, a security guard drives into the parking lot, going five miles per hour, with one of those twirling yellow lights on top of his car. My mom drops to her knees, trying to hide and warn Connie at the same time. But the light's on in the Corvette because the door's open. The guard drives up real slow and—"

"Slowly," Sissy says. "And you don't need the adverb."

Jaclyn closes her eyes. I'm pretty sure she's counting.

"Sorry. You can take the teacher out of the classroom, etcetera,

etcetera."

"Uh huh. Well, anyway, he sees the light, sees the door open, but doesn't see a person. And it's, like, two-thirty in the morning. So he pulls up and gets out of his car, sees my mom crouching down by a tire, and Aunt Connie under the dash. Before anyone can say anything he makes a 911 call to the Van Nuys police, who had to have been parked three cars down, because almost before Connie can say, 'It's not what you think,' the cops are there. And the only thing that keeps her from getting arrested on the spot is that her name is on the registration right next to Jock's.

"But the security guy goes to apartment 209, or whatever the corresponding parking stall number is, wakes up Jock—who isn't alone, if you get my drift—and says his wife is there, hot-wiring his car, and is that okay? So Jock comes out, and sure enough, there's Connie trying to explain to the police why she's hot-wiring this cherry of a car at two-thirty in the morning. And Jock's sporting this 'gotcha' grin, just listening. So about the time Mom and Connie are pretty sure the handcuffs are next, Jock says, 'Hey, beautiful. Forget your keys?' And he jingles them in front of her, still wearing that dumb grin. So she says 'thank you' as she snatches them out of his hand, and she and Mom get in the car and drive away. They laughed most of the way home, until the adrenalin wore off, then their hearts all but stopped."

"You mean he just let her take the car?" Sissy is suspect.

"He smiled, winked and waved goodbye. Figured he couldn't let that much creative effort go to waste. This was the same husband she was at a party with one time—"

"Wait. How many husbands has she had?"

"Just two. Jock and Elvis, who she's been married to since I was in college."

"Elvis? You can't be serious."

"I swear, I'm not making it up. And what a guy. When she tells this story he just shakes his head and says, 'I'm not leaving her. I like my car.'" Jac pauses till the laughter dies down then says, "They were at this party once, she and Jock, when this guy she knew in college happens by.

He was big man on campus, a real head-turner I guess. Anyway, he introduces her to his wife or girlfriend, whoever she is, and Connie turns to Jock with a sweep of her hand and says, 'And this is my husband ...' And she sweeps her hand again. And still again. But her mind is completely blank. She cannot think of his name. She gives him this look that says, 'Come on, help me out here,' but he's having too much fun watching her squirm. And, of course, when she's telling us this story she laughs like it's the most natural thing in the world to forget your husband's name. When he's standing right beside you. She's a riot, isn't she, Bree?"

"Yeah." She really is.

"You've met her?"

"Oh, yeah."

"I'd rather be the one cheated on than the one cheating," Ainsley says all of a sudden.

There's a very heavy pause, then Sissy says, "For heaven's sake, why?"

"All that guilt. I think it would be harder to forgive myself than someone else."

Well, you can imagine who's squirming now, though the look on Ainsley's face is anything but judgmental. She tells me with her eyes that she takes me at my word when I say I didn't sleep with Jeff, so it isn't me she means.

Still, my spirit burns.

"I suppose that makes sense," Sissy says. "But I'd have to make ... a statement of some kind before I forgave. I don't suppose any of you are old enough to remember Lorena Bobbitt?"

"Bobbitt?" Ainsley says. "Is there a punch line?"

Sissy gives this wicked chuckle. "Punch line? Oh, yeah. Google the name sometime." Then she winks at me. "It fits right in with your solution, love."

"Yeah?"

"Yeah."

Then I may not want to know. "Tell her about the mirror," I say to

Jac. I'm so ready to change the conversation.

"Ah, the mirror." Jac laughs for a minute, while Ainsley and Sissy wait for the story. "Well, Connie loves to shop for antiques."

"You should see her house," I say. "Ainsley, you'd love it."

"Oh yes, you would. Anyway, she takes me along one Saturday. Did I say she lives in the Napa Valley? They have the most amazing antique shops in that entire area. Quaint, you know? Well, we go to Yountville this one particular day. And shop and shop and shop. It's been a long day, at least for me, but Connie's not quite finished, which interpreted means she hasn't yet found anything to buy. 'Oh, oh,' she says, 'look at this darling place.' And it is. A beautiful Victorian house, a creamy white with shutters the color of raisins, hot pink bougainvillea hanging from baskets on the porch. Very inviting. So we go in and we're looking around at all the incredible furniture. The place is decorated beautifully, makes you feel right at home, and of course, nothing is marked, but then, it never is. You only learn the price after you've fallen for the piece, you know?

"We're not there very long when Connie sees *It*. The most beautiful mirror you've ever seen. Beveled glass in, well, I can't begin to describe how gorgeous the frame was. Let me just say even I began to salivate"— Jac squeezes my shoulders—"and you know me and antiques."

Yes, I do. Old, in any form, is not the least bit appealing to uber-modern Jaclyn.

"She has to have it, no matter the price. And trust me, price is not a problem for Aunt Connie. So, she's attempting to take the mirror off the wall when this woman walks into the room. And, oh, is she elegant. Exactly what you'd expect in a place like that. 'Excuse me,' the woman says, 'may I help you?' 'Hello!' Connie says. She doesn't even turn around, just catches the woman's reflection in the mirror. 'Yes! Thank you! Could you get the other side, please? It looks terribly heavy.' 'It is heavy,' the woman says, and she's very deliberate about it. 'And beautiful,' Connie says. 'It's exactly what I'm looking for.' "

In spite of myself I smile, because I know what's coming.

"The woman cocks her head like a sparrow. A confused sparrow at that. 'Excuse me,' she says again, 'but this is my living room.'

"Connie takes a step back and slowly turns to the woman. The look on my aunt's face is priceless. 'Your living room?' she says. 'Ah. Then you probably don't take American Express?' "

Jac's laughing so hard I'm amazed she could deliver the punch line.

Sissy gives her a sidelong glance that verges on appreciation, and sniffs. "Why have I never met this woman?"

Jac stops mid-laugh, meets my eyes in the vanity mirror and raises her eyebrows. "I'm sure we could arrange it."

"And Elvis. Is that his honest-to-goodness real name?"

"It is, though he's as far as you can get from the real thing."

"But handsome?"

Jac doesn't answer for a moment. "You know that old song, 'If you want to be happy for the rest of your life, never make a pretty woman your wife' ... ? Aunt Connie subscribes to that philosophy."

Sissy hits the brakes and I look out the rearview mirror on my side of the car to make sure no one's close enough to cream us. "Jaclyn Papier, are you telling me Elvis is a woman?"

And even I laugh at that.

Thirty-Five

I dread getting home. The best I can hope for is that David's gone. Maybe for good. Fed up, and done. We pull into the drive and only Sissy gets out of the car with me. So I'm on my own, I see. She goes around to the back of the Land Rover and opens the cargo hold. Ever efficient, she had A.J. load my two bags last, so all she has to do is pluck them from the top of the heap. She hands them to me, and with my arms full, making me defenseless, she hugs me. "Take care, love." She gives me a look that says she intends to see that I do.

"Bye, Bree," Jaclyn says from the backseat. "I'll call you."

Ainsley gives me a wink. "Love you."

I turn and face my house, but my feet feel as though they're planted in the concrete driveway.

"Go ahead," Sissy says. "It'll be fine."

"Nothing will ever be fine again," I murmur.

She gives me a sympathetic look, but it's all too clear she's not going anywhere until I'm inside the house, so I force myself to take one step, then another, till I'm at the front door. I try the knob, hoping it's locked as a sign that perhaps David really has abandoned ship, but it turns easily in my hand.

"It'll be fine," Sissy says again.

I'm quiet as I enter the house, and quiet as I close the door. I'd like nothing better than to tiptoe up the stairs and steal away into Kinsey's room, until my heart quits thumping, until I'm ready to face David, if he's there to be faced. I stand without moving for a full minute, listening to the intense silence, finding great comfort in it. But then, with a stealth equal to mine, David juts his head around the corner.

"Bristol." He sounds as startled as I am. "I thought you were going. Away. And not saying goodbye."

I know what he means about *away*. His eyes glisten and he swallows with effort. I have to look anywhere but at him. "So did I."

We stand at an impasse, but I feel the longing he can barely suppress, to reach out and touch me, his boomerang wife.

"Bristol. I'm sorry. Really, I—"

"Don't. Please don't."

He tucks his hands in his pockets and looks around the little entry of our house. "I'm glad you're home." And then he says, "You are home?"

I don't know why it matters all of a sudden that I be fair with him, but it does, and so I confess. "There's something you should know."

"I know."

"No, I mean—"

"I know."

"You can't know," I say, my jaws tight, but I can tell by the look in his eyes that he does. At least he thinks he does. And still he looks at me with longing. He takes his hands out of his pockets, but doesn't seem to know what to do with them. "We can survive this, Bristol. I know we can. We just have to want to."

The laugh I intend sounds more like a whimper. "Well, that's the problem, isn't it?"

"Last night I couldn't sleep." He gives me a look that's a blend of concern and apology." And you know what I was remembering? The ribbon you won at the fair, for that sketch of Ainsley just before she had the twins. It was a great sketch; the pose, the look on her face, the way her hand touched her belly, it said so much. Man, I was proud of you, of your ability, but you were unsure about it, didn't know how good you were. You never have."

"It was white," I say, "the ribbon."

He nods. "Third place. Out of, what, three hundred entries, maybe more?"

I look away and shrug.

"That's what I mean," he says. "If I had to characterize you in one sentence, Bree, it would be to say you don't know how good you are. At what you do, at who you are. You have no faith in yourself."

I close my eyes and whisper, "That's three."

"You've always shortchanged yourself."

"Four."

"Compared yourself to your sister—"

"Five."

"And allowed what Teri did to define you for all time."

My muscles tighten and I pull back as far as my suitcase will allow. Teri has always been off topic for us.

"You deserve better. In every regard." David takes a step toward me, closing the space between us by a few unwelcome inches. "I was wrong, Bristol, to go back on my word to you. And look what happened." The silence that falls pounds in my ears. "I can never undo the damage I've caused this family. And maybe we can't recover. But you know what else I was remembering?"

I want to tell him that I don't know and I don't care, and that I don't deserve better, in any regard, but I stand there looking at the empty space over his shoulder, and say nothing.

"I was remembering that time we went to Moaning Cavern in Calaveras County."

"The one that quit moaning in, like, 1930?"

"But they don't tell you until you pay. Exactly." He tries to catch my eye, but I still can't look at him. "Anyway, we were down there in the cavern and I was surprised at how pretty it was, you know?"

"We both were."

"And you were doing fine, at least on the outside. But then you started up that spiral staircase. After five or six steps—"

"I froze."

"Couldn't go up, couldn't go down."

"It was the worst feeling," I say, but then I think no, not the worst, not by a long shot.

"You stood there for the longest time, on the verge of hyperventilating. And I thought if I could get you moving, you'd be okay. So I coaxed you to take one step up. Just one. With me right behind you. And you finally did. Then I coaxed you to take the next one, and the next, and eventually we got to the top." He takes another step toward me. "I realize that cave is nothing compared to the one we're in now. Not as deep, not as dark. Not anywhere close. But all I can say is we have to take a step. We can't stay in this place, Bree. We'll die if we do."

I blink like crazy, fighting the deluge that's building behind my eyes. I can't swallow, can't breathe. I don't want to wipe at my face, don't want to give myself away, but I'm coming undone.

"We have to move toward the light, babe, or this darkness will swallow us up. We'll never find our way out."

I steal one glance at his face and then I can't look away, can't even close my eyes to sever the connection that's fixed like a magnet. And when he takes another step, I can't help it, I close the scant space between us and work my way into his arms. I say nothing, just wrap my arms around the small of his back. His touch is light, timorous even, as his arms encircle my shoulders. I hold him tighter, and he follows my lead. My head fits perfectly beneath his chin as I rest my temple against the hollow of his throat. It's like returning to the womb. The feel, the smell, the sound of that steady heartbeat, exactly like the womb. I could stay here forever. The pain on my own beating heart is fierce. Amazingly, the dam holds for now, but oh the ache of it, the effort. My throat is so constricted.

The feeling strikes, that sense of déjà vu, that I've been here before, in this exact place, emotionally.

I still bear the stitches of my episiotomy, my breasts are torturously engorged. They leak onto Davy's shirt as he holds me, but if he notices he doesn't complain, doesn't draw away as we stand entwined at the foot of Kinsey's basinet in the NICU. We'd already taken her home, had spent two terrifying nights as an expanded family, feeling our way in the dark as all new parents do. Kinsey slept incessantly, to the envy of every sleep-deprived person I knew who'd ever had a baby. But I could barely keep her awake long enough to feed her and she seldom needed a diaper change. Novice or not, I knew that wasn't normal. I called the pediatrician for the fifth or sixth time in two days, and the nurse assured me, again, that Kinsey was fine. But then, as if for no other reason than to pacify me, she said to take Kinsey's temperature. And I did. "Ninety-two point four," I said, reading from the digital screen. There was a long pause and then she said, "Again. Take it again. With a different thermometer if you have one." The urgency in her voice set me to trembling. "I don't." "Fine. Just take it." "Ninety-two point four," I said again. "Mrs. Taylor, wrap that baby as warmly as you can and get her back to the hospital. ASAP. The doctor will meet you in the NICU." Where Kinsey spent the next five days.

Popsicle Girl they called her. It happens to preemies sometimes, they said, that drop in body temperature, but as I stood in the haven of Dave's arms I knew for the first of many times that I was an unfit mother. No matter how much anyone tried to assure me, I knew it was true. I'd failed my baby girl in the first few days of her life, nearly killed her.

"A chilling moment," Davy declared days later, when the crisis had passed and the family had gathered for the second homecoming, and even I had to laugh. It was just the relief I needed. And for a while the self-doubt abated.

Until I proved beyond all doubt that I was right.

At length, David's chest expands against mine as he draws a breath to speak, but I silence him with a tighter grasp of my arms. I'm not ready to forfeit the safety of the moment. He responds with a tighter grasp of his own, and presses his lips against my hair.

This is right, a voice inside me says. This is true.

"It wasn't you," I finally whisper. "Not then, not now. It was all me."

"No. No, Bree. This wasn't your fault. There's only one person to blame, whoever it was that—"

"God." The word is again an accusation, but only for a moment, then it's this presence that stirs within that empty space deep inside my soul. It swells until it seems there's no room left for me, and just that quickly it's gone. But it leaves a tiny seed of something behind, barely there. Not hope exactly, but it could become that.

"I can't defend him," David says. "I don't have an answer. But I wake up every day with a prayer on my lips, and an inexplicable belief that he can bring Kinsey home. And this knowledge that he might not. Not in the way I hope for. The grief is profound, but so is the hope."

"I can't stop asking why. A million times a day I ask."

I feel him nod. "So do I."

I don't know why that surprises me, but it does. "What if we're wrong, David? What if this is all there is?"

"Then we're wrong."

His words bring a new flood of tears. "I can't bear to think I'll never see her again."

"Then don't think that way. It doesn't cost a thing not to think that way."

He's right, of course, but, Lord, how do you do it? "Will we ever get through a single minute of a single day without this pain? Will we ever laugh again?"

Even the thought seems a betrayal to Kinsey. But then I hear in my inner ear a giggle as infectious as the best you ever heard.

"Mama?" Kinsey sits beside me as I sketch, and swipes a cornflower crayon across a page in her Handy Manny coloring book.

"Yes, sweet pea."

"Will Grampa like my picture?"

"Oh, he'll love it. You wait and see."

"Can we wrap it in paper?"

"Well, of course we can. It's a present, and presents should be wrapped."

I let her pick, and she picks Strawberry Shortcake for Grampa's picture. He'll love that too.

"Will he have a birthday cake?"

"I'm sure Sissy will have a cake for him." Store-bought, but a cake.

"Will Sam be there?"

"And Eli, and Auntie A, and Uncle Grady. Everyone."

Kinsey smiles, because she loves a party. And she loves her buddy Sam.

When we arrive, there is a cake, of course. There are six candles on the bakery beauty, each one representative of a decade of life. But Kinsey can count to twenty and beyond, and something doesn't look right to her. "Are you six, Grampa?"

He smiles and tugs on one of her ponytails. "Not six, but sixty! What do you think of that, kiddo?"

She squinches her face as she looks from him to the cake and back to him again, thinking about his question. "People die when they're a hundred."

"Well then," he says, with hardly a pause, "we better get this party started."

And how we laughed.

Epilogue

I can't say it's been notably easier since that desperate weekend. Every day, every hour really, requires a conscious decision to take one step and then another. Sometimes even to breathe. But if there's a difference, it's that I don't feel so alone now. I no longer shut myself off from Dave or my family or ... well, God's still the difficult part of the equation, I confess. I thought he might surprise me on that first anniversary of Kinsey's disappearance and bring her home to us. But I forgot he's God, not Santa. I've always had better luck with the big guy in red than the one I can't see, feel, or hear on most days. The one with all the answers, wouldn't you just know? I continue to ask, and he continues his silence.

But it's not just Dave, Ainsley, Jac and Sissy who are urging me on toward the light, there's a divine draw as well. I know that without a doubt. I'm still angry, yes. It's no secret to God, but whoever said it, got it right: "Lord, where else can I go?"

We return to the beach house every anniversary of Kinsey's

disappearance, Sissy, Jaclyn, Ainsley and I. We currently have three getaways under our belt. Every year I want to fill my pockets with rocks, but every year I'm buoyed by these crazy women who love me—don't ask me why they do. They still have the ability to hope, and it's their hope alone that keeps me from sinking into the pit that nearly claimed me, since I no longer take the antidepressants—as if any of my family would let me after what happened. Sissy's convinced they led me to thoughts of suicide, or at least magnified the ones I manufactured on my own. She sees the commercials, with all those disclaimers. Well, I'm happy to let her think that way. But their hope has begun to ignite a spark of hope in me as well, minuscule to be sure, but still it's there. And in spite of little Zachary, whose story breaks my heart every single day, I cleave to every frail wisp of hope that comes from the happy-ending stories I read about, where lost children come home, decades later sometimes, like Jaycee Dugard and the three women in Ohio. Lord God Almighty, what they went through. But home is home. And home is where I crave Kinsey to be. Now that I can think clearly again—though "clearly" remains a very relative term in my world—I see how sad it would be for her to come home and find me gone. That's something I know from experience. And as long as I breathe I will be looking toward that day.

And I pray. Without ceasing, I pray. My broken starfish sits on Kinsey's pillow, a reminder in boomerang theology that things cast on the water sometimes do return. I'll drown for sure if I can't believe that.

I continue to press my memory for the things I so want to remember about Kinsey, like the last time she climbed onto my lap with her blanket after her bath, smelling like shampoo and little girl; or the last time I held her hand to cross the street; or the last time she kissed me with her little heart of a mouth; or the last words she spoke to me. They're not all forthcoming, these memories, but when I can remember unequivocally, I use my Last Will and Testament journal to record them in.

I read *What We Keep* every anniversary too. I kept the book, since my bequeathing became a moot point, and I think about Teri. I'm happy for Ginny and Sharla, and Marion, too, the characters from the novel, for though I don't fool myself into believing that my and Ainsley's story will have a satisfying end where Teri's concerned, I don't begrudge them theirs. Though more than once I've been tempted to search out her number, if that's even possible, and make a call. Because there's another side to the story, her side. I might not like what I hear, but I'm intrigued. For the first time ever, I'm intrigued.

My father-in-law is my pastor again, but there's been a change in him. He's still as kind, still as good, but his dogma isn't what it used to be, his answers not so pat. That makes his teaching much easier to swallow. "The older I get, the less I know" has become his mantra. There's a lot to be said for that.

Baby Talk is a big seller in the world of greeting cards. Regarding this, my emotions are mixed to say the least, though I am glad I never signed the contract with I'm Just Sayin'. But with every new card I design and order I fill, I can't help but ask, "Why, Lord? Why now and not then? When it mattered. But the why game is a treacherous one to play, so I do my best to give it a wide berth. Ainsley and I have built a flourishing internet business with Baby Talk. And on the back of every card is a *Have you seen this child?* message that spreads Kinsey's photo—the one with the strawberries on her sundress and the flowers in her hair—across the US. Canada and Mexico are next. That was Ainsley's idea, of course. Ainsley, the selfless one.

About the Author

Sharon K. Souza, author of *Unraveled*, *Lying on Sunday*, *Every Good & Perfect Gift*, and *A Heavenly Christmas in Hometown*, has a passion for writing Heart-of-the-Matter Fiction ... with a good dose of humor. She and her husband, Rick, are natives of Northern California. They have three grown children—one who now resides in Heaven—and seven grandchildren. Rick has traveled the world building churches, Bible schools, orphanages, and helping to strategically build the Kingdom of God in various countries and regions. Currently he ministers with Global Teen Challenge, helping TC centers around the world start businesses so they can be self-sustaining. Sharon travels with him on occasion, but while Rick lives the adventure, Sharon is more than happy to create her own through fiction.

Visit Sharon's website at www.sharonksouza.com.

You can also visit Sharon at the blog she co-writes with fellow authors Bonnie Grove, Patti Hill, Kathleen Popa, Latayne C. Scott, and Debbie Fuller Thomas: www.NovelMatters.blogspot.com.

Or visit her on Facebook at Sharon K. Souza, Author.

Also from Sharon K. Souza

Unraveled

Aria Winters wants off the nut farm. Literally. She wants to get as far away as she can from the Shunk-Winters family-run nut-farming business. So she takes her Bible school degree and heads to Moldova to teach English at a missionary school. Aria falls in love with all the children, but especially shy and beautiful Anya. When the unthinkable happens, Aria begins to question what were once the absolutes in her life. She returns to the family compound, where she tries to hide from life, and most especially from God. But just as the Moldovan sunflowers can't help follow the face of the sun, so Aria must face the true Son. Can she live with what His light exposes?

Lying on Sunday

After learning her husband died of a heart attack—in another woman's bed—Abbie is faced with a choice: She can give in to despair, or create a new life. Abbie does both. As she searches for healing, she fights to protect her daughters from her husband's infidelity. Then a shocking revelation threatens to undo everything she's accomplished. Will the power of the truth really set Abbie free, or is forgiveness out of reach?

Every Good & Perfect Gift

After thirty years of close friendship, there are no secrets between Gabby and DeeDee. Except one. Thirty-eight-year-old DeeDee decides she wants a baby. And while the friends believe they have faced their greatest challenge, an unexpected turn of events alters their lives forever.

A Heavenly Christmas in Hometown

Eustace and Spencer are not your ordinary investigators. They have been given the difficult assignment a long way from home just weeks before the holidays. Hometown's annual Christmas pageant is put on hold when cantankerous Andrew Parsons insists on enforcing the new ordinance enacting separation of church and state. Not only that, he's fighting to regain the property his late wife left her nephew. It seems Andrew has his own plans for that property, and it doesn't include a new church. Will Eustace and Spencer save the pageant, the property, and make it *A Heavenly Christmas in Hometown*?

A Heavenly Christmas in Hometown – the Play

A Heavenly Christmas in Hometown by Sharon K. Souza is now a full-length play, perfect for churches, Christian high schools and colleges.

The play takes 90 minutes to perform, and can use up to 30 cast members.

For ordering information contact Sharon at sharonksouza@gmail.com

Visit her website at www.sharonksouza.com

CPSIA information can be obtained at www.ICGtesting.com
Printed in the USA
LVOW07s2028230415

435823LV00006BA/820/P